THE SINGING

Algonquin

Books

of

Chapel Hill

1992

THE SINGING TEACHER

A novel by Susan Skramstad

TEACHER

Published by

Algonquin Books of Chapel Hill

Post Office Box 2225

Chapel Hill, North Carolina 27515-2225

a division of

Workman Publishing Company, Inc.

708 Broadway

New York, New York 10003

This is a work of fiction. While, as in all fiction, the literary perceptions and insights are based on experience, all names, characters, places, and incidents are either products of the author's imagination or are used fictitiously. No reference to any real person is intended or should be inferred.

Library of Congress Cataloging-in-Publication Data

Skramstad, Susan, 1942–

The singing teacher : a novel / by Susan Skramstad. — 1st ed.

p.   cm.

ISBN 0-945575-69-6

I. Title.

PS3569.K67B3   1992

813'.54—dc20   91-24308 CIP

10   9   8   7   6   5   4   3   2   1

First Edition

For my

mother and

for Skram,

Rob, and

Elizabeth.

Special thanks

to

Nick Delbanco,

Bob Walker,

and

Charlie Baxter.

Spin, my sister,

and sing on!

—*Götterdämmerung*, by Richard Wagner

THE SINGING TEACHER

Chapter One

My mother's call upset me a little, that's all, the one where she said she and Poppy weren't coming for Christie's graduation. It seems normal to me, to be a little disturbed when a person's parents do something so unexpected. But, repressing bad news is one of my specialties, so I put it to the back of my mind for later consideration.

My view on this graduation is pretty calm; it certainly doesn't make me feel like I'm over-the-hill of all things, which is what Frank says I feel. I'm worried about what to wear is all, and yes, maybe about whether Christie will like Bolton College or not, and maybe a few other things, but my age has never crossed my mind. I'm not humming, which he *should* notice, and I'm not thinking out loud; it should be obvious I've got my usual personality under control.

I'm even blow-drying my hair extra long to tame it, when mostly I write it off as a lost cause. Frank bought a roll of thirty-six to commemorate this occasion for the family album, and I figure fifty years from now we'll probably be featured in some antique-store window. Naturally I want to look my best.

So, I'm just bent over drying, and brushing, and hoping nothing comes along to mess up the day. That's about when Peter's feet enter my bird's-eye view, which is the floor.

"Mom, I can't go."

I figure if I stare at those thin knuckly feet, just bore into them with my most concentrated look, maybe they'll go away, so I just keep blow-drying full blast and staring, and I don't answer.

"No way," he says louder, "I can't go."

I can barely hear him, but I hear enough, and he knows I'm not deaf. Through the flailing and flapping of my upside-down hair I see his toes wiggle, meaning, he thinks he's got a chance to pull this off.

He flops onto the bed beside me. At sixteen, he is tall and dramatic, and has potential to be a decent human being one of these days, I hope soon.

"I'm sick," he moans.

I sit up, turn off the dryer and eyeball him. He doesn't look sick to me.

"Peter, your sister will be very disappointed if you're not there."

"No she won't." He eases himself into the pillows. His curly red hair, direct from me, is uncombed and out of control, and he's wearing pajamas which I know he put on for this heart-to-heart, since he always sleeps in his underwear. "She won't even care."

"Of course she'll care."

"That's your fantasy, Mom. She hates me."

I slide him a pained look; it's my specialty.

"Besides," he looks at the dog-eared western on Frank's pillow like he wishes he were propped up reading it right now, "the place will be packed. You can say I was there. She won't know."

"You *will* be there," I say, reaching up to touch my hair, which doesn't seem to have quieted down yet.

"Mom, I'm sick, I'm not kidding." He rolls onto his side, and groans into the wall.

Frank's in the shower, which is too bad, because he never feels conflict in a situation like this. Me, I worry about everything, like, is Peter *really* sick or isn't he? Should I let him stay home, or should I make him go? Should I have had children? That's the bottom line, really. Frank just doesn't get into this kind of thing.

I glance toward the bathroom. The door is open because the room steams badly, but the water's still on, so Frank can't have heard any of this. Wearily I address Peter's plaid back. "You're not sick, you just don't want to go."

"Mom, I'm telling you for your own good. Make me go and I can't be responsible." He rolls toward me, with a hand across his forehead.

"I'll take that chance. Your grandparents can't come, so we're all she's got."

"How'd they get out of it?"

"They didn't get out of it," I say testily, "they just can't come."

The truth is my mother sounded so down on the phone I didn't push it. All I know is, it has something to do with my father, and I'll find out tomorrow.

"Well, I can't come, either. I've got big-time germs." He leans forward to see what kind of effect he's having. "Pregnant women, old people; think about that, Mom."

I've stopped listening. I forgot to tell Christie about her grandparents, or maybe I repressed it. Since Frank's parents are dead, they're her only grandparents, and she's very close to them.

"Say they left early with me."

"What?"

"You asked what to tell Christie," Peter says.

"I did not."

"Accept it, Mom." He pats me on the back.

"Well, anyway, I can't. We'll see them tomorrow."

Frank and I are going to take Christie to Bolton College for a special freshman orientation. Since my parents live about halfway to Bolton, we'll stop by their house overnight. Peter was supposed to stay here by himself, so he must be planning on a miracle recovery as soon as graduation's over.

"Peter, get ready. You're going with us."

"I'll probably puke my guts up right when Detwiler starts to talk."

Ernie Detwiler is principal of Alden High School and no one's favorite.

"No you won't. Get moving." I turn the hair dryer back on to signal our talk is over.

I should have stuck with my opera career. Besides my great voice, this hair and an artistic life were meant for each other. It has not been an asset for someone who lives in a small town, believe me. One of my music students told me his mother said I was a witch; it must be the hair.

Besides, if I'd stayed with the opera I'd have had a job

until my voice cracked. As it is, well, where am I now? This graduation shows up as a real fork in the river of life, I can tell you. I'm questioning everything I ever did, everything I do now, and everything I may do in the future. Frank says it's a big waste of time, but then I'm questioning about Frank, too.

The thing that bugs me most is that I left the opera when I married Frank. Women don't do that kind of thing anymore; they just add on and on, and it all works out. I probably should have done that, but I didn't think of it.

And, there's a little more to it. My leaving the opera was a monumental flip-the-bird, if you know what I mean. I had been Mericilla Benson's understudy for *Aïda* for over a year. *Mericilla Benson*, and she got the flu. What a break! It's the kind of moment every singer dreams of. But our music director, Madame Carmen Perillo, supposedly my mother's friend, supposedly my mentor, picked Amy Vandercore to sing the role instead of me. It was totally unfair. Frank said it was because Madame was in love with Amy—that's Frank's idea of saying something really mean, and I appreciated the effort at the time.

Naturally I was particularly vulnerable to a stable person like Frank. He just goes along doing what he's supposed to do day after day, no highs, no lows, just steady as she goes. It's like Frank is the anchor and I'm a skiff blowing around and around in a high wind. It's been the same for our whole marriage; I keep blowing, but I never quite break away.

Anyway, when you're hurt like that, sometimes you do something a little abrupt. That's what I did; I quit the opera and left with Frank. And I took my costumes with me to sleep in. I sing a lot when I'm alone, I can't help myself, which probably means it was my destiny; and I can still break a glass with a high C at twenty paces—sort of an unusual skill in most neighborhoods. That's why Frank moved us to the country. Of course he never said that, he talked a lot about the beauties of nature, but I know Frank, and if I may say so, he's a little inhibited. And he doesn't know, or care, anything about the beauties of nature.

I sit up, flip my hair back, and look in the mirror. All this drying has made my hair crazy. We have the largest mirror in the world, and it barely holds the extent of my hair. Yesterday, when Christie told me curly hair would limp down if it was blown enough, I didn't connect with the fact that her helpful suggestion came right after I said her boyfriend couldn't come out with us after graduation. Pathetic. And she forgot I might try it today. Too bad. I guess this counts as another lesson in life for both of us. I guess I'll have to wear a hat.

When I scan the contents of my closet with graduation in mind, I notice that most of my clothes are a little odd. I could wear the black linen I bought for those times Frank and I go out with his lawyer friends, but Christie will be in black. I reach for the subdued silk print my mother sent me last year in her annual make-over attempt. I slip it on and look in the mirror. Frank's pictures will look better with the contrast, that's one thing in its favor. Besides, my mother will feel like her life's been worthwhile if I wear this dress.

Frank's out of the shower now, planted in front of the fogged mirror, irritated as all get-out that he can't see in it. I consider this one of the positive features of our bathroom, but Frank's no dreamer so I wonder why he doesn't wipe it off. Instead he just stands there. His eyes are a little red-rimmed; maybe he didn't sleep very well, either. Probably stress; Frank has a new colleague.

Her name is Melinda Jeffries, a recent addition to his law firm, and she's got a crop of gore red fingernails you wouldn't believe. My feeling is that she cultivates this look to set herself off from the secretaries, since obviously she can't type unless she hits all the keys at once. Why else would anyone but a werewolf have nails like that? The firm put her over Frank because he's got a daughter, so they figure he's committed to women's rights. Melinda's a real piece of work, and it's got him all confused.

He's got a terry-cloth towel wrapped around his middle and nothing else on—not how either of us look our best these days. He doesn't look old exactly, I'd call it more like soft, sort of slouched, or pouched, I'm not sure what it is. And his hair seems thinner than it was yesterday, maybe because he's parted it in the middle for the first time in his life.

"What do you think?" he asks, turning to show me, his face campfire red. Frank takes the hottest, longest showers in the history of the world, and it always looks like he's about to drop dead when he gets out. His feet are damp and wrinkled and slightly turned out. He definitely looks better in a suit.

"You decide," I say, and hand him a washcloth to wipe off the mirror. I'd like to help him out, but I just noticed the blue flamestitch wallpaper I hung two weeks ago is pulling away from the ceiling and needs my attention. I stand on the edge of the bathtub to press the paper back in place, but it flops back over my hand. This makes me want to rip the whole thing down and stuff it into the toilet. But I don't, because if Frank sees how irritated I am he'll have some comment, or even if he doesn't say anything I'll know exactly what he's thinking. His opinion is that I only get like this when I'm about to get my period, which is very wrong, and subtly denies my right to any *real* emotions. So I decide to let it slide down on its own, painfully.

Meanwhile Frank wipes the steam off the mirror and stares as if he doesn't recognize himself, which I sort of understand.

"Maybe graduation isn't the right time to change your look," I say.

He nods. "It was just a thought." He sounds disappointed, but he reparts his hair and combs it in the usual way.

Frank and I are having a crisis, but I think I'm the only one of us that knows it. Christie's leaving for college has obvious implications for us. Aside from the fact that we'll miss her, especially me, it's the beginning of a very big change. One more year and Peter will be gone too, and then it'll be Frank and me, alone together. I pat the damp towel that covers his rump; it's a beginning, but it doesn't feel all that natural to me.

Frank doesn't know this big change is why he parted his hair in the middle, but it probably is. It may even be why I didn't get the wallpaper on right when I'm practically a professional. My grandmother used to say we have to cooperate with the inevitable. I'm beginning to see what she meant. Today, I promise myself, I will begin to cooperate with all the inevitables.

I turn my back on Frank, and the steam, and the wallpaper, and hum my way into the bedroom with "Vissi d'arte," my favorite *Tosca* aria. It calms me. The scene moves forward. In my mind I play it out. Tosca picks up the knife and Scarpia's about to get it. But suddenly he turns into wallpaper, blue flamestitch wallpaper. Tosca stabs my wallpaper. As my grandmother also used to say, there's more than one way to cook a goose.

I sit in our old green armchair, and screw on large hoop earrings which my mother will hate when she sees the pictures, but put my personal stamp on the outfit. My hair is the next step. Sometimes for restrained occasions I pull it back into a twist, but in its present state of excitement it would spit hairpins like machine-gun bullets. I don't even try. Instead I dig around in the costume trunk until I find a turban; it's bright purple, not the best color I'll admit, but the only real problem with it is the huge rhinestone clip in the front, which will probably clue the world in that I didn't get it at a regular store. Unfortunately the clip can't be removed without putting a hole in the hat, so it stays. I shove my wild curls up inside.

I don't even think about checking on Peter; I'd only have to listen all over again to why it's inhuman to make a sick person go to his sister's graduation. He'll either be ready to go, or he won't, and that's all there is to it. For once in our lives, I want everybody to deal with their own problems and leave me alone.

I am longing, I have to say it, for a different kind of life. That's why I think so much about the one I've got, and not in the most positive light. I feel a little guilty about this, but I think many women wonder at one time or another what life would have been like without marriage, or at least without marriage to the present husband. Especially if a person might have been a world-famous soprano. I couldn't be the only one these longings jerk around on a festive occasion.

I might be a diva right now—what a word!—instead of a

music teacher. I could have homes in New York and Rome, a hideaway in Crete. I might never even have heard of this little town; the lady who thinks I'm a witch might have been my greatest fan.

"Lilly?" Frank calls. "Are you all right?"

I must have dozed off right here in the chair, because Frank's towel's gone and he's completely dressed and ready to go.

I look down at myself. I'm ready, too; at least I have everything on—my mother's dress, acceptable black patent pumps, small green bag, a gift from Frank and probably very expensive, and of course the turban that is slowly pushing up on my head like a popover in the oven. I hate the way I look.

"Sure," I say.

Frank has on his seersucker suit and looks like a jailbird, but it's his favorite outfit. His hair is still sopping wet; he likes to go places with his hair wet because he thinks it makes him youthfully dark. I told him once or twice he just looked wet, but then I gave up. Usually he dries out before we get where we're going, anyway.

"Don't forget the camera," I say, and tug the turban back in place. Then I hum my way out of the room.

Peter is hunched over on the living-room couch.

"You shouldn't make me go, you know."

I ignore him. His hair, which is as curly as mine, has probably been brushed. It's hard to tell.

"I brushed it," he says.

"OK."

His new suit has been on the closet floor since the junior prom, three weeks ago, and this isn't one of those situations where you can't tell. He's wearing a too-large shirt of Frank's, yoked around the neck with his pride and joy, a limp gray tie knitted for him as a home-ec project by Norma Hatcher, his first serious girlfriend. Even in all this childish disarray, his adolescent pimples look out of place and somehow appealingly vulnerable. I'm not 100-percent sure, but his face may be a little flushed. I decide not to kiss his forehead, because if he really is sick I don't want to know about it.

We move toward the door slowly. I guess none of us want to go, but for different reasons. The last high-school graduation I went to was my own. There have been a lot of bumps and jolts since then, and what I'm trying not to think about is that it won't be any different for Christie. Of course I don't want her to be bored, which I sometimes have been, especially after the bumps and jolts died down. It's a trade-off.

Outside, the brightness of the sun surprises me for so late in the day. Frank, who deals in facts, says, "Sure is hot." I give him credit for the effort, because he doesn't like small talk, and this situation calls for the smallest.

Christie hasn't been easy to raise. She's a little on the high-strung side, and very dramatic. It's a personality that I can really understand, and the thought of her going away hurts; sometimes more, sometimes less, but right now, as we leave the house, it has wrapped me up so inside that I can scarcely breathe. Even the hair trick is somehow endearing.

A person who's rock solid, like Frank, isn't a great help at a time like this. "She'll *love* college, Lilly," he says about every five minutes, which isn't the point at all. Sometimes being with him is like keeping shoes on when you're drowning.

"Just a few more blocks," Frank says.

I briefly wonder what Christie wore today. I bought her a dress and put a note on it that said, "From Dad." But she knows who it came from; she knows what the note means, too. She has taken to rifling through the old costume trunk for eye-grabbers to wear to school; I don't care, I just sleep in them, but Frank has a hard time with it. He's a little inhibited, I think I mentioned. Maybe I should toss the costumes, but I can't. I love them too much. It must be hard on Frank, living with us. Every now and then I think of that.

"Red light," Frank says.

"I shouldn't be going, I'm warning you," Peter moans.

I lean my head back on the seat and close my eyes. In a minute the car starts to move again. I sway, with each turn a little more disoriented, but the curves and bends are somehow comforting. I forget about the graduation and pretend I'm Gilda in the bag at the end of *Rigoletto*. Not a great moment in Gilda's life, I'll admit, and a real comment on her associates, but a beautiful opera with beautiful music.

Finally the car stops. "We're here," says Frank.

I open my eyes to find he's looking at me in a way I can only describe as curious. Maybe it's because I patted his toweled behind, maybe it's because he knows something's different and doesn't have any idea what to do about it. Maybe it's just because he's been my husband for a long time. One thing I'm sure of, he doesn't have any interest in knowing we're in a crisis.

"Sure is hot," I say, and pat his arm for good measure.

The inside of the auditorium makes me dizzy. It rises and falls on the flapping wings of hundreds of white programs that fan hot air across everyone's face. Frank's hair is still flat and wet; my dress is sticking to me, and Peter looks like he was dragged down a dirt road on his tie. Not a smile among us. Everyone else looks relaxed and informal. Probably they've graduated other kids, or maybe they've got extra daughters at home.

I wave at Dr. Felcher, the kids' pediatrician, but there aren't any seats near him. One of his grandchildren is in Christie's class. Horace Felcher is a great doctor; I go to him myself, even though most of the chairs in his waiting room are about six inches off the ground. He understands me, which counts for a lot. Years ago he taught me how to loosen all my muscles to keep from getting so tense; he calls it a Limp Lulu, and it really works.

Frank and Peter and I sit down in one of the empty side rows, and I put on my glasses so I can see the program. There's her name, Christina Tosca Blake, right where it should be, among the B's. I feel something warm spread through my heart and I'm glad to be here even if it is the hottest day of the year, and even if I am sometimes crazy enough to want her to stay with me forever.

I twist in my seat to see if I can see her. The kids are lining up in the hallway outside the auditorium and I'm sure they're even hotter than we are, under their long graduation robes. Maybe it's my opera training, but this many people in floor-length black usually means trouble for someone; I want to point this out to whoever's in charge. Of course, life's no picnic, maybe that's the point.

Anyway, she's by herself near the door, her long reddish gold curls cascade down her back; it's my hair, direct from my own mother, tamed by Frank's genes. For once her oddball boyfriend, Howard Woolfe, is not with her; blessedly separated by the alphabet, I guess. She sees me looking at her and waves. It looks like she, and most of her friends, have washed off the bulk of their makeup. The school must have made them do it. It's probably unconstitutional, but I'm grateful to whoever took the chance.

Clive Streeter steps up on a small wooden stool in front of the Alden High School band and raises his baton. He's the school's music director, as delicate as a mosquito and just about as much fun. Years ago, when we first moved here, I tried to be friends with Clive and get a chorus started at the school. But Clive thought I wanted his job so he told people I drank. No one believed him, of course, but it took some of the shine off working with him. Instead I taught voice and violin to kids whose parents wanted them at my house after school instead of theirs. I'm pleased to see he's losing his hair.

Clive's left hand rises dramatically in line with the baton hand and he holds the pose. There's a hush in the auditorium in response to his frozen position. All eyes watch the baton. It twitches, then swoops the starting beat of "Pomp and Circumstance" by Sir Edward Elgar, whose heirs and assignees must have made a fortune on it by now. The band saws away at it and the Alden High School senior class begins to move. They thump down the center aisle through the flapping sea of programs; most of them are hunched a little, as if they grew too fast.

Howard Woolfe appears toward the end of the line. His hair is long and blond, mashed underneath the tasseled mortarboard like ragweed. His eyes are popped wide open, like he's just seen an archangel or something; it's his normal look and it gets on my nerves. When he sees me he bows and winks as if he's got an uncontrollable twitch. It's supposed to be amusing.

Sweating, smiling, the kids file to their seats and stand in front of them. When the aisles are finally drained of graduates they sit in unison, a billowing black cloud. There is blurred movement on stage and when I put my glasses on I see it's Ernest Detwiler, Alden High School's principal. He moves forward and flicks the microphone with his fingernail. The thwack reassures him. He smiles at us and pulls the microphone so close to his mouth you can hear him breathe as he waits for silence. The program flapping slows in expectation. I glance at Peter. We both remember this is the part of the ceremony where he has threatened to puke his guts up. He smiles at me grimly.

Detwiler begins. "Ladies and gentlemen. I am pleased to welcome you to these commencement exercises. Let us stand and pledge allegiance to the flag."

Not a word about its being hot in here, and it's at least 100 degrees. He may be an android, which is what Michael Korby, one of my students, says. Michael says they're all over. Michael is definitely his own person, and one of my favorites.

We all stand and stumble through the words. The room has ceased fluttering because for the moment everyone has their program flattened over their heart. Fortunately Frank seems sure of the words so I follow his lead. After the Pledge of Allegiance I know we'll sing "The Star-Spangled Banner" and I'm ready for it. My family knows it too. Up front Christie's head sinks between her shoulders and Frank's body tenses beside me as we get to ". . . and justice for all." Peter sits down and puts his head in his hands.

There's no way my voice will blend with the others; I can't help that. I don't want to embarrass my loved ones, but I hardly ever get to sing to an audience anymore. As a compromise I decide to go through it fast and finish before anyone can locate me.

I take a deep breath and begin. People turn and look to see where the gorgeous, if I may say so, voice is coming from, but I'm careful not to catch anyone's eye. I'm much more certain of the words to the SSB than the Pledge of Allegiance, and hit the high notes right on. It feels great! I'm almost loud enough to drown out the orchestra and I'm way ahead of their tempo. Frantically they try to keep up, all except for Michael Korby, on violin, who's playing "America the Beautiful." Only a well-trained ear could pick it out in this heat though. Clive breaks his baton in a fit of pique, but since almost everyone is turned toward the back of the auditorium, I'm the only one who sees. I smile a mean little smile and almost lose my place.

All too soon the singing is over and we get down to the business of graduating our children. Christie's head reappears and when her name is called, she walks across the stage with her back as straight as an astronaut's. Her long red-blond hair shimmers like fire and I wonder why everyone in the place isn't holding their breath just looking at her. She turns, looks in my direction, and smiles her broadest smile; then she dips her head shyly, which she isn't, but it's a nice gesture she picked up from Princess Diana, and glides across the stage as smoothly as if she's on a track. The black robe forms the perfect backdrop for her hair so maybe I'm wrong about these gowns, although she's also a knockout in blue.

When Howard Porterfield Woolfe's name is called I'm surprised to learn he has won an award from the Art Department. He looks paler than usual, but it's Howard all right; his green high-top desert boots propel his black-gowned body across the stage like a wind-up toy. Maybe I should have said yes when Christie asked if she could invite him to dinner tonight. She wanted his mother, too, which unsettled me because I prefer to think of Howard as an orphan. But for just this once I didn't want to share her. I can't figure out why she didn't argue, not counting the hair trick, of course; I've never gotten out of anything so easily—she's a real talker.

The speeches are mercifully short. Ernie Detwiler wants to go home, you can tell by looking at him, and the class valedictorian starts to cry in the middle of her speech and has to be led away.

Frank whispers, "Poor kid."

He surprises me sometimes, like now. I pat his hand for old times' sake.

And then it's over. The black cloud rises and bobs its uneven way up the aisle, the fresh young faces like soap bubbles on an oil slick. Frank pats my hand back and we smile at each other. I don't know what he's thinking, but I'm wondering where all that time went. And what it will be like when it's just the two of us again.

"Are you OK, Lilly?"

"Of course I'm OK," I say.

"You're humming," he says.

"No I'm not," I say.

Christie runs up and the three of us hug as if it's been years instead of hours since we saw each other; but something significant has happened and we all feel it. She pats the purple turban, maybe even feels a little guilty, and turns to Peter, but he sidesteps out of her reach.

"Don't come near me," he moans. "I shouldn't be here."

"Why not?"

"I'm sick. Can't you tell?"

Christie turns to me and rolls her eyes. Then she looks behind me, a little frown, two lines, etch a delicate V in her forehead.

"They couldn't come," I say.

"Why not?"

She looks so disappointed I want to hug her again, but I know her first rush of enthusiasm for us has probably passed. "Grandma didn't say why. We'll find out tomorrow."

"Are they OK?"

"I don't know, darling. We'll find out when we get there."

Her frown deepens. "Didn't you *ask*?"

"Of course I asked. It's something your grandmother didn't want to talk about."

"But are they *all right*?" She's taller than me, more delicate, and *so* pretty.

"I'm sure they are, Christie. It's probably Poppy's feet bothering him again, or something."

She seems to accept this and takes my hand, pulling me along behind her. Flashbulbs are going off all over the place. The crowd is moving toward the gym for a reception and we follow along. When we get there, Peter hunches away from us and sits on the polished gymnasium floor, leaning against the cinder-block wall, legs straight out, feet pointing to the ceiling; Norma Hatcher's tie is unravelling around his neck. He's hard to miss.

Ordinarily this would bother Frank, but he's not totally normal today, and he's able to lose himself in his role as the recorder of the event. "Stand over there, you two." He directs Christie and me to an empty wall underneath a basketball hoop. The camera's up to his eye, and he's trying to focus. I don't want to tell him he's got the lens cap on. I put my arm around Christie and smile. I'm not sure I'll want to remember all this, anyway.

"Yo, Mr. Blake." Howard Woolfe hurries toward us, robe flying, his black tasseled mortarboard clutched to his head. "Yo, Mr. Blake, you got the lens cap on," he yells as he approaches. Anyone close enough to hear, which is most of the gym, smiles indulgently.

"Of course it is," says Frank, who likes Howard about as much as I do, but is more mature about it, "Mrs. Blake does not like to have her picture taken."

I'm a little confused here, but Frank continues before I can say anything, "She'll only pose with the lens cap on. When she's ready I whip it off and take the picture." He looks at Howard as if he's an idiot. Howard looks at me as if I am.

I glare at Frank.

"Ready, Lilly?" he asks, taking a real chance. "I'll be quick." He pulls off the cap with a flourish. "Smile, girls."

Our arms are around each other like long-lost friends; maybe I *will* want to remember this some day.

"You look like sisters," Frank says to make up.

Christie puts on her give-me-a-break expression, but she doesn't roll her eyes all the way back to the whites. That's her favorite look, has been since she was two—probably because I fainted the first time she did it. I don't know why she spares me this time.

Frank takes two quick pictures, then holds the camera out to me so I can take a few of him with his daughter.

"Take me and Howard first, Dad," Christie says. She's talking to Frank, but her glowing look is on Howard.

"Christie, I want to take you with your father," I butt in, wondering, as always, what she can possibly see in this kid.

"Howard has to *go*," she says, with a look that says this high school is her territory and I should be careful.

But then Howard steps forward. "No problem, Chris," he

says. "Let them do their thing. I'm easy." And he smiles a superior smile that says only he among us is an adult.

Naturally he gets his way. "Stand over there, Howard," I say, and point to the spot beside Christie where I just was. "Christina's father will take your picture."

I can't look at him, though, I'm too irritated. I bend down, take off my patent-leather pump, and shake it, like there's a stone in it or something. Actually, it's a stand-in for Howard's neck, and I really get into it. Frank nudges me, which brings me to.

Satisfied that I'm going to be OK, he turns and takes a couple of pictures of the two kids. Howard's about four inches taller than Christie and looks about ten years younger.

"Hey," Howard moves over to Frank and reaches for the camera. "How about I take the three of you together?"

Christie practically melts with the wonder of it all, and the scoreboard lights up once more for Howard Woolfe. I can see Frank thinks it's a nice idea too, but it kills him to admit it. When I walk over to Christie he gives in and hands over the camera; we stand on either side of our daughter while her boyfriend gets ready to capture the moment.

"I don't have any practice with that lens-cap trick, Mrs. B.," Howard apologizes, "but I'll be quick." He gives me a you're-nuts-but-I-can-handle-it wink, and lifts the camera to his eye. He twirls the lens frantically to hurry it into focus. "By the way, thanks for the invite, Chris. I'd like to have dinner with you guys, but I'm not feeling so great."

She doesn't even look guilty. I start to hum the intermezzo from *Cavalleria Rusticana*. Frank tightens his hold on my waist and I stop, but I feel the turban rising up on my head.

Howard adjusts the focus and points to the right of me;

there is no way I could be in this picture. "We went Mexican for lunch." He snaps the wall above us. "How do these Mexicans do it? I mean they eat it everyday. Don't they ever puke their guts out?"

This reminds me of Peter who is still sitting on the floor, leaning against the wall. Now his eyes are closed.

"Turn around, Mrs. B.," Howard calls.

I'm smiling like a shark, when Howard presses the button. The shutter seems to be stuck. He examines the camera, holds it upside down, shakes it. "Think you're out of film, Mr. B."

"That can't be." Frank reaches for the camera and looks it over carefully.

"Think so," says Howard, shifting his weight from one green desert boot to the other.

"Frank, didn't you put a new roll in?"

Frank looks down to where Peter is sprawled on the floor. "Peter?"

"I took a couple pictures of Norma's cat, Dad. You said I could."

Frank holds the camera out toward Peter. "We've only taken five pictures, Peter. This is a roll of thirty-six."

"No kidding." He shakes his head in amazement.

"Norma's cat?" asks Christie.

"It's pay for the tie." He looks proudly at his front.

"I thought *that* was Norma's cat," Christie sneers.

A large woman with crystal-cluster earrings approaches. Her blue eyes are as faded as sun-bleached paint. "There you are boy-o," she says, squeezing Howard. He submits to it pretty well, but he's looking at Christie with a pained expression over his mother's soft shoulder.

She was pretty once, I can tell that, and she's probably a nice person because there are no frown lines on her forehead. Christie told me a lot about Mrs. Woolfe once. Her husband died a long time ago so she raised all three boys by herself. Howard's the youngest. There is something behind her eyes that says it wasn't easy. She holds out her hand and I take it, but I feel like hugging her because I know what she must feel like inside. Howard is going to California for college, which thrills me, but must seem like an awfully long way away to her.

"I'm Nancy Woolfe," she says. "I've been wanting to meet you for a long time. Christie's such a sweet girl, I love having her around." Her hair is heavily mixed with gray and much too thin for her large face. The hand she gives me is damp. She and I probably graduated from high school in the same year, or close to it, thinking high school was the worst there was.

I start to cry. Since I have already been described as a lunatic by my husband during the lens-cap episode, this surprises no one but me. No one even asks what's wrong. Mrs. Woolfe pats me on the back and then leaves with Howard who keeps turning around to see if I've stopped yet. Finally they go through the outside doors which seems to make me feel better.

Then I remember Peter. "Frank, we'd better take Peter home. He doesn't look well."

"I thought we were going out to celebrate," Christie says. "This is my graduation, Mom." She's standing in front of me like Princess Diana herself, and all I can think of is what can a gorgeous creature like this see in Howard Woolfe and his flying-saucer eyes.

"Mom?"

I shake the vision out of my head. "We are, darling, we'll go anywhere you want. Just let us take Peter home first."

Peter rouses himself off the floor. "No way," he says. "I go to graduation, I go to dinner."

This little show of spunk reassures me. He just wanted to get out of graduation—as I thought all along.

Chapter Two

Peter distinguishes himself by waiting to throw up until he's halfway through the most expensive dinner of his life. As I look at his miserable, genuinely flushed face, I am squashed by remorse.

We straggle out of the restaurant single file, an unhappy family unit, weaving through a maze of elegantly draped, candlelit tables. The eyes of everyone in the place seem to bore into my back, as if they know whose fault it is. A tuxedoed pianist tries to cover our exit with a switch from a slow romantic number to wild boogie-woogie; his hands jump over the keys like water lilies in a dishwasher, but his eyes, too, follow us out the door. Melinda Jeffries, at a darkened corner table, with Alex Marsh, one of the other partners with the firm, looks elegant in a scarlet sequined dress with a neckline that plunges below the edge of the table. Alex is the only one in the place not watching us.

In the parking lot, Peter is sick again. It's obvious that Frank won't be going with Christie and me tomorrow.

"I told you," Peter mumbles as he falls into the backseat.

"Yep." I take off my turban and hold it by the rhinestone clip; it glitters under the parking-lot lights.

"Why did you come if you were so sick?" Christie asks. She's slouched next to Peter in the back, her legs stretched through to the front between the bucket seats.

"She made me," he groans.

"Who did?" Christie asks.

"Mom."

She raises her hands in a gesture of despair. "Why, Mom?"

"I knew you'd want him to be there, Christie."

She bites a hangnail. "I wouldn't have cared."

Peter sits up happily. "What'd I tell you? Do I know my own sister or what?!" He smacks her on the leg. This effort exhausts him and he flops back on the seat again.

Frank is quiet. He drives as if there's no one else in the car. He probably thinks we did it on purpose. This was not only a scene, it was a doozie, not to mention who was there. He's thinking we can never go back to that restaurant. He's probably right. He may even be wondering what his life would have been like if he'd never met us—there's no reason I should have a corner on that question.

The streets are lit by an occasional lamp, and we drive from one yellow pool to the next like a stone skipping across a pond, until we approach the turn-off to our house. There the night is blackstrap molasses, thick and sweet. We dip into it and bump over our country road toward the house in silence;

but it's not one of those comfortable silences, it's more like an everybody-has-a-gripe silence.

Our downstairs lights are on, we always leave them on when we go out at night; it looks as if someone's waiting for us, which is a nice feeling if you're a little lonely. Frank stops in the driveway and we all sit there for a minute. It seems that something should be said, but what? To whom? For one of us, me, there are all kinds of possibilities I suppose: sorry, to Peter for making him go to graduation when he was sick; sorry, to Christie for ruining her graduation dinner; sorry, to Frank for a honey of a scene. But I really don't feel like it.

Finally Christie sighs, pushes open her door and gets out of the car. She has on the green dress I bought, by the way, and she looks about as right in it as a palm tree at the North Pole.

I catch up to her at the front door, and give her a hug. "I'm proud of you, darling. Congratulations."

She hesitates and then hugs me back. "Thanks, Mom."

I shove the turban in my purse but my head still feels like it has a tight band around it. "This was all my fault."

"I know." She pats my hair. "Don't worry about it."

"That dress looks pretty on you."

"I did it for Dad." She shrugs her shoulders in a loose gesture. "He cares about these things."

I nod.

"I hate the dress, though." She reaches to open the door and then turns back. Under our porch light, her eyes look even greener than usual. "You couldn't have known Peter was really sick," she says.

"I *told* her," says Peter, dragging up the front steps. "What more could anyone do?"

Christie turns around and looks at him. "Peter, throw that tie *away*."

They go inside together, followed by Frank, who's still pretending he's alone.

I stay downstairs for a moment, making sure everything is turned off that should be off. I stand for a moment in the center of our dark living room and then, I'm good at this, it's a stage. The audience is hushed. I drop a deep curtsy and wait while the orchestra tunes up. We are in an encore situation. But suddenly, there's a commotion in the balcony.

"Lilly!"

It's Frank. "Peter wants you."

My audience is waiting; they can hear him, of course. For god's sake, Frank, they want to cry out, *you* take care of it for once. But they don't.

"I'll be right there," I say, and turn back to my waiting audience. "I'm terribly sorry," I whisper, "my son is ill. He needs me. We'll make it another time."

They are very quiet as they watch me go slowly up the stairs. I probably wouldn't have had time to travel with the opera anyway, what with one thing and another.

By the time I settle Peter with some Pepto-Bismol and a back rub, Frank's asleep. I brush my teeth, ignoring the once-proud sheet of flamestitch royal that is now slumped to the floor. A worn copy of *Last of the Breed*, by Louis L'Amour, covers Frank's face; the grizzled cowboys gallop wildly under an impossible moonlight. The book tells me he either tried to wait up for me, or he wants me to think he did. I get into bed and stare at the ceiling, wondering what it will feel like to lie beside him when there's no one else in the house. My mind is in a whirl.

I try a Limp Lulu. I don't want to think about Frank and me, not to mention my mother's call, which I admit scared me a little. Actually, being me, I've been expecting it; after all, my kids are almost grown, I figure it's about time my parents' problems start up. But this kind of thinking won't let me Lulu, so I tune into something neutral and potentially pleasant, like seeing Carole Williams tomorrow. Her daughter Melani is going to Bolton, too, and since they live in Lakeview near my parents, we'll go together. Christie is sort of divided about this plan, because she doesn't know Melani all that well, but I've assured her they'll get along, which I hope is true.

I've known Carole all my life. Aside from the fact that she spends most of her time making sure everything she has on matches everything else, she's probably my best friend. And Melani has given Carole her share of problems, which I can appreciate. Frank's worried Melani will be a bad influence on Christie, but he's deluded, considering his own daughter's temperament. Besides, it's the kids who never do anything bad that you need to be worried about.

At first, when the doorbell rings, I dream it's a curtain call. I have a dizzying out-of-body experience, heading for the stage. Frank turns over but he doesn't wake up. The bell rings again, unmistakable this time as a doorbell. About the time I figure it out, I hear someone run barefooted down the stairs. When the front door bangs open I turn to Frank.

"Frank," I shake him. Nothing. "Frank, there's someone at the door."

He turns to the wall. "Probably for Christie," he mumbles into his pillow.

I hand him the alarm clock. The glowing hands read four A.M. He sits up slowly and hands it back to me. He scratches his head.

"Frank, hurry up. Christie's down there." I'm sleeping in an old Norn costume from *Götterdämmerung* so I can't go. I have a strong feeling it's Howard. "What if it's Howard?" I say.

Frank pushes himself out of the bed and stumbles downstairs. It takes him forever to really wake up, and I'm pretty sure he's still asleep. I hope he'll keep his eyes open, at least while he's talking to them. The sound of mumbling reaches me, but I can't make out the words. Then he's back.

"It's Howard." He's already got his feet under the sheet as if it's OK that Howard's at our door at four A.M.

"What's he doing here?" I ask, sitting up on my side of the bed.

Frank's striped cotton shoulders rise, and he shakes his head in the well between them.

"Did you tell him to go home?" This, it seems to me, would have been a reasonable approach.

"Howard wants to say good-bye. That's all," he says.

"Good-bye? Good-bye for what?"

"Christie's going away tomorrow."

"Frank, wake up." I shake him. "She's going to orientation. She'll be back in a week." I pick up the clock again. "It's four A.M.!"

"Go to sleep, Lilly, it's four A.M."

"Frank you're so innocent." I get out of bed and start to pace. "It's no wonder I worry so much. Somebody's got to do it."

"Huh?" He leans back into the pillows and closes his eyes.

"I'm wrecking my nervous system, Frank."

"I know."

I move to the side of the bed and stand over him. "Why didn't he come over after dinner like a normal person, when we were all awake?"

Frank turns his head toward me, but he doesn't open his eyes. "I asked him that." He opens up and squints at me. "He got a message from the stars."

It looks like he's about to turn over, so I take hold of his arm. "It was not at all necessary for him to come over here at four A.M., Frank," I say, "stars or no stars."

"She's OK, Lilly. Go back to sleep."

"What do you mean, stars, anyway?" I ask.

He points at the ceiling with little jabs of his index finger, then closes his eyes and in a matter of seconds he's asleep. I'm not 100-percent sure he was ever really awake. Frank cuts down a lot on stress by checking out of awkward situations. I can't help but think my opera heroes could learn a little something from Frank.

I won't be able to sleep again tonight. Once I'm up, I'm up. Howard's mother's probably awake, too. She must have heard him go out. A mother never really sleeps. If I knew her better, maybe I'd call her up. We could play cards, something, until they get older. Sort of wait it out.

I start to hum. I can't help myself, it's much too quiet down there. One thing I know for sure—I don't want my daughter to sleep with Howard Woolfe, which is, of course, what I'm afraid is about to happen. And it's not because she's too young, either. She could be a hundred and five and I'd feel the same way. If I could, I'd march right down there and bring her back upstairs, but I can't do that; even I know she's too old to go for it. All I can do is hope he'll hurry up and leave for California.

I could sneak along the hall and peer over the banister but the boards between here and there are too creaky and Christie would probably hear me. Instead I tiptoe to the window that is right over the front porch. Their voices are faint, but at least they're talking. I stretch out on the floor and press my ear to the wall, but I can't quite make out what they're saying.

Suddenly there's a thrashing of sheets behind me, and the next thing I know Frank's sitting up in bed. He snaps on the light, his back as straight as a flagpole.

"Lilly, where are you?" he calls. He smacks around on my side of the bed trying to find me under the covers.

"Over here, Frank," I whisper, waving my hand to get his attention.

"Lilly!" he bellows.

"Here, Frank," I wave again.

"What are you doing down there?"

It looks bad, I'll admit it, me lying on the floor like this, but Frank looks a little out of it. "I dropped an earring," I say.

"Oh." He cocks his head to the side and looks at me with a sort of sleepy inattention. He nods as if he should have thought of that. Then he turns the light off and falls back with a thud.

I smile in the dark, but not for long, because Christie has seen the light. Her bare feet run as quickly up the stairs as they did down, only with more purpose. I'm hoping she won't see me, but of course the hall light picks me out the minute she opens the door. Her cheeks are very pink and her green eyes are blazing.

"What are you doing down there?" Her pointing finger pins me to the spot.

I look up guiltily. "Looking for an earring," I say.

"Ha!" She spins on one toe and then stomps down with the other, a sort of mini whirling dervish. She has on a ruffly, candy-striped nightgown my mother sent her a few weeks ago as a graduation present. Unlike Frank, her mind is not clouded by sleep or anything else. "You were spying on me, weren't you, Mom?"

I push myself up off the floor and walk toward her. "I wouldn't call it spying," I say and reach for her hand.

"Don't touch me," she jumps back. But then she stands still, lets her hands drop to her sides, and looks me up and down. "At least you didn't come to the door like that," she says. One bare foot is on top of the other.

"Of course not." I pat the tattered gauze of my Norn outfit.

"You were listening at the window." She has on her amazed look, and she's very good at amazed.

I don't feel as ashamed as I might. "No, I wasn't."

"Yes, you were."

"Well, if I was, and I'm not saying I was, it's just because I wanted to make sure you were all right."

"How could I not be all right?"

"You were with Howard."

"Ha! I *knew* you didn't like Howard."

"It's not that I don't *like* Howard, Christie, he's a little odd is all."

"And you're not?" Her eyes move significantly across the Norn costume.

"Has he gone?" I ask.

"How could he stay after *this*?" She flings a hand in my direction. "I'm so humiliated."

"I'm sorry baby, I've got a lot on my mind." I look at my motionless husband, who has nothing on his mind. I know I can't get back in that bed and lie awake all night beside him without hating him for the rest of my life.

"Why don't we just head out?" I say. "We were going in an hour anyway."

She looks at me as if she's about to say something probably better left unsaid, but she turns and leaves my room. Her light goes on and I hear her moving around so I figure we're going. I pack the rope ladder I always take to my mother's, the new preppy outfit I bought to impress everything-matches-everything Carole, and a few other necessaries like tooth-paste. Then, I pull on my favorite pants, the dark blue sweats with the elastic waist, and one of Frank's long white shirts. My hair is having a nervous breakdown, so I bind it under an old red-and-white scarf and I'm ready to go.

Frank has missed it all. I write, 'Call you tomorrow,' on a yellow Post-it and leave it on my pillow. I look down at him critically. His hair *is* getting thin, it wasn't my imagination, and there are lines around his eyes that don't show when he's awake. I pull the Post-it off the pillow, crumple it up and flush it down the toilet. Then I write another one, 'Call you tomorrow, I love you,' and stick it on the pillow. I hope it's true is all I can say. I grab Christie's backpack, which for some reason is sitting in a corner of our room, and go downstairs as quietly as I can. The last thing I want is for Peter to wake up right now.

Christie's already out in the driveway by the station wagon, a car that doesn't put our best foot forward, but holds a lot. Her suitcase leans against the back door of the car and she leans beside it; she's got her pillow with her so she can go to sleep in the car and not talk to me, I guess. She has on short lederhosen decorated with red-and-green sequins, and knee socks; the Gretel costume from Humperdinck's *Hansel and Gretel*. My mother will comment about it the minute we're alone. She's in Frank's mind-frame about Christie's fashion sense, but she wouldn't want to hurt Christie's feelings, so she'll dump on me.

Christie's suitcase isn't quite a steamer trunk, but almost; it takes both of us to load it into the back. I try to remember why I ever let her buy such a big one, and finally decide that I wasn't along.

We haven't been on the road five minutes before she breaks the silence with a huge sigh. "That was pretty bad, what you did back there." She's got a new way of raising her eyebrows that makes lines rise in the center of her forehead like a sergeant's stripes.

I nod.

"I don't believe you did it." She shifts, one leg curled up underneath her, and clasps her hands tightly in her lap.

"I worry about you, Christie, that's all."

"Worrying and spying are two different things."

"Not exactly," I say.

She turns away and presses her forehead against the window. "You don't like Howard, is all." Her breath makes a thin white cloud on the glass.

"I wasn't sure it *was* Howard. It could have been anyone." This is pretty much a lie, actually, which I hardly ever do, but I'm closed up in the car with her.

"Dad came down. Dad talked to him. Dad saw who it was."

"Dad was asleep the whole time. You know how he is."

I reach for her hand on the dark front seat. "Our house is pretty isolated."

She moves her hand away, and doesn't say any more.

To tell you the truth, I'm not sure why I don't like Howard, except that he's what my grandmother would have called a 'callow youth,' not to mention I adore Christie. Maybe if he was going out with someone else, Norma Hatcher say, he'd be all right. But Christie? No way. She's at such an inconvenient age. I want her to get just a little older before she has to take it on the chin. I don't trust him, I guess, it's as simple as that.

I do want to know why he came in the middle of the night, though, and not that silly explanation Frank gave. I take my eyes off the road just for a minute to look at her, and then look away. "Why did he come in the middle of the night, anyway?"

"The stars." She yawns and stretches.

"What stars?" I ask, feeling like I might have already had this conversation.

She jabs her finger at the windshield in the direction of the night sky. "Stars are stars."

"Christie, you don't have to act so superior. I know what stars are, I just don't know what you mean."

"Howard does everything by the stars," she sighs, flopping back boneless to indicate that it's a real trial, dealing with someone as dense as I am after dealing with the solar system of Howard's mind. She examines her fingernails, pushing at the cuticles.

I figure if I don't say the wrong thing she may go on, so I don't say anything at all.

She runs her hands over her ears, tucking her loose hair back. "He wants me to go to California with him."

It feels like my stomach has sucked my heart in.

"Howard's really smart," she continues. "It's mathematical, the star thing, and if you can figure it out, the stars tell you what to do and when to do it and you get what you want."

"Are you going?"

She sighs. "I don't know."

Now, when I'm upset I have two hallmarks—I'm a speeder, and I'm an eater. The only advantage to being such a worrier is that I never gain any serious weight.

Ahead I see the convenient neon glow of a fast-food cluster. "I'm hungry," I say, "let's get off here." Without waiting for her to answer, I sweep up the exit ramp and straight into a Dunkin' Donuts parking lot. The parking-lot lights fill the car and the sequins on Christie's outfit sparkle; she's got dark glasses pushed up on her head like two little bat ears.

"Just bring me something," she says, "I don't care what," and pulls a nail file out of her sock.

As I tug open the door to the shop, I look back toward the car. She's hunched in the front seat illuminated by the garish pink glow of a neon donut, working on her nails as if there's nothing more important in the world.

The waitress hands me my order, one coffee, one milk, a chocolate-covered chocolate donut for Christie and a glazed one for me. The sugar glaze makes my donut shine under the fluorescent lights. I take the first bite inside where it's light, so I can watch the glaze crackle all over the surface like crumpled waxed paper. That first bite is delicious and the fragile webbing of broken glaze is somehow beautifully satisfying.

Back in the car I hand Christie the carton of milk, and double-chocolate donut which is, I'm pretty sure, what this situation calls for. She doesn't complain. She may mention about going off to California with Howard as if it's no more interesting than going to Pizza Hut, but she's not my daughter for nothing. There's a big fork in the river of life up ahead, and she's gaining on it.

I put my coffee on the dashboard, but it steams the window so I hand it to Christie.

"I should go," she says, taking a sip.

"With Howard?"

"No, Mom, with Mickey Mouse."

I accelerate out of the lot. At whose knee was she supposed to learn common sense, I ask you, and the difference between Howard Woolfe and the rest of the world? Not to mention geography; who should have told her how far away California is?

Once we're back on the freeway, I get what's left of my coffee back from her. The asphalt rushes under the car like black rapids and the speedometer quivers around eighty-five. As soon as I see it, I brake and we slow like we hit a head wind, but my mind races on.

We have to talk about this. But I don't want her to think I'm prying. Should I tell Frank? I don't know whether I should tell Frank or not. But first things first, I've got to talk to Christie. I plan what I'll say, think over the options several times, and try to hear the words the way she'll hear them. I need to sound completely relaxed, but be able to give her a couple of different ideas. When my opening finally sounds OK in my mind, I speak up.

"So, you want to go to California with Howard?" It comes out very casually, considering my heart is plastered against my esophagus.

Nothing.

"Christie?" I glance over—she's asleep. Only a child could

drop off at such a moment. Or Frank. She's got her pillow balled up and holds it clutched against her stomach; the dark glasses have slid down her nose and her face against the seat back is turned slightly toward me. The corner of her mouth is flecked with little crumbs of chocolate, a drop of milk has traced a narrow streak to her chin. Asleep, she looks much younger than she is.

It's as if she's under a spell. Ever since Christie was born I have understood Wotan, King of the Gods, who put his daughter, Brünnhilde, to sleep and surrounded her with magic fire. This morning especially, I'd like to get in touch with him. If I could surround Christie with magic fire and keep her there for a few years, it would save a lot of wear and tear on both of us. I reach over and touch her cheek with my fingers.

It's still dark outside, nothing but the headlights of cars coming toward us, and the taillights of the cars ahead. There isn't much traffic, and I make good time. When the sun comes up, it reveals the beginnings of a cloudless blue sky. It's going to be a beautiful day, bright and sunny. The hum of the road is soothing and the quiet sound of Christie's faint breathing beside me makes the world seem surpassingly beautiful and, as long as she sleeps, uncomplicated.

She stirs and mumbles into the seat. In her sleep she brushes the hair out of her face with the back of her hand. A bump in the road jogs her awake. She looks confused, but only for a moment as she remembers where she is. With a yawn, she pulls herself forward, and leans against the dashboard. She searches the road. Then she flops back.

"Where are we?" She shoves the dark glasses against her eyes and stretches to the limits the car allows.

"You've been asleep for almost two hours."

She twists like a periscope looking for a landmark.

"But where are we?"

I hand her the map. "We just went over a river."

"What river?"

I shrug. "A big one—should show on the map."

"Mom, do you even know where we are?"

"Of course I do."

She sighs. Map-wise I have no idea where we are, but mental kinesthesia, an almost physical sense of where I am at all times, is one of my specialties. And she knows it.

Christie stuffs the useless map in the glove compartment and leans back. There's not much to see in terms of scenery right now—it's too hot even for the cows who usually dot the fields. They must all be in the barn. I picture dark, damp heat, and flies.

"What are you thinking about?" she asks.

"Nothing," I answer. Naturally, that's a lie. In addition to the cows, I'm thinking about Howard Woolfe and Christie herself, but I know better than to push it. Besides, I don't think she's forgotten it either.

She flips the sun visor down and examines herself in the mirror. "People think I look like you," she says.

"You're much prettier than I am, Christie."

"But you've got that great hair."

I think she means it, which is nice.

"I don't have your freckles," she says, running a finger lightly across her cheek. It's unclear whether this is good or bad, but she's right. Her smooth skin is unblemished.

"So," she says, "do you get along with Grandma?"

Christie is a master at subject hopping; from hair, to

freckles, to mother-daughter relationships, which is where I think we're headed. I turn on the radio and punch buttons until I find a classical music station. "Sure, why?"

"You're always jumpy when we're there." She spits on a napkin and wipes all around her mouth with it. When she looks up I see my reflection distorted in her dark glasses.

"I am?" I can't exactly say she's wrong, but the thought disturbs me. Frank said something like this to me once, too.

"You sure are," she says. "You even get hives."

"Don't be silly."

"I'm not being silly, you break out."

"I break out a lot."

"I know. It's stress."

"It has nothing to do with stress. I'm allergic."

"Allergic to what?"

"If I knew I wouldn't get hives." I rub my nose. "Your grandmother and I have a sort of formal relationship, that's all."

"What do you mean?"

"It's not exactly personal. When I was growing up, I told my mother what I thought she wanted to hear, and she didn't tell me anything. Sometimes it's hard to remember who I'm supposed to be when I'm there."

"I figured it might be something like that; we studied about it. Your whole generation was like that."

"We were?"

"Yep. You weren't the only one, Mom."

I must say I'm glad to hear this.

The radio begins to hop between stations, the violins invaded by bursts of a male voice hawking paint. The static takes over as we move out of range. I turn it off.

"We're personal," Christie says, "don't you think?" She has twisted a strand of coppery hair around her index finger and now lets it go. It uncoils in slow motion.

"Very." It's one of the reasons I'm going to miss her so much when she goes away. "We've always been open with each other."

"So," she says, "it's only fair I tell you I'm thinking about sleeping with Howard." She stares at me through the flat black plastic lids that close off her eyes.

I turn the radio back on. It's not, as I said before, that I'm against her sleeping with someone, although I know a little something about the consequences. Just not Howard is all I ask.

"I'm just being open," she continues.

A country singer has replaced the static and I leave the radio on that station rather than look for another one. If she'd only take off those glasses so I could see her eyes, I'd know better how to talk to her. As it is, all I can see is myself.

"I wouldn't if I were you," I say.

"Why not?"

"Because it isn't a great love, Christie."

"How do you know?"

"Because you're asking me."

"I'm not asking, I'm sharing my personal thoughts," she leans back with a satisfied smile, "so I won't get hives at your house when I'm old."

"I'm not old."

She looks at me like she has a Nobel Prize in patience.

"Well, do *you* think it's a great love?" I ask.

"Not exactly." She rubs her palms on her knees. "I think things through," she says. "I need to sleep with somebody pretty soon. I'm practically the only virgin I know, besides Howard."

A haymaker goes off in my head, because I would stake my trunk of costumes Howard's no virgin.

"Howard thinks it's a pretty good idea. He says we need experience."

"Experience for what?"

"So we'll know how to do it, you know, when the time comes."

I want to stay quiet, let that one hang in the air like the last leaf on the tree.

Naturally, given the situation, I have floored it. The climbing needle of the speedometer comes to my attention about the same time the cop does. His siren screams as he comes at me out of nowhere.

"Damn!" I say.

"Shit!" says Christie.

"Don't say that."

"Why not? You're about to get another ticket. This has got to be your millionth ticket."

She's exaggerating, of course. I seldom get an *actual* ticket. I have the kind of eyes that bring out the best in people. Even so, I have very strong feelings about the whole ticket-giving business.

"This," I say to her, indicating the policeman in my rear-view mirror, "is why there are so many crack houses and killers everywhere. The police have no priorities."

"Right, Mom." She has heard this before.

"Christie, this is something I know about."

I pull over to the side, outraged as always that a policeman would waste his valuable time on me, a woman just trying to get along. I hope he'll have the decency to turn off his flasher, which of course he doesn't. He gets out of his car slowly, and walks toward us as if he has all the time in the world, crunching gravel beneath his shoes like he hates it.

"God, Mom," is all Christie can say to help me out. She pushes her sunglasses up to the top of her head.

"Going a little fast weren't you, ma'am?" The policeman is young, very, and I have to twist my head practically off to see him since he stands behind my window. That, of course, is so I can't shoot him, which he should be able to see by looking at me I'm not going to do.

"I can't see you back there, officer," I say. "Will you please move where I can see you."

"Jesus, Mom!"

"Christie, this is all your fault. I'll thank you to keep quiet." I've got my purse upside down in my lap looking for my license.

"My fault?" She can hardly believe her ears.

"Your fault. You know I drive fast when I'm upset. I can't help myself. You might have saved the sleeping with Howard question until we stopped for lunch."

"Jesus," she says and rolls her eyes.

The policeman, who is, I repeat, very young, is willing to risk his life now to look in the window. He too has dark glasses so I've got no idea what he's looking at, but I can see Christie clearly reflected in his lenses and she's tapping her forehead to indicate I'm looney. I snap around to catch her at it, but her hands are neatly folded in her lap. She has replaced her sunglasses so all I can see is a reflection of him.

I turn back and hand him my license and then the registration which, thankfully, I happen to have with me. He crunches back to his car to call me in. I know I'm humming but I don't care. I hum louder. What's good for my nerves grates on other people's. So what? That 'so what' is a giant step in the right direction for me. I hum all the way through the citation, through seeing the outrageous amount, pocketing the ticket, and driving off. If only Frank had been here he would know that this ticket was not my fault.

Christie doesn't even mention it once we're back on the road. For a while we drive in silence. Then she clears her throat. "What about you and Dad?" she asks. "Was that a great love?"

Since I've been asking myself the same question for the last few months without success, I'm not anxious to get into this conversation, but maybe I owe it to her, woman to woman. Maybe there's something here that will help her. I finally say, "I don't know, Christie."

She nods. "It was a long time ago."

I guess she's right. Frank was the only one who understood what it meant not to get the *Aïda* part. He knew Amy Vandercore was a high-note cracker if there ever was one. I personally think Carmen Perillo was jealous of me, it had to be something like that, because I don't really think she was that way about Amy. She was getting old, is all; her voice was gone. I personally think she was totally jealous. But she had the power and she used it, and Frank understood how I felt. So, I seduced him thinking I might want to sue her. And that's the way it was.

We stop at a Kentucky Fried Chicken for lunch but we don't say much. I get a double order of mashed potatoes and gravy, and Christie orders six wings, extra crispy, and a chocolate pudding. When we get back in the car we both feel better. I start to hum and Christie doesn't even mention it.

There are fewer open fields now and more houses. Pretty

soon the small towns start to pop up, one after another. About this stage of the trip I'm always excited and I never know why, because I'm usually disappointed by the time I leave. But there's something so familiar about going home; it's the place I know best in the world. Once upon a time, everything came together here.

Chapter Three

We pull up to the curb in front of my parents' house, and sit quietly in the car for a minute. I look around like I always do, to see if anything's changed, but nothing ever has. The houses are a mixture of styles, mostly small bungalows, some colonials. The yards are neat, the trees large. There's a smell in the air, a mix of something like flowers and dust that I have never smelled anywhere else. It's a street of old people now; their children, like me, have all moved away.

My parents' house is toward the end of the block. It's a two-story shingle house, painted a faded green, with a center entrance and two bay windows, one in the dining room, one in the living room; they push out like frog eyes on either side of a brown front door. For years my mother has spent a lot of time at the living-room window, watching the comings and goings of her neighbors. No one's supposed to know this, of course, but we all do. There can't be much challenge to it these days.

An enormous oak tree grows from the center of the lawn, and shades my parents' entire front yard. My mother plants flowers around the huge trunk every year, impatiens or begonias; they're the only flowers that will grow in so much shade. This year it's impatiens, clouds of pink ones. The blossoms seem to have melted into each other in the heat, forming one shimmering, motionless ring around the tree. The grass in front is patchy because of all the shade, but even so the yard looks neat and pretty. I've always thought it was the nicest yard on the block.

"Grandma's watching," says Christie, tapping me on the knee.

I look toward the bay window just as the nylon curtain drops into place. I always tell my mother we'll arrive about two hours later than I think we will, but she's always there, anyway. Of course, she's too proud to let us know she saw us drive up, so we'll have to wait at the door for a while, probably longer than if we'd caught her by surprise.

Christie and I get out of the car. I unlock the back while she does deep knee bends to loosen up. I throw her backpack and my overnight bag to the pavement.

"What did you bring that for?" she asks from an impossible crouch.

"What did I bring what for?"

She points at the backpack. "That's Dad's."

"That's yours, Christie."

"It was on loan to Dad, for the trip." She turns toward the house and touches her toes.

"Dad's not here."

"Right, Mom." She looks at me from between her legs, her hair spread out on the sidewalk.

I unzip it enough to see shaving cream and a couple of westerns, and put it back in the car. Poor Frank. I bend over and strain to reach my toes.

Christie must feel successfully loosened, because she bounces up and hurries to the back of the car. "This is mine," she says, as she yanks at her suitcase. I shudder as it thwacks to the ground. A bedraggled scarlet plume is caught in the side. I can't remember what costume it goes to; I can only hope she won't wear it until we leave here.

The three cement steps to the front door bake in the sun. "This was the best spot in the neighborhood to play jacks," I tell Christie.

"You tell me that every time we come," she pats me on the back. "And you love the smell of hot cement." She has on kind of a crooked smile she often gets when she talks to me, sort of a cute-baby nod. I smile significantly at the sequined lederhosen she's got on, meaning none of us is perfect, but I don't think she gets it because she smiles back.

So, I ring the bell, and the day explodes into the snarls and howls of a mad dog on the other side of the door. Christie jumps, but I pat her arm reassuringly. This is the most recent addition to my mother's security system—Savage Dog, tape one. She ordered it from the *TV Guide*. It's the first time I've heard it in person, although she did play it to me over the phone. I guess I forgot to tell Christie.

My mother is probably standing just inside the door. I picture her leaning toward me as I lean toward her, while Savage Dog growls and snarls. We're each listening for sounds of the other. Her silence says that life is not so empty that she has nothing better to do than wait for her daughter and grand-daughter to arrive; mine says she's still my mother so I'm willing to go along with it.

Finally her voice, high-pitched and small, comes through the door, breathless as if she's just arrived from several rooms away. "Down, boy! Sit!" Chains rattle and bolts slide as she undoes a series of locks. When, at last, the door opens, she stands just inside, wiping her hands on an apron she has probably just put on.

"Well, look who's here," she says. She turns off Savage Dog, and disappears inside Christie's hug, like an edelweiss in the arms of a yodeler.

She looks shockingly frail; her gold-frame glasses seem the only solid thing about her. It's always like that, though, the sudden feeling of surprise at her size, how thin and white her once startling hair is, how visible the ropey veins in her small hands are, and then she's just my mother again.

She releases Christie and turns to me. Her eyes say I shouldn't have let Christie wear the Gretel outfit, but she hugs me anyway. We used to be almost the same height. Now her nose presses into my neck like a bird's egg. I hold her gently; her bones feel as brittle as a wafer. The only thing that never changes is her Evening in Paris perfume; she's worn it as long as I can remember. It makes Frank sneeze.

She pulls away and looks up at me. "Are you getting taller, Lilly?" she asks, shaking her head. "You should go see a doctor. Maybe it's the change."

My cheek starts to itch.

She turns back to Christie, a fluttery turn, a little unsteady. "I'm sorry we missed your graduation, dear," she says.

"Me too, Grandma," Christie says. "But it's OK."

My mother turns to include both of us in this conversation.

"It's not as if we didn't *want* to come."

Christie still can't believe her grandparents weren't there. "What happened?"

"Something came up." My mother looks past Christie's shoulder to the wall. "Poppy's not like he used to be."

"It was nice," Christie says.

"Mother, what do you mean, he's not like he used to be?"

"He's very forgetful."

This is a royal cop-out. "He's been forgetful for years," I say.

Nervously she touches her hair. "I didn't want to drive with him."

This sounds lame to me, but I don't think Christie wants to know any more. My mother's face is heavy with sadness. "OK, Grandma." She pats her gently on the back.

"Poppy's forgetful, darling. I don't like to get in his car anymore."

Christie nods. "OK, Grandma." She pats her back some more.

"But I don't like to say so."

Christie looks at the floor as if it's the most interesting floor in the world. "OK, Grandma."

"Is that what came up?" I ask.

"I guess you could put it that way, Lilly." Her hand quivers. I know there's more, she tells me that with her eyes, but I'm going to have to wait. "That's what came up."

The hallway smells as if nothing new has come into this house in a long time. I wish my mother would open the windows, open the doors, let the air blow through for weeks, months, whatever it takes to blow out this smell. But she won't, because of the "criminal element." You can't even get out without a key, much less in, and no one ever knows where the key is.

That's why I bring my rope ladder. Frank bought it for me. I guess he was worried, but it would have been nice if he could have said so, instead of saying it wasn't hard to outsmart my mother.

"The dog's pretty good," I say.

She beams. "Yes, isn't he." She closes the door behind us. "I got him from the *TV Guide*. I told you that, didn't I? They have other tapes, too; there's Howling Monkeys, Hissing Snakes, things like that."

"Depends where you live, I guess," I say.

"Yes, Savage Dog is perfect for me." She hands me a brochure from Rabid Protection Products. "You should look into this, Lilly, way out there where you live. Tsk, tsk, tsk."

I put the brochure in my purse. "Thanks."

The truth about my parents' house is, there is nothing here that would be of value to anyone except me, and even to me all that's of value here are my parents themselves. I personally think my mother is sending out the wrong message to the "criminal element," guarding her home like Fort Knox. But who am I? Maybe she's right, maybe we need Savage Dog at our house too. I don't think anyone would disagree that the world's gone crazy.

"Where's Poppy?" Christie asks, looking around. He's usually in the den with the TV on, but it's obviously empty.

"He's under the Lilly tree," my mother says, jerking her head toward the back.

The Lilly tree is a locust my father planted in the backyard the day I was born. Now it's tall and straight, and has a large canopy of delicate leaves that filter a lacy shade from the afternoon heat. It's probably more satisfying than me most days.

"OK." Christie finds the key, which for once is hanging where it should be, and unlocks her way out. The screen door slams behind her. That sound, the sound of a screen-door slap, defines summer to me. My mother crosses the kitchen to push the door shut. She locks it, and replaces the key on the hook. When she turns around she asks, "Why do you let her dress like that, Lilly? You should have thrown out those costumes a long time ago."

I've heard this before.

"I know," she says, "you've heard this before." She gets two cups out of the cupboard over the stove. "And you should have listened." The round O's of her glasses seem to widen her eyes as she looks at me. "How long can she dress like that before people stare? She's not a little girl anymore, you know."

She doesn't expect an answer, she's just getting that out of the way. There are more important things on the agenda. She places a tea bag in each cup, and pours in a steady stream of boiling water.

Even on the hottest days we drink tea together. My mother is always cold, and I have never told her I don't like tea, because it's the one thing we do together.

"How was the drive?" she asks, placing a steaming cup in front of me.

"Not bad." I stand up and poke through the cabinets.

"Haven't you eaten?"

I find a jar of peanuts and shake a few into my hand. "We stopped at Kentucky Fried a couple hours ago."

"Lilly, that's so unhealthy."

"It's chicken," I say. My parents eat chicken almost everyday.

"But it's *fried*, Lilly, *fried*." She shakes her head.

"Christie likes it," I say. "I try to humor her."

"You indulge her. She has no sense of good nutrition."

"That's not true," I answer, thinking it probably is. But KFC's not worth fighting about. "Besides, I like it too."

"Oh, Lilly." She despairs of me. Her hands are clasped on the table in front of her, the pale skin gathered like a walnut at her knuckles.

I want to hear what the problem is, but I don't, too, if you know what I mean. If my mother's actually going to confide in me, she must be desperate. She looks up, and I know she wants to tell me, but her gaze isn't steady and she turns away. Her brown eyes are watery and faded, as if the color has drained into her skin, which has a brownish cast, like weak tea. There's something brave about the thin little curls that can't possibly cover her pink scalp anymore. Especially when I remember what they used to be like, not all that different from mine.

She sighs, a sound like air bubbling out of an underwater balloon. "There's something wrong with your father," she says. She's not nearly as controlled as she looks; I can see that the whole huge lump of whatever it is, is caught in her chest. I can almost feel it myself. Christie and her clothes, Kentucky Fried Chicken, Savage Dog; it was good to have other things to talk about, even if just for a moment.

Now I feel cold. I walk over to the back door and look out to where my father sits with Christie at the far end of the yard. It could be so many things. My parents are older than some; they had me late. Sooner or later everyone wears out; it's just a fact.

"Is he sick?" I ask. I want to put my hands over my ears.

"No," she dismisses that with an impatient wave of her hand. "I should be so lucky."

I turn slowly away from the window, but my hand holds the cool brass of the doorknob. "Well, what then?"

"He's seeing someone else." Her voice is a wavery line in the air. "I don't know who."

I lean on the door and stare at her. "What?"

"Someone else, Lilly." She narrows her eyes as if seeing something bright. "They don't care what they do, I always said that, but no one paid me any mind."

My mother is talking about "loose widows," I know that right off; she has, for years, ever since her friend Evelyn Gray's husband ran off with a widow thirty years ago. It was one of those ideas she got in her head, like the "criminal element," and never let go of. It's been something of a joke between my father and me. The idea that my father himself might actually go out with a "loose widow" is crazy. My parents have been married close to fifty years. He's an old man. Who would my father "see"? Who would "see" him? I realize I've been holding my breath and I let it go. I laugh out of relief.

"It's not funny, Lilly," she snaps.

"Oh come on, Mother." I walk back and stand at my place across the table from her.

She sits very straight in her chair. "Why wouldn't your father have an affair?" Her eyes accuse me. She removes her glasses and rubs them with a napkin dipped in tea. "He's quite attractive for a man his age."

"Because men his age don't have affairs," I say, pulling out my chair and sitting down.

"Men any age have affairs." She reseats her glasses carefully.

"The question is, why would he?" I lean across the table and put my hand on top of hers, but we are both uncomfortable and she moves her hand away to straighten her cup in its saucer.

"I don't know why, Lilly," she says impatiently.

"Well, how do you know then?"

"It's obvious," she says, holding her hands tightly together.

"How is it obvious?"

"He goes out." She stares into her cup as if she can see him there.

"He has always gone out."

"Not like this." A small frown creases the shiny skin of her forehead and she nervously reaches up and touches her hair.

"He likes to walk."

"Not since his feet started to hurt." She raises an eyebrow. "That's five years at least." She is thinking I should have remembered this about my father.

"I know his feet hurt. He still walks."

Suddenly she gets up and goes to the window. "I don't want him to know I'm talking about him."

"He's with Christie, Mother."

"I know." She comes back to the table and sits on the edge of her chair. "He doesn't talk to me."

"He does talk to you."

"How would you know?" she sighs. "You don't live here."

"Pop just isn't much of a talker, Mother. A lot of men aren't." I toss Frank onto the pile of men who aren't.

"He was a talker when Bert was around." It costs her to say that.

Bert Foster and my father were best friends for seventy years, at least, until about three months ago when Bert died, as unexpectedly as someone that age can die. Poppy seems to have gotten smaller since then.

She nods absently. "That's what did it, I think."

"Did what?"

"That's when he went to *her*."

"Who?" I ask.

"Whoever she is, Lilly." She arches her eyebrow and leans back in her chair. "Maybe she makes him laugh, too."

By too, she means Bert of course. Bert was one of the most alive people I've ever known. He had a flushed face and a laugh you could hear a block away. We both look toward the back door, half-expecting to see him burst through it.

Bert liked to tell about how their two mothers bought a baby carriage together to save money. "They aired us out together," he used to say, smacking my father on the back. Poppy always coughed when Bert pounded him on the back like that.

Bert got married about the same time my parents did, but his wife died, and he made our house home base. "Never found another woman like her, Lilly," he once told me, but he was laughing like always, so I never knew if that was good or bad.

For years he came over almost every night for a drink, as regular as the mail, only later. My mother always stayed inside, while Bert and my father talked and drank bourbon out back under the Lilly tree. In winter, when they sat at the kitchen table, she went upstairs. I thought that was just how women of her generation acted. Now I see that whatever else was going on, she was probably jealous, too. I never understood that before.

And then Bert had his heart attack and died, boom, just like that. Poppy cried at the funeral. I never saw my father cry until that day.

She leans toward me and I notice a tremor she has never had before, as if her head is on a nervous little spring. Imperceptibly she quivers. She seems unaware of this new indignity, but her head's minute movements are obvious to me.

"How can he do this to me?" She moves uneasily in her chair.

"Have you asked him about it?" I concentrate on my tea cup.

"Be serious, Lilly, what would he say?" She tries to imitate him by lowering her voice. "'Yes, I'm having an affair.'" She leans back in her chair. "Never. Besides, what would I do if he did admit it?"

This is the first time my mother has ever asked me what to do, about anything.

"I'm not asking you what to do," she snaps.

"I didn't say you were."

"Yes, you did."

"Well, I'm sorry, I didn't mean to." I stuff an escaped clump of hair under my scarf. "Anyway, if it's true, which I doubt, you could work at it."

"Work at what?"

"Getting him back." I don't know how to stay in this conversation in a helpful way.

She looks at me like I've lost my mind. "I've been married to your father for almost fifty years." She takes a sip of her tea. "Lilly," she looks at me to see if I have brains enough to understand, "I've earned him."

She has a point. "Let me talk to him then."

"He won't tell you anything." She sighs. "Men lie."

"Since when are you so down on men?" I ask.

"I'm not down on men. They mean well." She gives a nervous shake to her hair as if scaring off a circling fly.

Just then Christie knocks at the back door. Her forehead is pressed against the glass, and she keeps on knocking. The part of her that's like me, wants to kick the door in. I get the key and open up. The screen door slams behind her. The smell of grass and sun come in the kitchen with her.

"What's the matter with Poppy, anyway?" she asks, leaning against the door with the flopped pose she has perfected. I've always thought she might have less bones than most people.

"There!" says my mother.

"What do you mean, 'There?'" asks Christie, her eyes half-closed as if she hopes we won't tell her, and if we try to, she'll close them all the way.

"What do you mean, 'the matter with Poppy?'" I ask.

"I told you, Lilly," says my mother. "You can't fool children and dogs."

Christie and I both look at her.

"Go on," she says, "tell your mother."

Christie looks confused. She hasn't followed much of this, but she does what she's told. "He's sort of spacey." She adds, "And he's got a washcloth on his head." A frown creases her forehead, a small V, like the one at graduation when she saw they weren't there.

"A washcloth?"

"Yes."

"Why?"

She shrugs her sequined shoulders. Without her sunglasses on she seems much more vulnerable, as if the eyes are the breakable part.

"Didn't you ask?"

When she shakes her head, her long hair shimmers.

"You mean, you sat out there and talked to him all this time, and never mentioned that he had a washcloth on his head?"

"Right." She doesn't look directly at me, and I realize that maybe I sounded a little sharp just then.

"Oh."

"I didn't want to embarrass him," she says defensively. "It's not as if there's anything wrong with it."

"You were probably right," I say, although it's kind of hard to imagine.

"He's sort of dreamy, Mom. And he asked me when graduation was going to be."

"What did you say?"

"I told him it was yesterday." Her lip quivers. "He looks so sad."

"You stay here and talk to Grandma," I say. "I'll go see what's what."

It seems cooler outside than in the kitchen, but then of course I don't have to be drinking tea out here. I wave but he doesn't see me. He's staring at something on the ground between his feet. The Lilly tree is all the way at the end of the yard. Grass has grown around the flagstone path so that the gray stones look round, and half their size. Bert and I helped my father lay these stones when I was a little girl. We were all pretty proud of ourselves, although my mother said we could have gotten them straighter. My father told her a straight line was not very interesting to him, and she either bought it, or gave up on us. As I get closer I see the washcloth.

"Hi, Pop." I bend down and kiss his cheek. It is like touching loose silk with my lips.

"Why, Lilly, how nice of you to drop by." He leans back in his chair and smiles at me.

"You knew I was coming."

"I know, dear, I know." His round, gold-rimmed glasses are exactly like my mother's; his pale eyelashes seem magnified behind them. "Did I know?" He cocks his head sideways like a sparrow, listening for something no one else can hear. Then, without waiting for me to answer he says, "Look at these ants." He points to the dirt between his slippered feet. Two tiny black ants are hauling a large crumb, bigger than either of them, toward a mound of crumbled earth.

My father stares at them. "I wonder where they got that," he says. His face is slack and there *is* something dreamy about him; it's the word I would have chosen, too. As if he has removed himself. "Sometimes I bring them things. They're not partial to chicken, though."

I pat his arm. "So, how're things, Poppy?"

"Fine, darling. All we ever eat is chicken around here, you know."

I nod.

"They don't like it, though," he nods toward the ants. "Chicken, I mean."

"Guess not," I say.

"Chrissie has grown into a lovely young woman." I don't

correct him on her name. I've always been sure he knows what her real name is, he just likes his version better. "Dresses funny, though."

"Gretel," I say, "from Humperdinck's opera."

"I thought it might be something like that." He shakes his head. "We missed her graduation. I don't know how that could have happened."

"It's OK, Pop." I sit down on the ground beside his chair.

"No," he says, "it's not." He looks up. "How's Frank?"

"He's fine, but Peter's sick so Frank stayed home with him. He sends his love."

My father's head dips down as he accepts this gift. A breeze, the first all afternoon, flutters the thin half-sleeves of his white shirt. "Not very sick, I hope."

"Just the flu," I say.

"That's good." He smiles, vaguely. "You missed Bert," he says.

It's downright cold out here. "Bert's dead, Pop."

"Oh, yes, that's right." He shakes his head. "Sometimes I forget."

I nod.

He ruffles his thin hair. "Knew him all my life." He stretches his legs out in front of himself and crosses his ankles. "Hard to remember he's not around anymore."

I nod in agreement, because I know exactly what he means.

"By the way," he says, "do you ever get a chance to sing anymore, Lilly, like you used to?" Shadows from the Lilly tree play games with his glasses as he looks at me.

"Not much. Sometimes in church. And at Christie's graduation I sang 'The Star-Spangled Banner.'"

"Solo?"

"No, me and everyone else. All you could hear was me, though."

He chuckles. "Solo," he says. He looks away, and hums a tune I vaguely remember. "Remember when I used to sing 'Summertime' to you when you were little?"

I nod. He was off-key then, and way off-key now, but when he tells me what he's humming I can pick it out.

"Pop, why do you have a washcloth on your head?"

He looks surprised. "It's hot out here, Lilly." He reaches under his chair and pulls out a small saucepan of water. Two ice cubes float lazily on the surface. "Ice melts too fast, though. I emptied a whole tray in here just a few minutes ago, while your mother watched for you. She didn't even turn around."

He slipped that in, that part about her watching. He's telling me that I mean a lot to her, no matter what it feels like sometimes. I know that.

He pulls the wet rag off his head and splashes around in the saucepan, then squeezes it out and puts it back on his head. It looks like a good idea to me.

He smiles when he says, "Chrissie didn't ask about it. Don't know if she didn't see it or what."

"She didn't want to embarrass you."

"Oh." He looks toward the house. "She think I didn't know I had a washcloth on my head?"

"She just wondered about it."

"She didn't ask me."

"She asked me."

He crosses his knees. "What'd you say?"

"I came out here."

He nods. "Your mother been talking?"

"About what?"

"Oh, anything?"

"Nothing in particular," I say. "Why?"

"Just wondered." He leans back in the green metal lawn chair. The washcloth is firmly plastered to the top of his head, a corner hangs over his right eyebrow. I can't see this man having an affair, but something *is* different about him and I don't know what it is. He seems at ease, but preoccupied. I think he's forgotten I'm here.

"I'm going to go help with dinner," I say, standing up.

He just nods.

When she lets me in the house I tell my mother, with a look in Christie's direction, how much I'm looking forward to spending a few days with her after I drop Christie off at school.

"Yes," she says, "we'll have a good talk."

Right.

Then I explain about the washcloth. Christie looks relieved. "I knew it was something like that." She smiles triumphantly, and goes upstairs.

I call Carole and we make arrangements to meet early. There's no point in talking now; we'll have plenty of time after we drop the girls off. Orientation begins at noon, so I say I'll come by around seven-thirty A.M.

As I wash lettuce for a salad I look out the window above the sink. I see my father get up and limp slowly out of the yard. My mother doesn't seem to know that he's gone, at least she doesn't mention it, but we both slow our preparations for dinner. I send Christie to Peg-Mel's grocery two blocks away, to get a lemon. No one ever asks what you need a lemon for, I figure; if it comes to that, I'll squeeze some over the salad. The truth is, I hope she'll run into him at the grocery sneaking red meat or something. But she returns with the lemon and says nothing, so I guess not.

About seven o'clock he comes home. I'm sure I smell whiskey on his breath but I don't say anything about it. My mother barely looks up from her plate. Christie chatters away while we eat, she has done that ever since she was a little girl. Her conversation bubbles up around us like an aerator in a fish tank, as she darts from one subject to the next, and I wonder what it will be like at home when she's gone. I picture what it would be like here, tonight, at this table, without Christie and me.

As I crawl into my old bed in my old room, I wonder if my mother could possibly be right, if my father really could be going to some woman's house. I know that my mother believes it. I think the real reason they didn't come for graduation is that she can scarcely move.

If he is, going out on my mother that is, I'm sure it's not something he's happy about. He's too straight-laced, like me. Neither of us look like we're straight-laced, but, underneath, where it counts, we have always been pretty boring people. One of us still is, and that's me; I'm not sure about the other of us, and I guess that's what I have to find out.

I close my eyes and dream of being taken away by a great adventure. The only thing I can come up with tonight is the usual prince; he leaps into my bedroom window and steals me away, right down the rope ladder. Singing. I've gotten pretty good at princes, and he's one of the best I've ever done—about twenty-five years younger than me, but then so am I, if you follow, and he's so crazy about me he can't take his eyes away, except when he has to fight off the red knight who wants me for himself. There are the usual chase scenes and the kung-fu fight scenes. It's pretty exciting, and my hair looks great.

But I have trouble sustaining fantasies for long; it's a real personality flaw. Tonight I can't help but wonder what it will be like at dinner with the prince, fifteen maybe twenty years down the road, when he's totally used to me. As I drift off to sleep, an ancient red knight totters across the room toward me and the prince keeps on eating.

Chapter Four

My plan of leaving quietly in the early morning light is wrecked when the station wagon won't start. It grinds and grinds, but nothing happens. I'm frantic. For one thing my parents are asleep, and it's important that they *stay* asleep, because the outfit Christie has on is so weird there is no way I could explain it to my mother. So, I just keep grinding, and humming, and finally it happens—the engine roars to life.

"God, Mom," says Christie.

Smoke pours from the tail pipe as we pull away from the curb, so about a block from the house I turn into an empty bank parking lot and rev the engine, blowing all that smoke to kingdom come. Frank's Taurus would have kept the family image up better, but I thought we might need more room. Besides, I'm not a snob about cars, and I'm used to this one's sag. I figure it's almost as old as Christie; it deserves to drive her to school.

I touch my bandanna to make sure it's on straight, and then double check myself in the rearview mirror.

"You look fine, Mom," Christie sighs.

I can't return the compliment, but I do my best to smile.

I wore the green bandanna today, to bring out the color of my eyes. Can you believe I thought of a detail like that? It's because of Carole. Carole notices everything, and every time I see her, no matter how good I think I look, she says I don't do enough with myself. But Carole only likes her own look. Once I figured that out, I could work with it. For this trip, for example, I bought a special outfit: plaid shirt, khaki slacks, boat shoes. I feel like an impostor. But my theory is that she'll be so dazzled by me today that tomorrow she won't even see my sweats.

I've known Carole Williams forever. She knows things about me that even Frank doesn't, like how good I was at hopscotch, and how much I hated the Girl Scouts, the kind of things you can't really *tell* anybody, because no one cares, but that are important to the scheme of the whole person. She's sort of the way Bert was to Poppy, I guess, except we haven't known each other as long yet. And—significant difference—Bert never found fault with anyone.

In the high-school yearbook we look young and eager. Under my picture it says, "Born to Sing," and under "Most Likely to Succeed" I came in second to Billy Birdwell, who was president of our class and wanted to be president of the United States. They were counting on me and Billy. I won't even tell you what happened to Billy, it's too depressing.

Carole wanted to be an actress, but she was too together,

I could have told her that. She didn't get listed under "Most Likely to Succeed" at all, even though she was prom queen, which made up for it at the time.

Now, when I see her waiting on the front steps of her house my heart does a little hop. Even though Carole's got control over her life with a capital C, and mine always seems to be going haywire, she's still my best friend, and we haven't seen each other for almost a year. The only thing that mars her perfect image is that brief episode when Melani was little. I like to remember it when Carole's acting too superior. It had to do with matches.

"There's Carole," I say to Christie.

"I can see her, Mom," she says, checking her reflection in the flip-down visor mirror.

As I said, Christie has mixed feelings about Melani coming with us. They used to play together when they were little, but they haven't seen each other in quite a while. And, she may be a little jealous of my friendship with Carole, which predates her. In honor of the occasion she wears Madame Butterfly's wedding kimono, and a light Kabuki makeup.

From here Melani looks like a clone of Carole, except that her dark hair is very long. She stands up and gives a shove to a huge suitcase, which slides down the front steps like a Dumpster on skis. It seems she's bringing at least as many, although probably not as interesting, clothes as Christie.

She and Carole look like mom and the perfect child, from the summer special issue of the Land's End catalog. It's times like this when I like to dwell on Melani's checkered past, which involved our garage.

As we get out of the car, Butterfly's kimono flaps open, and I see Christie's got on her SOCRATES T-shirt and jeans, an obvious backup outfit. She's probably testing the waters with Melani, or me; who knows? Carole and Melani are a little taken aback by Christie, I can tell. It's more the white face than anything else I think, but neither of them says anything. As we get closer, I notice Melani's eyes, the bluest eyes I've ever seen.

Carole hugs me, and I hug her back and then we stand apart and examine each other, while Christie and Melani hang back. This is the moment I wore my green bandanna for, the moment for which I bought this special outfit, that I personally feel makes me look like an idiot.

Carole, on the other hand, not only looks at home in her clothes, she looks terrific. Among other things, she's got on *shorts*, bright yellow shorts, not the kind I wear, that bag to the middle of my folded-over knees, but real shorts. And they look good. I'm clobbered by depression right there in her driveway. But I'm honest. It's one of my nicest characteristics.

"You look great, Carole," I say.

She pats me on the shoulder. "You do too," she says, and her eyes fill with tears. Carole always was a crier, it's just one of those things, and after years you get used to it. The attacks never last long, though; she doesn't have the attention span for it.

"Like my hair?" She pats the side of her neatly layered cut with long scarlet fingernails reminiscent of Melinda Jeffries, or a *Cosmopolitan* cover. Her hair used to be brown, regular brown. Today it's dark brown, not regular dark brown, but tar-pit brown.

"Passionate Abyss," she says. She turns toward Christie and Melani, seeking their approval, too.

"Nice," Christie says, staring. She's in her usual boneless pose, hand in pocket, with her weight on one foot and the other leg casually out in front. The kimono falls down her back like a cape, and her jeans are so tight I can't figure out how she'll ever get her hand out of her pocket.

"What do you mean, Passionate Abyss?" I ask, focusing on Carole.

"I enhanced my hair."

"What do you mean 'enhanced' it?"

"*Enhanced*, Lilly."

"You mean you *dyed* it?" I'm aghast.

"Just a little adjustment." She sticks her head under my face. "You should try it."

"You *dyed* your hair?"

"What's an abyss?" asks Christie.

"It's just a hole in the ground," says Melani. Now that I'm closer, I notice she's wearing huge dangle earrings, definitely hooker jewelry; they would never make it on a Land's End daughter.

"Sure, why not?" Carole flips open a compact and smiles at herself.

I can't think of any reason why not, exactly; it just seems, well, unsettling for Carole to have dyed her hair. On the other hand, it's done wonders for her. She looks like she's been sleeping for at least a month. Her eyes are a little more faded than the rest of her, but they're OK.

I stand up straight because Carole always said she hated being short. It doesn't give me all that much confidence; short or tall, she looks better than I do. As I said, I'm truthful, even when it kills me. So I have to acknowledge it again. "Carole, you look great!"

She grins. "I know." She pirouettes in front of me.

"You look nice too, Lilly," says Melani. Her bright blue eyes are soft and sensitive, but she doesn't stand up quite as straight as she probably should.

"All new clothes," offers Christie, for no good reason I can see.

"These old things?" I look down at my yachting outfit. "I pulled these out of the bottom drawer. You were so young when I got them you don't remember."

"They're new," she repeats to Melani.

Carole doesn't seem to be paying attention to any of it, she's so taken with herself. And I can't say I blame her. She has on a white T-shirt that just meets the waist of her shorts and forms the perfect background for her Deep Hole hair, or whatever it is. I, of course, even as we stand there talking, feel the one button on my one pair of nonelastic-waist pants, separate, and drop to the sidewalk, where it rolls around and around in ever smaller circles. It can only be overlooked if someone is being polite.

"Lilly, your button." Carole bends down and retrieves it for me.

"I knew I shouldn't have worn these old pants," I say with a look in Christie's direction.

She and Melani seem to have hit it off, though. They have left us and are dragging Melani's suitcase to the car, talking a mile a minute. They leave it by the rear door, thinking, I guess, that it will hop in by itself.

Carole wants to tell me something, I can feel it, and I know that whatever it is I'll wish it was happening to me. The mean part of me taps me on the shoulder and says, 'just don't ask, Lilly,' but the resigned part of me knows that sooner or later she'll tell me anyway, so I might as well cooperate. "Well?"

"Well, what?"

"Come on, Carole, out with it. What's up?"

She laughs deep inside her chest, a laugh I've never heard before; it must go with the hair. "You know me so well."

That seems to be all I'm going to get for the moment, because she turns and glides, that's the only word to describe it, back up the front steps and disappears into the house. She returns with a huge suitcase.

"What's that?" I ask.

"It's my suitcase." She grabs it with both hands and bangs it down the front steps. Over her shoulder is an enormous brown leather purse that could easily double as an overnight bag; I would have packed in it.

I touch the suitcase with my boat-shoed toe. "We're only going to be there one night."

"I like to change clothes." Now I do know Carole's got a real thing about clothes, so I shouldn't be surprised. In fact, if there was a word for nympho that referred to clothes, it'd be perfect for her. But this is a little much, even for my old pal.

Right then, Jeff Williams, number 44 on the Lakeview High football team of 1959, pops out of the open front door like a cardboard cutout in an FBI training maze. He's wearing a short-sleeved Hawaiian print shirt and blue jeans. His loafers are scuffed and comfortable-looking. He pauses at the top of the steps, blinking as if he just woke up; it's his contacts, though. Jeff's contact lenses never fit him right. The sun catches his various gold hangings, as he comes toward me grinning. "Lilly, Lilly, Lilly."

To Jeff, Lillylillylilly is my name. It always has been. He's got a new bald spot about the size of an egg, and he's put on a little weight, but he looks pretty good. I allow him to hug me for old times' sake.

He stands back and pats my head. "Love those curls, kiddo, always did."

"Thanks," I say. "Some people think I should dye my hair."

"Enhance." Carole suppresses a yawn. "*Enhance* your hair, Lilly."

"I like red hair," Jeff says.

"So do I," I say.

Carole brushes off the toe of one of her new, fang white tennis shoes. "It could be redder. I've always said you could do—"

"I've got my hands full with Christie."

"Yes," Carole nods, "I didn't think of that."

Jeff looks toward the car. "Is Christie over there? I haven't seen her for years."

Is he ever in for a surprise. He walks across the driveway like he's on springs. The car's too far away for us to hear what they're saying, but, judging from the way Jeff shifts his weight from foot to foot, bent, looking in the car, it's probably a nice conversation. After a few minutes he turns and comes back to us.

"She's almost as pretty as her mama," he says. He must actually think she's sickly, or maybe a vampire, but I guess if you sell cars all your life, you learn how to keep a straight face.

"Melani has beautiful eyes," I say to return the favor.

"Contacts," smiles Carole, turning away. "The color's a little off, though."

I want to tell her petite back that the beautiful blue may not be real, but the gentleness of the eyes is.

Jeff takes my hand between both of his and squeezes it. "You're right about that," he says.

I can only hope I said it nicely. I adjust my bandanna.

He hangs one of his huge arms around my shoulder again and I get the feeling he's showing Carole something. I don't think he wants to make her jealous, it's something else; it's as if he's reminding her we're friends, that we've been friends, the three of us, for a long time. We have a history.

He's much softer than he was during his high-school football years, and the old heartiness seems a little forced. Actually, he looks a lot like his father. I remember Mr. Williams, a cheering section all on his own. I used to give him my program after every game, so he'd have an extra. After high school Jeff joined his dealership, and they cheered themselves down the field of car sales until they owned businesses all over the state.

"How's old Frank?" he asks, folding his arms across his chest; his hangings make him gleam like an overweight sun god.

"He's fine," I say.

"Still doing law?" he asks. He scratches his head which leaves his hair ruffled around the bald spot like weeds around a duck egg.

I nod. "He likes being in court."

"All that power," Jeff nods sagely.

I don't resent it. He's right.

"Compensates for Christie and Peter and me," I offer.

He laughs. "Lillylillylilly, you're a card."

Jeff's eyes keep wandering to Carole, who moves restlessly from one delicate foot to the other. When he looks at her, the rest of us disappear, sort of like my prince fantasy.

"We should have done this in a day," I say to her.

Carole has turned away from the sun, so the three of us are facing the same way in an uncomfortable little line. "I'm glad we're staying over," she says, "we need to see a little of Melville."

"And gab." Jeff slaps us both on the back. "I know you gals. Once you get together, you'll talk your heads off."

"We haven't done that for ages," sighs Carole, looking at me like a long-lost friend.

"Tell it to my phone bill," I say, just to set the record straight for Frank's sake.

"Lillylillylilly, you're a card."

It's odd that Jeff thinks I'm a such a riot, because I never say anything really funny to him. That's not to say I'm not a funny person sometimes, but it's always when I tell Jeff something perfectly true that he falls down laughing. This morning I ramble on and on, mainly because he seems uncomfortable about saying good-bye, and I don't know what else to do. Carole doesn't help at all. In fact, she makes me nervous because she's straining from one foot to the other, like a hot-air balloon on a gusty day. Finally I run out of things to say. Jeff slaps me on the back again, and says, "Lillylillylilly, what a life, eh?" He really appreciates a talker.

"Yup." I nod.

"We'd better go," says Carole. "We'll be late."

Since we've allowed time to change several flat tires and then look around Melville a little before we drop off the girls, there is no way we can be late, but I say OK.

Jeff nods and picks up her suitcase; he heaves it, and Melani's, into the back and slams the door shut.

"Heavy," he says, his broad face flushed. He hitches his

pants up but they weren't going anywhere. "What do you need all that stuff for, babycakes?"

Carole leaves the open car door to pat his cheek. Her fingernails are a true masterpiece, I can't help but notice, maybe even better than Melinda's. "We have to dress so the girls can be proud of us," she says.

He beams down on her like she's a goddess.

I try to imagine this conversation between Frank and me, the looks, the touches, but it's easier to imagine a prince climbing up my rope ladder.

"I didn't bring much," I say.

"Lilly, you don't do *enough* with yourself." Carole pats her hair as if it was the waggy little rump of an adorable puppy.

"I do the best I can," I sigh.

"You could do a lot more," she says.

"If we run into anyone you know, you can say I was raised by wolves."

She ignores me and turns back to Jeff. "Jeffy, don't forget to feed Muffin."

Jeff pats her head. "Don't worry, Lambie, I'll feed the puddy tat."

I hit the ignition thinking, car, don't show me up now. She kisses his cheek and twists away. "OK, Lilly," she says, and flaps her hand at me like I'm a chauffeur or something.

I let out the clutch and we jerk away from the curb. Puddy tat? Carole tinkles her fingers out the window at Jeff, the flutter of a hummingbird's wing.

"Bye, Daddy," calls Melani, waving out the window. I see that she too has long and beautifully sculpted fingernails. It makes me want to drive with my teeth.

What could Carole be saving up to tell me? What could she possibly get that she doesn't have already?

I get a clear flashback of Howard Woolfe; of the scene at the restaurant; of Frank asleep with his mouth open as Christie and I leave—and my stupid yellow Post-it on the pillow. Why is my family so unfamily-like? I've put a lot into them. Giving up the opera would have been easier on me if I'd gotten a normal family in exchange. I grind the gears.

"Really, Mom," Christie leans forward. "What's your problem?"

I gun the engine and the car lurches forward.

"Mom!"

"Accelerator stuck. Suitcases OK?"

The girls look behind them. "Fine," they say.

"All the weight's in the back," I say, bouncing a significant look through the mirror to the luggage.

"I need all that," Carole says defensively.

"We won't even *see* the girls after this morning."

She eyes me. "We're going to college," she says. She turns away from me, and looks at the girls in the backseat. "I never went to college," she says, which everyone in the car knows. "Neither did Lilly." She pats my arm.

"I went to music school, Carole, like I *wanted*."

"That's not *college*, Lilly." She sighs and examines her fingernails in case I've missed them. "I wish I were going."

I can tell from her voice she's not kidding.

"I bet Lilly does, too," she adds.

"No I don't."

"Yes you do, Lilly." She curls one tiny leg up under the other. If I did that my head would go through the roof.

"It wouldn't be all that great, Mom," says Melani, patting her mother's arm. Her unnaturally blue eyes do look fake, once you know, but I can tell she's trying to be nice so I smile at her in the rearview mirror.

"Yeah," says Christie. "All that studying." She flops back in the seat and groans.

"I'd love it," says Carole, who got through high school copying my papers. "I love to know things."

"You do know things, Carole," I say. She's obviously headed for outer space.

"But not the *right* things, Lilly."

"Like what?" I ask.

"Like anything," she says unhelpfully. "Lilly, we are ignorant."

"I am not ignorant."

She looks at me. "Do you read the newspaper?"

"Of course," I say.

"You probably don't read the right paper."

"The *New York Times*? The *New York Times* is not the right paper?"

"You don't read the *New York Times*, Lilly."

"Of course I read the *New York Times*. Why would I bring it up if I didn't?"

"Dad reads it, actually," says Christie.

"We both read it," I snarl.

"Don't get so upset, Mom. He tells you what's going on." She drums her fingers on the armrest in time to some noxious teenage sound in her head. "You're probably pretty well informed, considering."

"Considering what?" I narrow my eyes in the rearview mirror, but she's not even looking at me. She's watching in fascination as Melani braids her hair with gimp.

"I should have gone to college," Carole continues with a sigh.

"So go now," I say.

"It's not that easy."

She's sitting very still beside me and if I could see her, head on, I know there'd be tears in her eyes again. I look sideways, as close as is safe at sixty-five miles an hour in a car that's dragging its rear end down the highway. She is definitely not happy. Her hands are folded in her lap like white tulips except the knuckles look knobby. In fact, her hands don't look as rested as the rest of her.

"I have to get control of my life," she says almost to herself, and the tulips quiver briefly in the bright yellow pool of her lap.

"Carole, that's nuts. If anyone has control of anything it's you. Look at you. You look wonderful."

She's pleased and flashes me a big wet smile. "Yes I do, don't I?"

"She plays tennis," Melani calls from the backseat. She's wrapped the extra gimp around the door handle and is digging into her purse for something. "Morning, noon, and night."

I look at Carole, who, if memory serves, is about as athletic as an eggplant. "This may be a stupid question," I say, "but how can you play tennis with those fingernails?"

She fans her fingers out in front of her. "Do you like them?"

"They're OK I guess, but how do you hold a racket?"

"Oh, I just pop them off."

"Off?"

"Sure. They're fake." She starts to bend one back.

"Never mind," I say.

"Are you sure, Lilly? It's really interesting. There's Velcro underneath."

"No thanks."

"OK." She clasps her hands back in her lap. "You should get some of these. They're not very expensive. I have them in lots of colors."

"Maybe I will," I lie, just to shut her up.

"Of course, there's more to looking good than just fingernails, and tennis," she says. "I've changed my life. No red meat, no liquor, no cream, no cheese, no sweets, just good, good food. And a little jog. I jog six miles a day."

Now I *am* depressed. I can't do that. I don't even want to do that.

"I'm serious about this," she says, in case I was going to say something mean. "I subscribe to a lot of magazines." She bends over and pulls a bunch of health magazines out of her purse. "I brought some of them along, Lilly. It might help."

"Help what?" I ask, wondering even as I ask it how I could have been so stupid as to let those words out.

But she doesn't have a chance to fill me in, because Melani whips a mirror out of her pocket, examines her small, white teeth, and says, "She also had a face-lift."

I take my eyes completely off the road and stare at Carole.

"Mom!" Christie screams from behind me.

I'm approaching the car in front of us at about ninety miles an hour. "I see it Christie," I say peevishly.

I brake, drop back, and then glance at Carole again. It's no wonder she looks like a cover girl for *Seventeen*. I could jog my brains out and never look like that. "How could you have a face-lift without telling me?" I ask her.

"I thought you might try to stop me." She licks a scarlet fingernail, and polishes it against her shorts.

"Why would I try to stop you?"

"Because, quote you, anyone who gets a face-lift is crazy."
Her voice quivers.

"I never said that." I glance at her sideways again, quickly.
"When was it?"

"That you said it?"

"No, that you did it."

"Three months ago."

"Three months! Carole, I've talked to you two or three
times in the last three months. Why didn't you tell me?"

Carole sniffles, and a tear rolls down her new cheek.

Christie stares at Carole. "Mom, you're making her cry!"

"I am not."

"You are too. Look. She's crying."

"That's just something she does, Christie. It doesn't mean
anything."

"Mom!"

A sad sound catches in Carole's throat.

I'm defeated. "OK, OK."

"You get used to it after a while," says Melani, putting
her mirror away. She smiles at me so I'll know *she* doesn't
blame me.

Carole dabs up the tear with a cotton ball. Melani talks to
me in the mirror. "She made me do tennis so I wouldn't get
in with druggies." She glances sideways at Christie and they
fall apart laughing.

"What's so funny?" I ask.

"Jocks are all druggies, Mom," Christie explains, adjusting
her kimono.

"No they aren't," I say.

"OK, they aren't," says Christie. She turns back to Melani.
"Then what?"

"The coach is a health freak," says Melani. "You wouldn't believe what we eat now." She wrinkles her nose.

"Bad?"

"The worst!"

"We eat some pretty yuck stuff too," offers Christie, "and it's not even healthy."

This seems like a good time to count. I do that sometimes when I can't sleep, or when I'm trying to think about a neutral subject. I've only gotten to about ten, when Melani leans closer to Christie and lowers her voice.

"There's more," she says.

Naturally I break off counting and listen.

"The coach hit on her. It was a riot." She laughs her little blue-eyed head off at the thought. "Of course, my mom didn't get it."

This I personally doubt. Carole's not looking at me but I know her so well I can feel her wanting to—it's as if she has her hand on my arm. For something to do, she bends over and centers the pink footlet bobbles that hang from the back of each new tennis shoe.

Melani swats the window with her gimped braid. "He's cute too."

Christie is interested. "No one hits on my mom," she says.

"Maybe you just don't know," says Melani.

"Nope. No one." She leans over the seat and grabs a package of Certs out of my purse.

Melani reaches for one. "The coach says he needs her on the team."

"That's a joke, Melani." Carole sounds bored. "Don't eat those things." She pulls a little brown bottle out of her purse, and holds it over the seat. "Vitamin C is much better for you."

"See," says Melani, "vitamin pills everywhere." She takes a Cert and hands Christie the package.

"I have to go to the bathroom," says Christie.

That's good as far as I'm concerned, because I need to get off the road before I get another ticket, not to mention I'm starving. I look for an exit.

"There's a McDonald's." Melani points at the golden arches, a neon M in the sky. M for mother, marvelous mothers. I have always known that's what the arches stand for. It's the only way I can eat the food.

I turn off the highway and head for the M like a homing pigeon. Carole pulls a magazine called *The Healthy Heart* out of her purse and starts to read the section on fast food aloud. We leave her in the car.

I eat a Big Mac inside, and order fries and a strawberry shake for the road. The new in-shape Carole has me worried. She has really gone crazy. And she is *serious*, there's no question about it. The way I figure it, if a person's going to get serious, they should get serious about the homeless or the national debt or something. Besides, I can't help but feel a face deserves to sag after a while; it wouldn't be fair to jack it up just when it thinks it can relax.

Chapter Five

Melville looks pretty much how I expected it to look; a typical college town, or at least what I'd always thought of as a typical college town. There are narrow streets that need repaving, old houses that need repainting, and big trees, lots of them.

The closer to the center of town we get, the more shops there are. Small storefronts exhibit offbeat clothes and belly-dancer jewelry in their windows, neon lights blink SALE, posters beckon—all clues to the new arrivals to leave the recreational spending hours open.

Melani and Christie press against the car windows like little kids. This is one of those land of Oz kind of places they never thought they'd be lucky enough to live without their mothers. They get quiet, though, the more we drive around.

The town advertises its connection to the college, a little overboard even, but it's a relief to me. Bolton banners, charms, T-shirts, mugs, underwear, key chains, nightgowns, sweats, jackets, jewelry, headbands, wristbands, shoes, watches, and umbrellas are for sale everywhere. Connie's Pet Fit blinks in neon that Connie has Bolton sweatshirts for any size dog, and the undertaker has a Bolton bumper sticker on the coffin in his window. Either there isn't any town-gown rivalry, or they're overcompensating.

"Isn't this exciting?" coos Carole.

No one answers her.

We drive down Fuller Street, the main drag. Hundreds of old sneakers dangle above us from the telephone wires.

"That's a fraternity prank," announces Carole. "Fraternities do that kind of thing."

"Keep your eyes open for the auditorium," I say, hoping to find the place we're supposed to take the girls without too much trouble.

"That's sexist, Mom," says Melani, batting the back of her mother's head affectionately with her braid.

"How is it sexist?" Carole twists to look at her daughter.

"A sorority could have done it," Melani says. "Why not?" She looks at Christie. "I want to be in a sorority."

"Me too," says Christie, who has told me at least a hundred times she would die first.

"Those are big shoes, Melani," says Carole. "They are obviously men's shoes."

"Maybe they raided the boys' gym," says Christie, looking at Melani, who nods encouragement.

"Whoever did it," I say, "obviously does not pay for their own shoes."

"God, Mom, you sound like Dad." Christie is buffing some of the makeup off her face with a sock.

Carole has been twisting around in her seat, and now she spots what we're looking for. "The auditorium!" she says, and points down a side street that goes off to the right. I turn at the next corner.

As auditoriums go, it's perfect. It even has a dome on top. It's made of some kind of stone, and it's covered with ivy. Frank would have made me pull it all off, the ivy I mean, if that were our house, which fortunately it isn't. I have always liked ivy.

This is where the new students are supposed to gather for announcements and instructions. Five sceni-cruiser buses, their luggage hatches open like whales scooping krill, are parked in the circular drive in front of the building. Each one is marked with the name of a dorm and there are already lots of bags on the sidewalk.

"There's Hooperman," shouts Melani, pointing to the third one in the row of buses.

This is the dorm Melani and Christie have been assigned, so I pull over to the curb. For obvious reasons the amount of luggage we have to dump does not bother Carole, who could use a sceni-cruiser of her own, so she helps the girls drag it out. I stay with the car in a very illegal parking space, protected from the law as nowhere else by my fragile status as a freshman mom.

When they come back they're hot to explore.

"Park the car, Mom," Christie says, "we want to walk around."

"Isn't this great?" says Carole, practically bouncing up and down in her seat. "C'mon, Lilly, park."

The visitor parking lot turns out to be behind the Bolton Student Union, and Melani and Christie decide they want to check out the snack possibilities in the Union. That's fine with me. When we get out of the car, Christie leaves Madame Butterfly's kimono behind.

Carole practically faints with delight when she sees that they have a health-food section. She orders a poppy-seed juice, and goes off to save us a table. The girls move to another station for coney dogs and Cokes; I get coffee. Carole has all her health magazines and brochures, order blanks, everything, spread out on the table when we get back, but we just put our stuff on top of them, since there's nowhere else to put anything. I'm sure that deep down she wishes she had my coffee, but she *wants* to believe in all this other junk. It worries me. In my personal opinion, she's not enjoying the aging process.

"Vitamin C?" she asks, holding out a handful of her little white pills.

What can it hurt? I take one.

"You need two, Lilly," she says.

I take another.

The girls ignore us both, because it is definitely not cool to be with your mothers, especially when one of them is handing out vitamin C.

The Bolton Union is practically empty. Except for a few family groups like us, the main cafeteria area is quiet. The brown Formica tables are shiny and clean, waiting for September when everyone comes back to school. The kids eye each other. They are all pretending to be at least seniors, I can tell; there's not a freshman in the room, including our two. The whole place quivers like a bowstring about to let fly.

As I look around I feel the same pang I felt at graduation, for so much innocence. I take a huge sip of my coffee, and burn my mouth. It's a coping mechanism. "Damn!" I say, sticking my tongue out and sucking in air. As a kid I dug my fingernails into my hand in a painful situation (like the dentist). In adulthood I've replaced it with hot coffee drinking, especially for pains in the heart.

"She does that all the time," sighs Christie.

But Carole's in la-la land, and doesn't comment. She still wants to go to college.

"Well?" she asks. Her eyes are open wide with wonder. Looking critically, I think they opened wider in the old days.

"Well, what?" asks Melani.

"Well, Bolton, of course," says Carole. "Isn't it wonderful?"

"It's OK, I guess." Melani wipes chili off her mouth with a neat little paper napkin swipe.

"OK?" Carole stands up and strides over to one of the tall windows that look out on the campus. She pulls aside the curtain and turns to us. "Look at it, girls. Is this a college, or is this a college?"

"Mom, sit down. *Please*," Melani whispers under her breath.

The other "seniors" are so happy this isn't happening to them, they can't take their eyes off her.

"Don't worry, Melani," I lean over and pat her hand. "No one will think she's your mother. Face-lift." I give her a wink.

She smiles weakly.

"Darling," Carol calls, "come over here and look." She

leans forward on the ledge. "That must be a classroom building. Maybe you'll have classes in that one."

"I might be wrong," I say, and get up. I cross the room and join her at the window. "It's nice, Carole."

"Nice?" She turns and stares at me incredulously. "God, Lilly."

"Carole," I whisper, "you've got poppy seeds in your teeth."

"I do?"

I nod.

She looks stricken. "Get them out," she says, "get them *out!*" She puts a finger in each side of her mouth and pulls, baring her teeth completely. Behind us, Melani is under the table pretending to wipe up a spill. Christie's down there with her.

I pick out the poppy seeds and lead Carole back to the girls. They have to come back up to their chairs now that our feet are under the table, but they keep their eyes down.

I look around at the mostly empty tables and imagine them covered with term papers, half-eaten food, and bike locks. The girls will be here a long time, and they'll be so different when they come out. "You'll be here a long time," I say out loud. Something inside me is stretching like elastic about to break.

"Yes," Christie sighs.

"Food's good," says Melani cheerfully.

"We want to share this experience," says Carole, her eyes filling with tears. "We want to hear your plans."

"What plans?" asks Melani, licking the tip of her little finger and shaping her eyebrow.

"Be careful," says Christie. "My mom goes nuts when you share plans."

"Huh?"

"On the way here," Christie has their attention, "she got a ticket because of it."

"A *speeding* ticket?" Carole asks in a tone that makes me want to put the poppy seeds back in her teeth.

"That's ridiculous, Christie," I say. "Besides, we're not in the car now."

"Don't upset her in the car," Christie continues, stretching her long legs out and admiring her ankles. "She gets millions of tickets."

"I almost never get an actual ticket," I say.

"You got a *ticket*?" Carole leans toward me.

"What did you tell her, anyway?" asks Melani.

"Didn't *you* ever get a ticket?" I ask Carole.

"Tell you later," says Christie.

"Of course not," says Carole.

"I don't believe it," I snap.

"Caffeine's making you jumpy, Lilly." Carole smiles. Then she looks around dreamily, and she's off again. "These are the best years of your lives, girls. Don't you think so, Lilly?"

"Maybe."

"I'm sure they are. We missed them." Her dark hair reflects the lamp hanging above our table.

"Missed what?"

"Our best years."

"We had best years, Carole, they just weren't college years."

"What were they then?" she asks and leans forward.

Fortunately Melani breaks in. "Is it time to go yet?"

I look at my watch, but before I can say anything, Christie pushes her chair back and jumps up.

"Howard!" she cries.

Howard? My heart stops.

She runs off and I reach into my purse for my glasses.

"Someone she knows?" asks Carole. She squints toward the two-person blur across the room.

I put on my glasses and bring them into focus. "Yes," I say.

They are walking hand in hand toward the table. Christie's wide, beautiful smile lights up the room.

Here in the Bolton Union, Howard, whom I now understand is an artist, looks even more out of place than he did at home. Bolton College is a sophisticated environment only in the sense that the facilities are good and the faculty distinguished. The students are mostly from the Midwest. There are few eccentricities apparent here, hence the leaving of Butterfly's kimono in the car. Howard, wearing a large question-mark earring, the usual green high-tops, and today, for some reason known only to himself and his muse, a kilt, stands out.

"Yo, Mrs. Blake."

I remove my glasses. It doesn't help; he's still there.

"Yo, Howard," I say.

Melani is absorbed in Howard's appearance, and who wouldn't be? Carole is unreadable.

Christie says, "This is Howard Woolfe." She adds, proudly, "my boyfriend," and smiles up at him as if he's quite a catch.

Carole nods, Melani smiles. Howard gives Melani the eye. He winks approval. She twists a loose strand of her long brown hair around and around a finger, watching him with her turquoise blue eyes. For a brief moment I think maybe he'll . . . but no, I can't wish that. Even under the present circumstances, and even a person with as little conscience as I, can't wish that. Howard needs to be taken out, capital O-U-T, OUT, not moved over to someone else. California should do it, if we can only get him there.

"Why are you here, Howard?" I ask, pleased at how controlled I sound.

"I knew you were worried about Christie, Mrs. Blake. I could tell by the way you broke down at graduation and all."

Carole touches my hand. "You broke down at graduation?"

"It was partly him," I say before I can stop myself.

Christie looks at me like I'm a squid, but Carole understands.

"That's OK, Mrs. Blake. I'll grow on you." He hangs over Christie like Spanish moss. "I've come so you can relax."

"That doesn't do it for me, Howard," I say, resisting the urge to scratch a very annoying spot on my neck.

"When you think about it, this is the best thing that could happen, me showing up I mean."

"You should go home, Howard," I say.

"I know you're just trying to be brave, Mrs. B.," he says. "Everybody knows how you feel about Christie leaving." He leaves Christie's side and squeals a chair across the floor to straddle it beside me. "I like to help people out. I'd be a good psychiatrist."

I scratch both elbows at the same time. "Does your mother know where you are?" There is something painted on his knee. The letters are upside down, a personal message to himself.

"Nah, she wouldn't care."

"I think you're wrong, Howard."

"You think I should call her?" He tugs at his ear. "I'll only be here a week."

"You're staying the whole week?" Christie sneaks a look at me, but her green eyes don't give much away.

"Yep." He grins. Then he lowers his voice. "I hitchhiked out here—some real weirdos picked me up."

"Nobody wants to hear, Howard." His knee says CHRISTIE TODAY.

"*I* want to hear," says Christie.

"Then ask Howard another time. We all know it's dangerous to hitchhike."

"But do people know *why*?" asks Howard. "I do, if anyone wants to know."

"Everyone knows. You were crazy to do it," I say. I'm pushing my short, stubby, unpolished fingernails into the rim of my styrofoam coffee cup.

"Most people've only heard about it." He sits forward on his chair. "I mean, I *know*."

"Howard," I say, "it upsets me to think that anyone, especially anyone your age, would get into a car with a stranger." Across from me Christie's sort of low in her chair. I think she's trying to kick me, but she's too far away.

"Strange is right! You just wouldn't believe what's out on the road." He shakes his head so that the question mark swats his cheek. He must like it, because he keeps on doing it.

"Howard," I push my chair back.

"OK, Mrs. B. You're sensitive. I remember about the camera and all. Don't want to shake you up." He pats me on the shoulder.

Carole comes to my rescue just when I'm about to show

him strange. "Where are you staying?" she asks.

"Ah." He leans back and laces his hands across his stomach. "I got a deal. There's this shack in front of the library. Some guys built it, but they have to take it down every night at eleven unless someone's in it—if they don't it's considered a billboard or something so it's illegal. I offered to sleep in it for 'em."

"What's it for?" asks Melani. From this angle, her contacts reflect the plaid shirt she's wearing.

"Protest," says Howard. "It's a protest shack. I knew what it was the minute I saw it."

"What are they protesting?" asks Carole.

Howard shrugs. "Didn't ask." He looks at each of us in turn with his moon-eyed look. "They're real committed, though."

"What if it isn't something you believe in?" asks Melani.

"Oh, I believe in it all." He examines his hairy leg. "I'm thinking of becoming a vegetarian."

This may trick Carole into thinking he's a regular guy, which would be terrible because I want her on my side. But I can only worry about one thing at a time.

"You have to be in there from eleven P.M. on?"

"Yup. But anyone can visit me." He grins broadly.

"Except for Christie and Melani," I say. "They have to be in the dorm at eleven. There are activities."

"Sure," says Howard with an open wink at my daughter. I close my eyes and enjoy a brief fantasy of sending him to the moon with a super kick in the butt.

"What time is it, Mom?" Christie manages to sound perfectly normal.

I look at my watch. "Time to get you two where you're supposed to be." We all stand. "Howard, you really shouldn't have come." I say. "Christie won't have any free time. She's supposed to learn about Bolton this week."

"I know, Mrs. B. Don't worry about me. I'll just be her little shadow." He picks up the leftover half of Christie's chili dog and downs it with one bite.

I suspect Christie is looking at me, but I don't look back. "Let's go," I say, and start walking.

"Wait up," calls Carole, grabbing her handbag and stuffing the brochures inside. She hurries after me.

We walk in a straight line, more or less, toward the auditorium, with me in the lead and the others straggling behind. I'm moving at a pretty good clip because I want to deposit my daughter in other hands, hands that have, I hope, every minute of her time planned.

Somewhere along the way Howard disappears. I want to pretend he's not here at all, but then we pass the shack, it must be the shack, a lean-to made of scrap lumber, cardboard, and old newspapers, right in the center of the campus green. A message painted on the side in white reads, 'WHAT DO RAIN FORESTS, WHALES, NUCLEAR WASTE, AND THE HOMELESS HAVE IN COMMON?' No answer is given, so it's unclear whether or not there simply is no answer to this complex question, or there wasn't enough space to answer it.

An old Doris Day tune slips in and out of my mind—"Que Será, Será" and I start to hum, overcoming its basic blandness with a flair all my own. Moments into it Christie's tugging at my sleeve.

"Jesus, Mom!"

I put my arm around her. "OK, OK." I walk slower and hum quietly, switching to "Over the Rainbow," a good place for Howard.

There are lots of parents and their teenage children in the lobby of the auditorium by now. It's hard to tell the mothers from the kids because most women, it seems, have either been working on the bod, or know how to dress it pretty good. And they are *all* wearing dark glasses, Carole and me included. Inside the auditorium, when we take them off, the differences are easy to spot. It's all in the eyes. I wonder if Carole sees it. You could fall into the eyes of most of the mothers, and there's something there, like with Mrs. Woolfe, that makes you want to cry.

There are fewer fathers here. Most have a soft midsection over their belts and a lot of them are losing their hair, but on the whole they seem a more contented bunch. They joke with the kids and ignore the wives. Men are more reality oriented, in my opinion, which makes life a little easier to take. I never deal with the exact situation at hand.

Like this thing with Howard. What's the worst that could happen? I can't pinpoint it, exactly. When I really think about it, I know that Howard's only a slightly eccentric young person. His skin probably does not zip off, he's not a lizard-person like on TV, and I probably won't have a lizard grandchild.

Anyway, we're herded into the auditorium for a pep talk about separation. The hall is dark, cool, and red velvet. I could stay in here all day, because I'm not ready to separate, but of course the parents are soon dismissed. We make arrangements to meet our kids back here on Friday at three P.M. There's a lot of rustling and coughing and talking, and then the parents straggle out, a little more slowly than they straggled in.

As we pass his shack, Howard leans out and waves. He has the nerve to grin at me. It's like my nightmare has followed me into the light of day. Probably behind him, in the darkness of his shack where I can't see it, he's swishing his tail. It's just something I know is happening at this very moment.

Chapter Six

I need to talk to Frank before I get carried away with this lizard thing. He's a good check on my imagination, since he doesn't have any. Today I'm able to see that his way may not be all bad.

Carole remembers there were some pay phones at the Union, so we head back there. On the way we're stopped by a man in brown Bolton coveralls, with LARRY printed on the pocket in neat blue letters. He tips his Bolton hat brim, and I see he's wearing gardening gloves, covered with dirt, so I guess he must be on the grounds crew. I'm about to tell him how nice everything looks, when, "Ma'am," he says to me, "auditorium's back that way," he nods in Carole's direction, "for orientation."

It puts the cap on my day. Carole pretends she didn't hear.

It's kind I suppose, but maybe she's a little embarrassed too. "She's very high-strung," I say. "Can't handle crowds."

"Oh," he says, stealing a sideways look at her.

"We're going to get her bear. She left it in the car." Carole glares at me. I smile. There's nothing to say.

The telephone booth is dark and sticky. It's not somewhere I want to stay for long. I just want to tell Frank about Howard. But no one's at home. I dial the number three times, but the phone just rings and rings.

I can see it all, and I know it's my fault; the phone booth fades and I'm standing in the middle of my living room looking down at Peter and Frank. They can't answer the phone, they're dead, of course. Frank caught whatever Peter had and they never thought to call a doctor because I always do that for them. There can be no other explanation. By the time I make up my mind to call the office, I've got myself in such a state my hands are shaking.

Polly Wagoner, Frank's secretary, answers the phone on the fourth ring, chewing. She's irritated because she hates to answer the phone when she's eating, which is most of the time.

"Blake, Hayes, Marsh, and Johnstone," she says, and swallows somewhere between Hayes and Marsh.

"Hi, Polly," I say. "It's me."

A cellophane wrapper crackles like a campfire at the other end of the line.

"Who?" she says.

"Me, Lilly Blake."

"Oh, Mrs. Blake. All the partners' wives say 'it's me.'" She lowers her voice to a whisper. "Even Mrs. Johnstone. The new one. Naturally I recognize her voice."

Naturally.

Harvey Johnstone's post-midlife crisis involved dumping his wife of thirty-five years and marrying Lucille, the hat-check girl at Heidi's. She could give Christie a run for her money in the wardrobe department. Harvey looks like he's been struck by lightning. I ask for Frank.

"He's not in," she says. "Haven't seen him all day."

This is bad news. "Have you heard from him?" I ask.

"Nope," she says. I hear a nail file at work in the background.

"Any idea where he is?" I ask.

"Nope. Wish I did, though. He's had a lot of calls."

I think about asking her to check the house, but if they aren't dead it would be pretty embarrassing. "Well, give him this number, OK?" I read it off the crumpled paper I forgot to leave for Frank, "790-0452. The area code's 218. It's the motel, in Melville."

"Sure, Mrs. Blake."

When I hang up, my damp fingers have added another layer of prints to the sticky phone.

Carole is seated in a booth on the other side of the room. "Lilly, you look terrible! Come sit down—I've got something for you." She waves her hand across the table, pleased with what she has done for me. There are two thin sandwiches on paper plates in front of her, their contents some kind of twisted green stuff that hangs from the edges of what look like flattened bricks. It would take a rack of ribs and a couple of pieces of chocolate-chip cheesecake to give me comfort now, but I'm touched.

For once we are quiet. In fact, I almost forget Carole's sitting across the table from me. My mind hops up and down like a pogo stick; Christie loses her virginity to Howard; my mother and father get divorced after almost fifty long years; Frank and Peter lie side by side on the living-room floor. I put my head in my hands and try to shut them all out.

Carole tugs at my sleeve. "Maybe we ought to go check in, Lilly. The motels are full this week."

"OK," I say, but I can't put much enthusiasm in my voice.

She balls up the waxed-paper wrappers from our sandwiches and tosses them in the gaping mouth of a huge trash can by the door.

The station wagon looks old and tired as we walk toward it. I could have it painted, but Frank says that's a waste. I decide not to mention this to Carole, for the obvious reason.

The motel is clean and bright with a restful pale beige carpet on the lobby floor, and the smell of room deodorizer in the air. The young girl behind the counter is cheerful and efficient, and she's about Christie's age. Her name, Noreen Kelly, is pinned slightly askew on her collar. She's pleased I have my confirmation number. "Most people don't," she says. "You'd be so surprised." She has curly brown hair and wide dark eyes, and she smiles at me as if I've really done something good.

Of course, I only have it because Frank taped it to his car keys. HIS car keys! Great. I've not only got his shaving stuff, I've got his keys too.

"Who's Frank?" Noreen asks.

"Oh, nobody," I say, guiltily pocketing the keys.

"If there's anything I can help with," she says, "give me a call."

"Do you go to school here?" I ask.

"At BC?"

"Uh huh."

"Yes?" There's a flicker of suspicion in her eyes and I'm reminded she doesn't know me. I could be one of Howard's highway weirdos, just in off the road after a killing spree.

I look as foursquare as possible; my outfit helps. "My daughter's going here," I say.

"Oh." She sounds relieved. "I'm taking summer school."

"Do you like it?" I'm thinking she would be a nice friend for Christie, who right now doesn't even *know* anybody but Melani.

"It's OK." The girl hands me a comment card. "For when you leave. What's your daughter like?"

I realize she's a little hard to describe, and I don't answer right away.

"I mean, is she tough? You've got to be tough to stick it out here."

Carole is over looking at a rack of pamphlets about places of interest in the area, like caves and waterfalls and pick-ur-own strawberry farms. There's no way we have time to go on any field trips, but she never could keep her eye on the ball. "What do you mean tough?"

"The place is big." Noreen shrugs. "Easy to get lost in."

"I see." My voice is quivery, even I can hear it.

"But she'll be fine. Most are."

I put the comment card in my purse. "She'll be in the dorm," I say.

"They say the dorm's real wild." She blushes, and scratches her cheek with her NOREEN pin. "Sorry. I didn't mean to say that. I live at home."

"You do?"

"My parents make me."

"They do?"

She nods. "It's OK. I'm sort of a boring person."

"I'm sure you're not a boring person," I say. "How far from campus is your parents' house?"

I'm thinking Christie might move in, and I'm just getting into it when Carole leaves the rack, grabs my arm and the room keys, and pulls me away.

"Thanks," she calls over her shoulder. She hands me a pamphlet on the zoo. "This looks nice, doesn't it?"

I give it back to her. "Carole, did you hear what that girl said?"

"Yes, I did, Lilly, and I'm not going to discuss it with you."

"Why not?" I ask.

She's got the key in the door of Room 123. "There's no point to it, Lilly, that's why. They're coming to school here and that's that."

"But did you hear what she *said*, about the dorm?" I ask pushing past her into the room.

"Of course I heard. I also heard her say she was a boring person."

"So what?" I ask.

"If you're a boring person, you couldn't possibly have any idea what it's *supposed* to be like in a dorm," she says, "especially if you don't live there. What's wild to a boring person would be mild to someone like you or me."

"I'm a boring person, Carole," I say.

"No, you're not." She snaps the words shut like a change purse. "You just don't worry enough about how you look."

I flop down on the bed and watch Carole unpack, which is a major project. I don't mention all the clothes again, but unless she changes every hour or so, she's not going to use them up by tomorrow, or even the day after.

"Don't you want to change?" she asks.

"No thanks," I say.

She slips on a pink sleeveless dress with a full skirt and a wide black patent belt, a little dressy I think, for wandering around Melville, but who am I? Her shoes have stiletto-thin heels, the kind that could split a flea. When she goes into the bathroom to redo her makeup, I kick off the boat shoes, which hurt, and put on an old pair of round-toed tap-dancing pumps from the senior class production of "Singin' in the Rain." Christie took the taps off before she gave them to me.

The town's so small that once we're back in the car I find I already know my way around pretty well. We park at the edge of campus and walk into the area of classroom build-ings. It doesn't really look so bad to me, and I begin to relax. There's a little stream that runs through the campus and lots of green; grass, trees, bushes, flowers. It's beautiful. The old stone buildings look as if a whole lot of impor-tant things are going on. The new ones show they're serious about progress. And the ivy is everywhere, creeping all over the place. Ha, Frank!

Somehow, we end up back at the auditorium. Maybe it's because that's where we left the girls, but we're drawn to it like a magnet. It's so quiet inside I can close my eyes and hear the ghosts of all the parents and all the children who have come through these doors over the years.

Carole tugs at my shirt sleeve. "Lilly, stop humming. It gives me the creeps."

"Sorry." I didn't even know I was humming, but I can't shake off my sadness. I hear Rigoletto's cry once more, as he discovers Gilda in the sack. The dark humid interior of the auditorium seems to have swallowed my daughter; no amount of pushing it aside will bring her back. You don't have to tell me that's overdramatic. I know it—and I don't care. Change is hard on me.

We cross the lobby and go through the double doors into the heart of the theater itself. The ghosts are all around, but I make a big effort not to hum or do anything strange, because Carole's jumpy enough already.

We walk down the side aisle and up the steps onto the empty stage where just a little while ago a psychiatrist from the student health service gave the parents mass therapy on letting go. The parents around me didn't look like they were going to have a problem with it, but Carole and I probably looked OK, too.

We sit on the stage facing all the empty seats and it strikes me that this is where we both always wanted to be. Maybe that's what brought us here, not the girls at all. We sit quietly for a long time, but our silence is OK, the way it used to be.

Finally Carole leans back on her hands and starts to swing her legs out in jerky motions over the orchestra pit. She's winding herself up to tell me whatever it is that's on her mind. I'd almost forgotten about it, what with one thing and another. While I wait, I try to think up something I can tell her back in case, by some fluke, this *isn't* good news; that's always been part of our friendship, the exchange of secrets. It's a trust thing. Even so, I won't tell her that Frank and I may lose what's keeping us together when our children go, because I'm not ready to say it out loud. I can tell her I'm tortured about Howard. She's seen him.

She goes first. "I'm having an affair," she says. She looks directly at me, and I'm sure she can see she's rocked my little boat.

"An affair?" The ghosts in the auditorium are holding their

breath. There's no sound except the sound of Carole's voice across the empty seats repeating what she's just said. I can't hum, now of all times, but I've never had such a need for music from inside. Carole doesn't look upset, exactly. But then, drama is to her like humming is to me, and this is definitely dramatic.

She waits for a comment, confession, declaration, something. But I can't say anything for fear a hum will slip out. Finally she adds, "Lots of people have affairs, especially at our age."

Before I commit myself to this proposition, I want to be sure she's not kidding. It doesn't look like she's kidding. I'll let her say one more thing.

"It's not a crime," she continues, and she sounds sort of snippy. Definitely serious.

"I never said it was."

"You looked it."

"I did not." I try to look sincere.

"Yes you did, Lilly. You are very judgmental."

"You surprised me, is all. I always thought you were happy with Jeff."

"This doesn't have anything to do with Jeff," she says, and leans back on her hands.

"Whoa, Nellie," I say and leave it there. I examine my tap shoes, knocking the toes together.

Carole, however, is not one to let things lay. "What do you mean, 'Whoa, Nellie?'"

I sit back and look at her. "I mean, how can you say this doesn't have anything to do with your husband?"

"It *doesn't* have anything to do with my husband."

"How can you *say* that, Carole?" I sit up straight.

"You don't even like my husband."

"Of course I like your husband." I'm astonished to hear myself say this, and even more surprised to realize it's true. Big, slaphappy Jeff has finally gotten to me. Besides, even if I didn't like Jeff, which, I repeat, I do, I would still find all this a little hard to take.

"You're jealous, I think," she says. She looks close at her fake fingernails, and I pray she won't start pulling them off. I'm very tense. "Anyway, I haven't actually done it. I'm about to."

"You mean, you haven't . . . ?"

"Not yet. I bought a new nightgown." She smiles, thinking about it. I bet it's a honey, too, this being Carole Williams.

"I don't want a new nightgown," I say truthfully. "So why am I jealous exactly?"

"You're jealous because somebody wants me."

"Somebody wants me, too."

"Only Frank." She dismisses him with a shrug.

"What's wrong with Frank?" I ask, tugging the corners of my green scarf back into place.

"He's your *husband*, Lilly." She almost falls off the stage, she's so superior.

"What's wrong with that?"

"There's nothing *wrong* with it. It's just so *boring*."

Me and Noreen at the motel, peas in a pod. I knew it. "You just said I wasn't boring," I say.

"Well, maybe I was wrong." She looks out over the empty seats.

"How do you know nobody else wants me?" I ask.

She shrugs.

"Christie doesn't know everything," I say slyly.

"She doesn't?" Carole stops swinging her legs.

"Of course not. She just thinks she does."

"Are you saying you *are* having an affair?" She really perks up.

"No. I'm just saying she doesn't know everything."

"Lilly, you're so middle class."

Neither of us says anything for a minute, then we both start to laugh. "Why are we fighting?" she asks and hugs me.

I can't think why, and I'm laughing right along with her, but I'm not all that happy inside.

"I need your help, Lilly." She leans forward and taps me on the arm to make sure she has my full attention.

"How?"

"You have to tell Jeff we decided I should stay to keep an eye on the girls," she says.

"I can't do that."

"Sure you can. Tell him Howard showed up." Her fall-into eyes plead with me.

"Why didn't *I* stay?"

"Because you had to get back to your parents' house, dummy. Everyone knows what's going on."

"What do you mean?" But I don't look at her.

"It's a small town, Lilly." She nods like she's some kind of sage.

I decide I don't want to get into this so I move the conversation back to her territory. "You have to call him, Carole. I break out when I lie."

"You break out from everything," she says. I know she's angry with me. I reach over and touch her hand. "An affair isn't going to help you, and it will hurt Jeff."

She looks back at me. "In the first place, I don't need any help," she says. "Besides, Jeff will never know." She doesn't sound like she believes it.

"Of course he'll know. It's a small town, remember?" I draw my legs up and sit cross-legged on the stage. "And you packed enough clothes for a week. He isn't stupid."

"Yes he is," she bursts out.

"No, he isn't. And, even if he never finds out, you know, and I know, and this guy, whoever he is, knows, and that does something to Jeff."

"You're so . . . so . . ."

"Middle class," I supply.

"Well, I'm sorry to say it, Lilly, but it's true."

We sit quietly staring out over the theater. It seems significant that this real-life drama is being played to an empty house.

"I'm hungry," I say.

"Figures," she says, but she swings her legs up onto the stage and pushes herself off the floor. "Maybe you'll understand when you see him." She smooths her too-dark hair back. "He's gorgeous."

"I'm not going to understand, Carole. This is crazy." I want to tell her I think she's too old for this, but since she's obviously undergoing some kind of age-related crisis I decide not to do that. This morning's psychiatrist would have done well to tell the parents the various guises the stress of losing a child to college comes in. If Carole and I are typical, he had a whole auditorium full of women about to lose their minds. Men are good at setting their emotions on autopilot; that's how they get through life. I think it wouldn't hurt the rest of us to take a page out of their book. I've done a lot of agonizing in my life, and I can't see that anything much has come of it.

In the lobby I tell Carole I need to try Frank again; he needs to know Howard's here.

"You're not going to mention about me, are you, Lilly?"

"Of course not." And I'm not, either. Talk about middle class; first he'd be amazed out of his mind, then he'd overreact. We'd fight, and I'd end up telling him she was right to do it. And maybe she is; what do I know?

I call home, because I don't want to seem overanxious by calling the office again. Still no one answers. I'm thinking if Frank's alive, he has his nerve.

The crazy half of me thinks maybe I *should* ask Polly to go out to the house, but it isn't a very good solution. If no one answers the door, she'll never think to look in the window to see if they might be lying on the floor. And I can't *tell* her to do that, obviously. So, what would I gain?

When Carole and I leave the auditorium, I'm surprised the sun's still shining; it seems we were in there for hours. My watch says it's only five-thirty P.M.

"You'll meet him tonight," says Carole, pulling my wrist over to look at my watch, which has hands big enough for her to see.

"Meet who?"

"Todd. He's coming by to get me around eight o'clock," she says.

"Todd?"

"That's his name, Lilly. Todd Conway. He's English."

He's real, is what he is. I finally feel it. And I'm starting to get angry about the whole thing. So much for innocent girl talk and catching up on our lives. So much for friendship. I'm a cover story for an assignation. I can't believe it.

Frank doesn't use people, which I realize doesn't have anything to do with anything, but it *is* a point in his favor. And he, gone who knows where, is suddenly the only person I want to talk to. Since he knows nothing about my growing enthusiasm for him, he won't know he's supposed to react in huge brush strokes when I finally reach him. Naturally, that will piss me off, and the whole thing, Frank's rise and fall, will have been played out in my head. Actually, that's how it usually is; no one has much control over what I think about them, because I make everything up. It's a problem for all concerned.

An awful thought suddenly occurs to me which is, what if this Todd person is staying with Carole and me at the motel? This is, after all, the age of the co-ed dormitory, etcetera. I can't actually figure my old pal Carole setting me up for something like that, no matter how with it she wants to be. She's basically as boring as I am in the alternate lifestyle area. Maybe *she's* not staying with me.

"Of course I'm staying with you," she says. "Todd and I are just going out for a little while." She pats my hand, which irritates the heck out of me.

"You're having a date with this guy?"

"Why not?" We're walking down a street with a million little shops on it, and Carole can hardly keep her mind on the conversation.

In front of a store where I think the dresses are too preppy even for Carole, I ask, "Where are you going on this date?"

"I don't know." She's looking in the window. "The movies probably."

"Carole, give me a break. You're going to the movies with a guy you're about to sleep with?"

"Why not? You want to go in here and look around?" She starts toward the door. "After the movie we'll probably go to a bar."

"No, I don't want to go in there," I say. "Carole, you can't stay out late. You never could."

"I'm in better shape now," she says, joining me back on the sidewalk.

"You're not in any better shape than you were at seventeen, and you're not seventeen anymore. You just look it."

"No kidding?"

"No kidding."

She laughs and hugs me. "So he'll find out I can't stay up late, so what?"

"You won't be very exciting to be with."

"And?"

"It may ruin the . . ." It's hard to say it.

"Affair? That ought to thrill you."

"If you're going to do something as stupid as this you might as well enjoy it, I guess."

We're standing in front of Big Banana's Pizza Palace, when the door opens and a group of five or six kids come out. The air around them, and now us, smells of crispy crust, stringy cheese, tomatoes, onions, and peppers. I nudge her inside.

The interior is dark and it takes a minute for our eyes to adjust. Each table is set with a small red globe with a candle inside. The effect is warm, homey; romantic if you are a young couple, kind to the face if you are not. Carole looks spectacular in here, so I figure I probably look OK. I'm in love with these red-globed candles. They would be useful in the bedroom; and if I replaced the fluorescent light in the bathroom with these little globes, I wouldn't have to rehang the flamestitch royal.

The problem with so much atmosphere *here* though, is the same thing that would be its most positive feature at home; it's hard to see. But it's only the little things I can't see, like I probably won't be able to read the menu. Howard Woolfe, on the other hand, is perfectly clear. He has moved his candle to the side of the table so only one side of his face glows pink. This is so he can lean across toward the woman who is with him, caress her hand, as he is doing, while she fondles his earring, without getting burned by the glass candle globe. This is no girl he's with. She's not my age, but she's not seventeen, either. I notice he has a big bandage on his knee.

"Hurt yourself, Howard?" I ask.

He is not happy to see me. "Yo, Mrs. B.," he says.

I stare at the person he's with. Her glasses reflect the red globes. "Oh, sure," says Howard, "this is Samanda." He has dropped her hand. "She came by where I'm staying for a look-see. A lot of people drop in that way."

Samanda doesn't smile, but she doesn't not smile, either. She just looks at us.

"Samanda's a street person," says Howard.

"Really," says Carole.

Samanda looks over at Carole. "Actually," she says, "I live in a box. There's a whole group of us."

"Well, she's right about that," says Howard, twitching in his chair. "There is. Her box is over by Hunter Creek."

"It's true," says Samanda. "That's my address." She has

one of those swamp-weed perms, and perfectly round lead-rimmed glasses. "A double-door refrigerator was in my box once, from Sears. It makes you think."

"Sure does," says Howard. "I tried it out. It's cool." He slaps his bandaged knee and laughs like a jackal.

"I've heard that one before," Samanda says with a yawn.

Carole, who has always been interested in unusual life-styles, asks, "What do you do if it rains?"

"Oh, the rain doesn't hurt it," says Samanda. "It's in my tent." She turns to Howard. "Got that at Sears, too," she says. "It's the store of the people."

"Oh." Carole is clearly disappointed.

Samanda reaches over and takes Howard's hand again. "Arthur says I can stay with him tonight, though, just for a change."

Howard clears his throat. "It's my middle name," he explains looking at me.

That's not the way I remember it from the graduation program, but I don't say anything.

"That should be fun," says Carole, smiling down at the yellow hair standing straight up on 'Arthur's' head like little haystacks.

"It was the least I could do," he's looking at the table. "Samanda's a graduate student." It looks to me like he's trying to pull his hand away, but he's being too discreet to have any success at it.

She smiles. "Yes. I'm a poet."

Howard nods. "It's true. She's twenty-five."

Carole looks interested. "A poet? That's wonderful. Why don't you live in the dorm, by the way?"

"Oh I wouldn't live in there, it's too closed in. I like the outdoors." She lets go of Howard to pick something out from under a fingernail. "In the winter I move to a condo."

"Besides," says Howard, "it's too wild in the dorm." He shakes his head. "That's what everyone says, Mrs. B. Sorry you had to hear it here."

Samanda continues, "There's a whole lot of box people," she says. "In the summer we all live together; in winter we separate."

Howard nods. "Samanda's the editor of their newsletter."

"It's called *Box Flocks*," Samanda offers, "for the biblical overtones."

"I'm thinkin' of moving in," Howard says.

"What about California?" I ask.

"Yeah, well, that too." Samanda has recaptured his hand.

"Let's go sit down, Lilly," Carole tugs my sleeve.

"I guess we'd better," I say. "Enjoy your evening, *Howard*." I smile a sweet gotcha smile. Howard just smiles back at me with those weird eyes of his.

Carole and I are given a booth. We can't see Howard and Samanda from here, which pleases me, because I'll be able to concentrate on Carole in case she has any more bombs to drop.

"Are you going to tell?" Carole asks.

"Christie?"

She nods.

"I won't have to. The women in our family are born with a psychic side." I reach for a menu. "I mean, she won't know, know, but she won't be surprised when she finds out."

Carole accepts this. "Didn't take him long, did it?" she says.

"Maybe that's what it was about him," I say. "I never liked Howard."

"No kidding."

The menus are tall and thin and grease-stained. I can almost make out the words but not quite, and my glasses are back at the motel, of course, so I'll have to wing it.

The girl who comes to take our order is dressed like a banana. She tells us her name's not Chiquita, and then practically falls down laughing. When she finally catches her breath, she says, "It's Chipizza," which starts her off again. I think she's kind of cute, like Christie, so I chuckle, but Carole just gives a cool smile. Of course, to be fair, she has other things on her mind.

Since I have no idea what's on the menu, I'm a little self-conscious about ordering, but I ask for a mushroom pizza, and Chipizza doesn't blink, so it must be on there. Carole orders a small green salad with oil and vinegar on the side.

When the food arrives I want to dump that stupid salad on Carole's head. The little banana unloads her tray. "Enjoy," she says with a wide smile at me. She ignores Carole, who picks up a lettuce leaf as if she were a little woodland bunny and nibbles at it. I have to look away from her, because for a moment that's what I see, a rabbit sitting across the table from me, a vitamin-crazed rabbit. I lift a piece of pizza off the serving tray and slide it to my plate. The cheese stretches out like a wide rubber band.

The pizza is delicious and I begin to relax. I've ordered wine too, red, perfect with mushroom pizza. I decide to ignore Carole, and pretend I'm not in Big Banana's, or in Melville at all; I'm in Milan, at a quaint little bistro frequented by artistic people, having a little snack before I go to La Scala to dress for the stage. Paparazzi are hanging around outside waiting to snap my departure for a quick buck from *People Weekly*. I'm wondering what would have happened if I'd decided to marry Frank back in the good old USA when Carole interrupts me.

"You *did* marry Frank, Lilly."

"What?" I look at her like she's crazy, but if my life gets any more stressful I'll have to wear a gag.

"I *said* you did marry Frank."

"I know who I married, Carole." I offer her some wine, but of course she won't touch it.

I bend over and shove in a huge bite of my pizza. This mouthful is still attached to the plate by two strings of cheese, one out of either side of my mouth, when someone slides into the booth opposite me and next to Carole. I look up to see a gorgeous guy give Carole a kiss on the cheek. She looks surprised. This must be Todd, in the flesh.

When he fixes on me I see Carole's point. His hair is a little too long, but it's too long in a blow-dry designer kind of way, the macho huntsman look. He is tanned like Jeff and Frank could never be. It's a work-in-the-outdoors-never-read-a-book-killed-a-grizzly-with-my-bare-hands tan, and it looks like he stores his tennis balls in his upper arms. He's wearing a striped T-shirt with short sleeves; the sleeves are stretched to the max, which I personally think is overkill. And his eyes are shifty, as well they might be under the circumstances.

He holds his hand out to me across the table, which is pretty dumb since I'm still attached in every possible way to my plate. Miraculously, the pizza detaches itself from the cheese that dangles like drool from my mouth. I sit up to take his hand and we shake. My fingers are very greasy, which is not my fault. If he had any manners at all, which he doesn't because he picks up a napkin and wipes his hands off, he'd pretend not to notice.

"This must be Lilly," he says to me. His accent is royal-family nasal.

"I'm Lilly," I nod.

"Carole talks about you all the time."

"That's nice," I say. "I just heard about you today."

He nods. "Yes, until now it's been our secret." He looks at me with his dark eyes until I'd swear he flexes them. "So, what do you think?" he asks.

I look at Carole. She knows what I think, which is not to say the guy's not a work of art. But her eyes plead with me to be nice, so for old times' sake I force a smile and shrug as if I barely notice this kind of thing.

Carole doesn't want to push me too far, which is smart, so she takes the conversational ball. "What are you doing here, Todd? I thought you were going to pick me up at the motel."

"I got to town early, so I decided to check the restaurants." He winks at me. "I know a lot about you," he smirks. "You're very trim. I'm surprised."

Carole looks at the wall.

"She wants to go on a date first," he says to me.

"Yes, I know." The English are known to be frank, but I think this is going a little far.

He turns to Carole. "I'm going to take you to the movies, dollbaby."

Carole's pink dress seems pinker. She's not looking at me but she is, if you know what I mean. All I can wonder is how she can pick two guys that call her such stupid names.

"*Fatal Attraction*'s just up the street," he says. "It's supposed to be worthwhile."

I'm about to think this relationship's going nowhere, since the guy doesn't even know this is a no good preaffair date choice, when Carole brightens. "Great," she says, so she must not know it, either.

"So go," I say in my heartiest voice. "I'll take care of the bill and see you at the motel later."

"OK."

Todd stands up, way up, and holds out his hand to Carole who slides out of the booth. It's hard not to notice the veins that rise up on the backs of his arms.

"I'll have her in by eleven o'clock," he grins down at me and slides his arm around Carole's patent-leather belt. I feel at least ninety.

After they go I ask the waitress for a doggie bag, which feels right. I pay the bill and leave. All the way back to the motel I think about Carole in the movie theater, watching a movie about fooling around, while an English tennis pro snakes his arm around her. I can't figure how she separates all this out. Todd is gorgeous, no question about it, it's the word I would have used too, but we're supposed to have outgrown that by now.

But then my other side sits up and taps me on the shoulder. Maybe Carole's doing the right thing. Maybe a person should try all kinds of things, taste of life's many fruits, so to speak. Maybe a person should even take a gander at affair-having while they still can, just so they know what it's like. A lot of people have done it, so there must be something to it.

When I get back to the room I settle down for serious work on what's left of the pizza, and a thinking session with myself.

One thing's for sure—everyone around me's having a sort of a last hurrah, and I can't help but wonder if I'm missing the boat. I think about it from a soap-opera point of view: My husband and invalid son have disappeared; my eighty-one-year-old father is unfaithful to my mother; my oldest friend is going to bed with a tennis coach; my daughter's boyfriend consults the stars on matters that pertain to her; and me?— I'm pretending to be an opera star every two minutes. Whoa, Nellie.

Chapter Seven

The phone wakes me up, and when I reach for it I knock the grease-stained Big Banana's bag off the night table.

It's Frank, a person far too mature to turn to food just because of a little stress. "Hello, Lilly," he says. He sounds well, which doesn't really surprise me.

"Frank, where have you been?!" I hang off the side of the bed and snap up the Big Banana's bag.

"Now, Lilly, I know you've been worried, but—"

"I have not been worried, I've been mad." We both know this is the same thing. "Where's Peter?"

"He's in bed. It's after ten o'clock."

"I know what time it is, Frank. What I don't know is, where was he when I called the house today? I couldn't get either of you." I crumple the greasy bag into a small wad, and pitch it across the room, about a foot short of the waste-basket.

"That was probably when we went to Dr. Felcher's. He sends his best by the way."

This makes me sit up. "Why did you go to Dr. Felcher?"

"Peter's sick, Lilly. When you're sick you go to the doctor."

Frank likes to lecture me, little short lectures, the kind of reading on a situation a person should write down and carry in their wallet. It has never particularly bothered me, but tonight I'd just as soon he'd skip it.

"And?"

"And they sent us to the hospital." He rustles papers around as if he's looking for something. "I've lost his prescription."

"The hospital?" I'm sitting on the edge of the bed now.

"It's a nasty flu." Frank clears his throat like a consulting physician. "It can turn into pneumonia; they had to check it out."

I feel like a beetle. "Oh." Between this news, and the grease-stained bag screaming pig out from the middle of the floor, I feel a huge guilt trip coming on.

"Don't feel bad, Lilly. Dr. Felcher says there's no way you could have known. Everyone had this a long time ago."

"I could have believed Peter," I whimper.

"Don't be silly," he says.

"Thank you, Frank."

I hear the chair creak as he settles back. "He asked me to read to him."

"No kidding."

"I haven't done that since he was about six years old."

"What did you read?"

"Just his history book. He has a test on Monday."

"Did you have to cut the pages?"

"They don't make books like that anymore, Lilly." More paper noise. "I'll find it. Just some cough medicine, don't worry."

"I'm not worried." I'm worried about getting the Big Banana's bag up off the floor is all; it's crazy I know, but I feel like Frank can see it, and I know he wouldn't approve.

"Melinda asked after Peter. She saw the whole thing, you know."

"I know."

"She and I are doing Alex's divorce, that's why she was with him."

"Right, Frank."

"I am right, Lilly. I know what you're thinking, but you're wrong."

"Maybe."

"You should get control of your imagination before it gets control of you."

"Right, Frank." Where's my pencil?

He sighs deeply. "Lilly, did you take my things with you?"

I slide off the bed and crawl toward the crumpled bag. "Christie's backpack?"

I feel him nodding. "Yes, Frank, I'm really sorry. I thought it was hers."

"Oh, that's OK. What about my keys?"

"Keys?"

"Yes, I can't find my car keys, the ones I taped the motel confirmation to."

"Gee, Frank, did you look in your top drawer." It's not as if I'm 100-percent concentrated on this conversation, because half of me is wondering if this phone cord will stretch as far as the greasy bag.

"I've looked *everywhere*."

"That's too bad," I say. "Just use the spare set until I get home. I'll help you look then."

"I'm already using the spare set, of course, Lilly. I want my own keys."

"We'll find them, Frank, I'm sure."

He lets it drop. "So, how's it going?" he asks.

I could really entertain him, given the last few hours I've lived through, but Howard's the high spot. "Howard's here," I say.

"Howard Woolfe?" He's incredulous. "What's he doing there?"

I've almost reached the Big Banana's bag. "He wants to help keep an eye on Christie, so I can relax."

"What do you mean?"

"You convinced him I was crazy, Frank, with that camera thing." The telephone cord barely stretches far enough, but with a big reach I get the paper in my hand. "Not to mention I cried."

"Lilly, are you OK? You're breathing funny."

"Thinking about Howard does it," I say. I toss the bag into the can where it lands with a satisfactory thwack.

"I'm sorry about the camera."

I shrug to the wall. "That's not what made me cry, anyway."

"Bring her home," he says.

"Who?"

"Christie. Bring her home."

"What?"

"You can't leave her there with Howard, Lilly."

"She's not exactly *with* Howard. He's staying somewhere else." I'm back on the bed now, and I stick my legs under the covers.

"On campus?"

"Sort of."

"Then it's too close."

"Well, it's a protest shack. If it's got someone in it, it's not a billboard or something and the campus security people leave it up." There's a terrible mirror opposite me, and nowhere else to look. I close my eyes and pretend I hear clapping at the end of an aria, from say *La Traviata*, considering I'm in bed. "Howard's in it."

"Lilly, you're not making sense."

"Frank, I'm just telling you the facts. You're the lawyer." I open my eyes and stare boldly at the mirror. "But there is good news. He's met a girl who lives in a box; only in the summer, though. It may be our big break."

"Lilly, are you sure you're OK?"

"Right as rain, Frank. Christie's in a dorm with Melani."

"That doesn't sound much better." By now his face will be flushed.

"You don't even know Melani."

"She set our garage on fire."

"She was only three, Frank."

"Once a pyro, always a pyro, Lilly. I see them in court." He's tapping his fingers on the table, I can hear him. It's a habit he has.

"OK, Frank."

Really, this has nothing to do with Melani. He must know that too, because he asks, "How's Carole?"

He would never understand.

"Lilly, are you OK?" he asks.

"Sorry Frank, I was thinking about something else. Carole's fine. She's right here."

"Let me say hello." The chair creaks as he leans forward in it. I can see our hall clearly, with Frank sitting in semidarkness and Peter asleep upstairs.

"Well, I don't mean here, here, exactly. She's in the bathroom."

"Oh, well, tell her I said 'hello.' "

"OK." If I can only get close enough to the toilet I'll flush it with my foot; it would be a nice touch. I slide off the bed again.

"Lilly," Frank pauses.

"Yes?"

"What would you think if I took some riding lessons?"

"Horseback riding?"

"Sure, why not?"

"It doesn't sound like you."

"Yes it does. We have a lot of land out here, I'm thinking maybe we should have a horse."

"You've been reading too many of those westerns, Frank."

"That has nothing to do with it."

"I'll be home Friday, we'll talk." I'm halfway across the room when the cord yanks me back so I can't reach the toilet, but it doesn't matter. Frank believes Carole's here anyway, he's very trusting. It's only me that sees life as an art form.

He clears his throat. "Actually, Lilly, I'm renting a horse now."

"You're what?"

"I'm renting a horse. I've been riding around out back; I may ride her to work as soon as I get the hang of it. I got the idea when I couldn't find my keys."

"Frank . . ."

"It's exhilarating, Lilly. People seem to be paying more attention to me."

"I'll bet."

"By the way, your mother called and told Polly you weren't coming home for a while."

"Of course I'm coming home."

"That's not what she told Polly . . ."

I get back on the bed. "That really makes me mad, Frank. She didn't tell me I wasn't coming home."

"Now, Lilly."

"How long am I supposed to stay, anyway?"

"She didn't say. What's the problem?"

"I don't know yet, at least I don't know exactly." The motel has left a little rectangular sketch pad and a small pencil on the bedside table. I draw circles. "She's imagining things."

"What kind of things?"

"She thinks Pop has another woman."

"Your father?" Frank says this on the inhale, and then holds his breath.

"Yep."

Frank doesn't have any comment on this, so I tell him a little more. "He *is* going somewhere, I just don't know where yet." I tell him about my father slipping out the back gate, but I do not describe the old man I have seen in my father's chair.

Frank sighs. He misses his own parents, and he thinks I don't appreciate mine. "Can I do anything, Lilly?"

"I don't think so." Right now I don't see what anyone can do.

He changes the subject. "What about Howard, then?"

Now I sigh. Sometimes it's an affectation, but this time it sort of creeps up on me and heaves out. "It'll work out," I say.

"I don't know, Lilly. I think you should bring Christie home."

"I promised Mother I'd come back, Frank. And, if she's expecting me to stick around until I take care of her problem, I'd better go back now."

"You can't leave Christie there, by herself."

"Why not?"

"Because of Howard, of course." His fingers drum steadily on the table now.

"She's not by herself, Frank. She's with a whole bunch of other kids. I have to go back to Lakeview, tomorrow."

"I don't know, Lilly."

"Samanda may save the day."

"Who's Samanda?" I picture his fingers lifted, halted mid-drum so to speak.

"The girl in the box. The one I was telling you about." I lean my head against the wall. "Her name's Samanda."

He doesn't have much to say about that. We say goodnight, and I picture him smoothing down his few remaining strands of hair as he walks up the stairs. It's really a new twist to have Frank more upset about something than I am. What I am coming to in my thinking, though, is, somewhere along the line Christie has to be responsible for herself, with or without Samanda; with or without Frank and me. If Howard is what she wants, Howard is what she'll get. And there won't be anything I can do about it, or Frank either for that matter. It seemed unnecessary to mention Howard's California invitation, and I'm glad I didn't. Frank's agitated enough.

He's got a tone I don't recognize, and this business about the dumb horse is outer space, pure and simple.

I close my eyes and pretend I'm Brünnhilde, but it's Christie I see, surrounded by the magic fire. In a little corner of the tableau Melani sits lighting matches. Todd is a tennis ball that Carole bounces on her racket, and Howard is walking stupidly into the dragon's lair.

Just as Howard's about to get it, Carole walks in. The vision skitters right out of my head, but I like the idea; I'll come back to it.

I look at Carole hard to see if her date's been successful, and more important, if she's still in the dating phase. "How was the movie?" I ask.

She pulls the pink dress over her head and drapes it across a chair. Then, without answering, she goes into the bathroom. She practically brushes her teeth off. When she comes out she has changed into a slinky peach-colored affair with lots of straps that could be worn either to bed or, with the right jewelry, to the White House. I'm in my old Norn costume, probably a lot more comfortable, but that's all I can say for it.

"I know you don't care about the movie, Lilly, so why ask?"

"I'm showing interest in your life, Carole. What's wrong with that?"

"The movie was fine," she says, buffing her nails with a purple sponge thing. I don't see any of the glow I think I should be seeing, but I don't dare ask.

I yawn, something I perfected when I understudied Brünnhilde, and pull the covers up. "Good," I say folding my arms.

"You don't have to be so disapproving," she says.

"I'm not disapproving," I say.

"You are." She points at me. "You're rejecting me."

"I am not," I say hotly.

"Look at how you're lying there, Lilly, with your arms crossed on your chest. It's body language. I've read all about it."

"It's crap," I say, but I uncross my arms. "You didn't seem to want to talk, that's all." I arrange my pillows more comfortably, and fold my hands in my lap. "That's a pretty nightgown," I say.

That gets her. She beams at me with her unused face. "This is nothing," she says. She opens her side of the dresser and pulls out a white box with gold lettering, slanted finely, across the top. It is a very elegant-looking box. She opens it and pushes aside layers of tissue, to reveal a filmy little number, all veils and translucent glistening material, sort of pearl-like, if you could give the color a name. "Three hundred dollars," she says, and holds it up by its straps. "It's the one I was telling you about."

It doesn't look all that different from my Norn costume in its original condition.

"This is what you're going to wear when you do it?" I ask.

She nods. "What do you think?"

"It's pretty."

"I look great in it." She holds it against herself and looks in the mirror. "I looked for it for days. You'll think this is silly, but . . ."

"What?"

"Well, I didn't decide to do it until after I found the nightie."

"You didn't?"

"No. The nightie decided me. I look so good in it."

"Good color for you," I say.

"It's the hair," she says.

"Maybe."

She folds the nightgown and returns it to its box with, the only word for it is, awe. "I can hardly wait to wear it."

"It's sort of like a prom dress, I guess," I say.

She looks at me suspiciously but decides I don't mean anything nasty by that.

"Do you like Todd?" she asks. She stands in the middle of the room, cradling the elegant box.

"What's not to like? I just met him. He thinks I'm your mother."

She ignores this. "He's a terrific tennis player. You should see his serve." She walks to the dresser and puts the seduction nightgown back in the drawer. If we had a safe, she'd use it.

I nod. "I especially like the nightgown," I say. "You can tell about a nightgown right away."

"He was a pro for a while," she rattles on, she wants to talk about him I guess, "but he didn't like so much travel. He wants to settle down, have a home."

So. He wasn't good enough to make it, I think to myself. Uh oh. I can tell by her eyes I didn't think it to myself.

"Of course he was good enough to make it," she snaps. "He just wanted a home, like I said. The English are very domestic."

I roll my eyes.

"Lilly, you're impossible. It's not your business what I do, anyway." She picks up her hairbrush and starts to brush her hair back from her face.

"Carole, I didn't do anything." I look as earnest as I can possibly look.

"Yes you did."

"OK, OK, but I want you to be happy."

"Everybody wants me to be happy. It's why I'm so miserable!" She drops the hairbrush and starts to cry. Carole doesn't bawl like I do, she never did, she cries beautifully. It's something I've always envied.

I get up and put my arm around her. "Come on, sit down. Let's talk." I take the brush out of her hands and put it back on the dresser. Then I lead her over to her bed. She sits on the side, and I sit on the edge of mine opposite her. I hand her a couple of tissues from the box on the bedside table, and she sniffles into her tissues for a few minutes. When she looks up, she takes me in for the first time. "What do you have on, anyway?" she asks.

"My Norn costume." I hold out a gauzy edge for her inspection.

She nods and dabs at her eyes. I remember how long we've known each other. Who else would accept that without comment?

I decide to try to clear a few things up right away. "I'm not thinking bad things about you, I'm just worried for you, Carole."

She sobs quietly. "How did we get here, Lilly?" she asks.

"What do you mean?"

"What are we doing old and alone, crying in a motel room?" She gestures around the room, as if that says it all.

This seems pretty exaggerated to me. For one thing, I'm not crying, for another, there are two of us here so we're not alone, and I prefer to think of the forties as middle-aged.

"Carole," I say, "you're tired, that's why you feel bad."

"That's why we both feel bad," she says. "We're tired."

"No, I feel bad because my daughter's boyfriend has followed her here, because my father doesn't have both oars in the water, and because my mother's flipping out."

"What about Frank?" she asks, not noticing I've left her out of this pretty picture.

"I haven't had time to think about Frank," I say. "Besides, why should I think about Frank?"

Carole puts aside the sodden tissue and gently uses her pillow to blot her face. "Are you glad you married him?"

"Of course I'm glad I married him. That's a silly question." I push myself back into the middle of the bed, and sit there like a righteous pond flower.

"No it isn't, Lilly. We had dreams. Where are they now?" She starts to cry again.

I'd be more upset if I didn't know Carole so well. I'm pretty sure she's having a great time.

"We changed our minds about what we wanted," I say, "that's all."

"But look at us now."

One of us, at least, and that's her, is looking pretty good, so here we have positive, actual proof that looks don't count on the happiness scale. Or money.

"That's not Frank's fault," I say, "or Jeff's."

"Who else's fault could it be?"

Whoa, Nellie. I hold my hand in the air like I'm stopping traffic; this is important. "I get it," I say.

"What?" She looks interested.

"You want to punish Jeff." This seems pretty obvious, now I've heard the ruined-life theory.

She takes a minute to think this over. "No," she says, and she's positive too, "that's not it."

"What is it then?"

"I want to sleep with another man. I don't want to die practically a virgin. I'm forty-seven-years old and I don't have any experience." From her bed she can see herself in the mirror, too, but I can tell she doesn't mind it.

"What kind of experience?"

"Sex experience, of course." She pats a curl into place.

"You sound like Christie." I'm thinking this conversation was bad enough the first time. "Who told you you don't have any experience?"

"Well, Todd for one."

I pull my hair back and hold it in a ponytail with my hands, like a slipped mountain climber clinging to a weed in the rock. "I'd say he has a conflict of interest, Carole, wouldn't you?"

"Maybe so, but you can't deny it. A fact's a fact. You're the same too, Lilly." She rips another tissue out of the box. "Life has passed us by." Outside a siren punctuates this remark.

"No it hasn't."

"Yes it has." She blows her nose.

"What about Melani and Christie?" I let go of my hair and it bounces forward. "I'd be sorry not to have had my children and that's a fact."

"They're leaving." She's removing her fingernails, one by one, and laying them in two neat scarlet rows on the bedside table.

"They're just going to school," I say, watching in fascination.

"But it's the beginning. Admit it, Lilly. There's a very lonely future ahead."

Since I've come up with this too, I can't exactly deny it, but somehow I never made the leap to lay it all on Frank. Or did I? I'm pretty disappointed in him.

"Frank says it's a beginning," I say.

"Typical!" Carole swings her legs up onto her bed and gets under the covers. "Jeff says that too. It's some kind of male line or something. They use it when we start to get restless." When she reaches to snap off the light, I see the Velcro strips, like fuzzy little caterpillars, on the back of each fingernail. "I called Jeff and told him I wasn't coming home," she says from the dark, "so you won't have to do it."

"What did you say?"

"I told him Christie's boyfriend followed her here and you couldn't stay so I was going to keep an eye on her."

"What did he say?"

"Jeff never says much. He did wonder where you were going to be, since you're her mother. He's a very domestic person."

"Thanks a lot." I get under the covers.

"It's true, Lilly, I will keep an eye on her."

"You won't have time for my daughter," I say. I turn the sheet back at the top, over the blanket, and pull it right up to my chin, tucking myself in, a neat package. "Besides, she's going to be fine."

"Good-night Lilly." She moves around on her bed, and I'm sure she has turned her back on me. She used to do that when we had sleepovers and she didn't want to talk anymore.

"Good-night," I say.

I lie on my back staring at the ceiling. My life feels like a river with no current. Everyone else's is in chaos, which seems, I hate to say it, a little more interesting.

Maybe I should take more chances. But everything's going so fast, too fast; that's the trouble. What I think I really want right now is to be the one inside the magic fire, at least until I get it all figured out.

Chapter Eight

Carole's already dressed when I wake up, and her fingernails are back on, now a pale coral color from some hidden fingernail stockpile. She is wearing a sundress that doesn't look all that different from her peach nightgown. The shoes are wedgies, very high, with the wooden wedge part carved into palm trees and painted bright colors.

"I bought these in Hawaii," she says when she sees me looking at them.

"They're nice."

She hooks on little painted zebra earrings, and admires herself in the mirror. "Cute," I say.

"We're going to the zoo."

"Zoo should be fun."

I realize now what she was up to while I was being told

about the problems of being a student at Bolton College; she was checking out places to go on a date. That was before I knew anything about Todd, of course, so in retrospect I might have been a little insensitive. Even so, it seems she should have paid attention to that conversation no matter what; and she should be listening to me now, because I'm her friend. But I don't think Carole has heard much of anything over the last twenty-four hours, and I'm sure she doesn't understand yet that college, not to mention life in general, isn't always a flyby.

She slips six or seven silver bangles over her wrist and walks across the room with a sound like a Slinky tumbling down a flight of stairs. It brings back memories, happy ones. Don't get me wrong, I'm not wishing for any little children around; but we had some fun times, the kids and I, and, even Frank.

"I love zoos," she says, smiling at me.

"It's supposed to be a good one," I say, as I pull on my sweatpants.

She sprays a cloud of perfume in the air and walks through it. It's sobering to see there's even a right way to put on perfume. Of course, Frank's allergic, but I could mention it to my mother. The effect is more subtle than, say, her splat-it-on-the-neck technique.

"Thanks, Lilly," she smiles at me from the mirror as she combs her eyebrows with a tiny silver comb I couldn't even get a grip on.

"It's OK." I pick up my overnight bag. "I'd better hit the road, I guess."

"I guess so," she says. "Wish me luck."

I smile, but I can't really get into it.

Actually, I'm happy to leave. This is all getting too confusing for me, and nobody wants my advice, which I have plenty of. It's like a daytime TV coloring book; Carole dresses, Todd flexes, Howard waits, and Christie longs. I'm glad to leave them all to it.

It's raining today, a gentle rain, but steady. The wipers sweep the water aside with very little sound; they have a pleasant rhythm. I slip a Solti recording of the Verdi *Requiem* into the tape player, and sing along with "Agnus Dei" and "Libera Me." It's a tremendous release. The music comes up from deep inside me, like oil out of a well. It feels good, and rich, and I wonder how it happened that I don't earn my living this way. By the time I'm within fifteen or twenty minutes of my parents' house I feel almost ready for them.

I told my mother I wouldn't be here until tomorrow, but as I pull up to the curb I see the curtain drop back into place. Behind it a bright red dress moves and disappears. It's the same dress she had on yesterday, a dress with so much color it fades her out completely. But it's not the kind of thing I would mention, which is odd considering she wouldn't have a problem telling me something like that; in fact, she lives for the moment.

I repeat the exercise of ring, knock, wait, this time in drizzle. Savage Dog, of course, howls and snarls behind the door; by the time she finally opens up, I'm starting to enjoy him. I'm ready to clip his little rectangular body to a leash, and take him for a walk.

She has changed out of the red dress, and into a night-gown. I'm supposed to think I've woken her up, I guess. Someone must have given her this nightgown, a ruffled white sack with pearl buttons at the neck; it billows around her backless slippers like a parachute. She wouldn't have bought this for herself, it's much too nice; and it's way too big for her. I myself have never given her a nightgown, probably because my subconscious thinks she never sleeps. Her thin white curls stand practically straight up, probably from yanking the dress off and putting the nightgown on in such a hurry. I struggle to remember that Savage Dog and this nightgowned woman are part of the real world, my very real world. I try to think of them as adorable.

"Lilly, what are you doing here?" She keeps her hand on the doorknob as if she has to hold on to keep from falling down faint with shock.

"Visiting you," I say, trying to get in.

"But I didn't expect you until tomorrow."

I can see in her face that she isn't ready for me, either; she has already come as close to her problem as she cares to for the moment, and now she wants to back away. In fact, if she weren't such a lady, she'd probably tell me to go away.

It occurs to me that maybe the reason she wanted me to stay with her for a while was that she wants company, not because she thinks I can help her. Now that she sees me, she loses enthusiasm for the idea, I can tell.

"Plans changed," I explain. "Carole decided to stay the whole week with the girls so I came back here." I shift my overnight bag to my other hand, hoping she'll notice there's only a puddle out here to put it down in. "She can handle whatever comes up."

"What could come up?" she asks, squinting up at me. "You girls are such worriers."

"There's a lot to worry about," I say. None of which I can tell her about.

Now she notices the rain. "You're wet," she says, shaking

her head at my foolish ways. "Come in and have some tea." She moves out of the way. I step quickly into the hall, and shake some of the rain out of my hair. "Where's Pop?"

She gestures impatiently toward the den. The silver glow of TV light answers my question.

She starts toward the kitchen. "Are you coming?"

"In a minute, I want to say hello."

She snorts. "He'll forget you were there five minutes after you leave. It's a waste of time."

I think she expects me to follow her. "Maybe so," I say. "By the way, why are you in your nightgown?"

"I just got up, Lilly." She rubs her eyes sleepily with the back of her hand, like a child. "Why else would I have this on?"

A shadow crosses the den's silver light and my father appears out of the darkness, and stands in the doorway.

"Lilly, my dear, I thought I heard you."

He is using his cane today so his feet must hurt bad, but from the grin on his face you could never tell. He beams at me.

I hug him gently and then stand back. "So, how are you, Pop?"

"Fine, darlin', fine." Behind him a game show explodes in a frenzy of bells and applause. "How are you is the question?"

"I'm good."

"Where's Chrissie?" He cocks his head to the side.

"*Christie*." I'm a little scared now, or I would never do it.

He looks apologetic. "Never liked that name—too churchy. You don't like me to call her Chrissie? You should have said."

"No, Pop, it's OK." My muscles relax a little. "She's at the college, for orientation."

"But you were just here yesterday."

"That's right. I dropped her off and came back to spend a little time with you and Mother."

Through this whole conversation my mother stands in the doorway to the kitchen. I'm surprised she hasn't broken in to hurry me off to our cup of tea, but I'm pleased that for once she hasn't interrupted.

"Margaret," says my father noticing her, "Margaret, look who's here."

She raises an eyebrow, she really is good at that. "Who do you think let her in, Gilbert?" she asks. She's my idol in the eyebrow-arch department. She leans against the doorway with her arms folded.

"Doesn't she have a key?"

I shake my head, hoping he'll give me one, which would save me a lot of trouble.

"Of course not. She's married now."

"Oh." This seems to make sense to him, but maybe only because he's immediately onto something else—the way she's dressed. His forehead rises up like ripples on a pond as he notices she's standing there in her nightgown. "What happened to your dress?" he asks.

"What dress?"

"The one you had on this morning," he says, his hands knobby on his cane. "The red one."

"I didn't have a dress on this morning, Gilbert. I just got up," she says, sort of humphing while she says it. "Can't you tell that?"

"You had the red dress on a minute ago, the one with the black belt," he says, scratching his head. He's not challenging her, he's just trying to clear up a little something.

"I did not," she says emphatically.

"I could have sworn you were just in here with the red dress on." He looks sad and shakes his head slowly from side to side. "Maybe that was yesterday. I don't know." He looks over at me. "I get confused sometimes."

I nod.

"It's pretty, though, isn't it," he says, "the nightgown. I think I gave it to her, Lilly."

"Lilly did," my mother says.

"Oh," he sounds deflated. "Well, maybe it was another one I gave you. It's nice, Lilly," he says to me. He turns back toward the television, where the contestants are squealing with joy. "Go on and have your tea, darling, we can talk later."

"OK, Pop," I say. I watch as he makes his slow way back to the den and eases himself into his chair. When I turn toward my mother she's gone. She probably can't look me in the eyes because of the nightgown situation. But I'm not going to confront her on it; there's no point.

I'm surprised she doesn't notice how failed my father is. Maybe she's just too mad at him, or maybe she sees him too much to notice change; maybe she doesn't care. It could be that she's afraid; that's something to think about. Sometimes people keep quiet about the things that really worry them; instead, they talk their heads off about everything else.

When I get to the kitchen, I find her over by the sink, looking out the back window. Mrs. Potter, next door, is in her yard, working in the flower beds. She's hunched down, like the print I have in our guest room, of a little gray figure in a rice paddy. She barely moves among the flowers, just twitches from time to time as she pulls a weed, or touches a petal. The theme for this year is yellow, and there are so many bright yellow blossoms springing from the ground it looks like the sun has landed in her yard.

"She hates flowers," my mother says. She sounds angry. "What's she doing out there in the rain? She's too old to be on her hands and knees."

"They were his special project," I remind her.

"Well, he's dead two years now. What if she falls over and hurts herself? What am I supposed to do then?"

"Don't watch, Mother," I say, and move her away from the window.

"She could catch cold," she says.

I pour out the tea for both of us, thinking I may like it better if I'm the pourer. My mother takes her cup and drinks from it in tiny little gulps, like she's anxious to finish it before someone grabs it away. The lace top of her nightdress obviously irritates her neck and she scratches it from time to time. The skin beneath her chin looks patchy and dry and sags like loose cloth. The sight of this uncontrollable looseness must be hard on her.

"Did you notice my flowers, out front?" she asks. "They are doing rather well."

"Yes, they look nice."

"But I always plant the same things, don't I? Impatiens and begonias." Her hand flutters between us, plucking at a napkin in the center of the table. "Never anything else."

"You don't have much choice with all that shade. You're doing the best you can do. It looks great to me."

"I'm bored with it, Lilly," she says, "bored with it all. Same tree, same shade, same flowers. I want a different look. I want a garden of sunshine, lots of flowers."

"You have lots of flowers."

"Pink." She sighs in disgust. "I want something very different. Yellow would do."

"Then you'll have to cut down the tree," I say.

"Don't be silly." She frowns. "Someone will develop a bright plant to grow in the shade. Something yellow, or even orange."

"Is someone working on that?" I ask.

"Of course." She is positive, and tugs at the neck of her nightdress with both hands. "Someone is working on everything."

I get up and open the cookie tin she keeps on top of the refrigerator. There are Fig Newtons inside. I offer her one but she shakes her head. I take two and come back to the table. Each time she takes her eyes off me I dunk the cookie in the tea; it's like a sweet little sponge. When she offers me a second cup I shake my head.

"I'll go up and get dressed then." She waits like I'm supposed to give her permission, not a healthy sign given her usual personality.

"OK," I say.

"And, Lilly," when she turns at the door, her head quivers on its tiny spring, "I don't want to talk about anything right now."

I knew that. I gather up our cups and saucers and carry them to the sink. As I wash them I look out the window to the end of the yard, where the Lilly tree is. I grew along with the tree for a while, but after a certain point, only the Lilly tree was getting better. I turn away.

This would be a good time to check on Peter.

When he answers the phone I hear the TV in the background; some woman is screaming her head off. Peter doesn't sound too thrilled to hear from me.

"Dad went to work," he says, factual, like Frank. I never noticed it before. "That lady picked him up."

"What lady?"

"The new one, that one he works for. What a dog."

Good old loyal Peter.

"You mean he left you?"

"Relax, Ma. He's got that problem with Mr. Marsh. He's coming home for lunch." Alex Marsh, Frank's law partner, is the one being divorced by his wife, Maxine. He has asked Frank to represent him. Maxine is a lawyer, too, nicknamed Queen Ballbuster by her husband. Frank's a little afraid of Maxine. Probably today he's genuinely happy to have Melinda take the lead role.

"Are you OK, Peter?"

"Sure. I'm fixing lunch. Listen." He's holding the receiver over the pan so I can hear the splatter of grease. "Hot dogs," he says. "I'm going to put peanut butter and bacon inside. What do you think?"

"Sounds good."

"I made it up."

"You're a genius, Peter."

"Thanks, Mom." Something scrapes across something. "The Hatchers want me to go to their cottage tomorrow."

"That's crazy, Peter."

"What's crazy about it? I think it's pretty nice of them."

"It is nice of them, but you have been very sick."

"I was a little sick, it's true, because of wearing myself out going to graduation."

A great hiss of steam followed by a loud crash interrupts

this inspired guilt trip. "Oops!" he says.

"Peter?"

"It's OK. No sweat." He drags one of the kitchen chairs loudly across the floor. For a minute the phone is completely silent. "Did you know about Dad's horse?"

"He told me."

"He's thinking of buying one, maybe this one."

"He's not really thinking about it, Peter."

"Sure he is. He's been thinking about it for a long time. Every time he reads one of those cowboy books, he talks to me about getting his own horse."

"Why doesn't he tell me?"

My psychic side sees him lifting his shoulders in a shrug. His voice is muffled, like he's holding the phone with his neck. "Garage makes a great stable."

"I'm sure it does, Peter, but this is just a phase. Don't encourage your father."

"Right. Listen, Dad and me are doing great." In a sweeping gesture of generosity he adds, "Stay as long as you want."

"Take care of yourself," my standard sign off.

He clears his throat. "Mom," he says, "it was nice of you not to ask what that noise was."

"Thank you, Peter."

"You wouldn't want to know, really." Water runs full blast in the sink. "But I can fix it."

"Fix what?"

"Oh, nothing." Something else drops to the floor. "I'd get a lot of rest with the Hatchers."

"Forget it."

The water's still running, the hot dogs still frying, and the girl in the background is still screaming her brains out. I know how she feels. "Good-bye, Peter," I say.

When I hang up the telephone, I half-expect my father to come out and join me at the kitchen table. He must have heard my mother go upstairs; maybe *he* will tell me what's going on. Obviously I can't go in there and just bring it up. I feel him listening, wanting to come out, wanting to talk, but not wanting to, too, if you know what I mean.

It is my mother who joins me eventually and pours another cup of tea.

The day moves slowly through the lazy summer hours. My mother gets out her new half glasses and shows me how good they are for reading. Then she puts them away. She doesn't really like them, and she's mastered the trick of slipping her regular glasses down her nose and looking over them, so she doesn't need them, either.

We take a walk around the neighborhood, but she talks very little and she seldom looks me directly in the eyes. She looks at every house we pass as if she's trying to see through the walls. And she sighs, over and over.

When we pass St. George's Episcopal, three blocks from home, I think of Bert buried in the small cemetery behind the Sunday school building. His funeral almost finished me, and I look away. When I was little, Bert sometimes took me to church with him, especially if he was reading a lesson or something. It took hours to get away afterwards because so many people wanted to talk to him. Sometimes I felt like they were lined up in the aisles just to hear his big laugh, and I was very proud to be with him. My father wasn't outgoing like that, and he never went to church. They were a strange pair really. Bert brought out the fun side of Poppy, the part he was usually too quiet to show. When they sat drinking bourbon and laughing under the Lilly tree, the whole world seemed safe to me.

I tell my mother I don't want to see the grave and we walk past, but I feel like I'm turning my back on a friend, and silently promise to come back, by myself. She never particularly liked being with him, anyway.

We turn at the corner of Hazel and Walnut, my crossing station when I was a safety patrol. Carole had the crossing on the other side of the intersection. The little kids always came with their mothers so we weren't needed much, but we got to wear a special orange belt that said we were important. I think that's the only time in my life I ever got respect.

My mother has dropped a little behind me and I slow down.

"You don't have to wait for me, Lilly," she says. But of course I do, and I'm conscious of it for the rest of the walk.

Back at the house, we fix lunch, tuna sandwiches made with yogurt instead of mayonnaise because my parents are on a low-everything diet, and a glass of skim milk. Carole would be in heaven here.

Before we start to eat, my mother lines up six pills, all different sizes and shapes, at her place, and six more, with the sandwich and milk, on a tray. "Vitamins," she says when she sees me looking. The center of the kitchen table is a nest of brown plastic bottles. "Gilbert has his on a tray," she says, and takes his lunch to the den.

There is no point in protesting this so I ignore it, and when she comes back we eat in relative peace.

For years, the after-lunch routine has included a nap, which today I'm happy about, since I have a lot of thinking to do. My father, apparently, is allowed to leave the den at rest time. The three of us climb the stairs together, like we always do when I come for a visit. I break off at the top and go to my old room.

Actually, my old room isn't my old room exactly. It isn't even the way it was when I moved to Chicago for the opera. It's younger. Somewhere along the line, my mother brought some of my dolls and stuffed animals up here from the basement where I had carefully packed them away. She put old dance corsages around my mirror, and pennants I've never seen before on the walls. I guess I disappointed her by growing up; maybe that's what it is that Christie senses in me when we come here.

As soon as my parents are quiet in their room, I tie on a scarf and sneak down the stairs. I fix the door so I can get back in—hoping the criminal element won't pick now, of all times, to strike—and race off to Peg-Mel's for a Snickers bar. I leave the wrapper in Peg-Mel's trash and eat the candy on the way back. It tastes even more delicious after a tuna-and-yogurt sandwich.

Back upstairs I stretch out on my bed and try to empty my mind. I have skimmed these last few days like a smooth pebble across a deep pond, one skip, two skips, three skips on the fragile surface. Since I'm not sure how deep it is, I mean to ease in slowly, so I won't drop in suddenly over my head.

The change in Frank makes me especially uneasy. He's looser and he's tighter, and I can't quite figure it out. On the one hand, for a man who gets embarrassed by a perfectly good singing voice, not to mention a snappy teenage dresser, to be riding around his yard on a horse as if that were as normal as the sun coming up in the morning, seems to me a little odd. On the other, his laissez-faire attitude toward Christie is gone with the wind. He's actually more worried about her than I am. My anchor seems to be losing its grip.

I once played Kate, the American wife of Madame Butterfly's faithless suitor, and even at the time I knew she was the only sane one of the bunch. I've never associated myself with her before; maybe because I wanted to be Butterfly. Now I notice her role—small, but important, very important. The only reason there's a future for any of them at the end, except for Butterfly herself, of course, is because of Kate. Good old Kate.

Chapter Nine

stay in my room a reasonable amount of time, about an hour by the Donald Duck clock on the bedside table, pleased to have discovered certain heroic Kate-like qualities in myself. Then, needing to satisfy a nagging curiosity, I slip quietly downstairs. I want to try on my mother's life for a minute; I want to see what she sees out the front window. I think maybe if I can understand what she feels, I'll know how to talk to her better.

There's no chair by the window, but there are four deep circles in the rug, like the paws of a large animal pressed into the wool. The old floral wingback by the fireplace seems the most likely to me, and I drag it over. It fits perfectly.

I can actually see through the nylon without moving the curtain back, but there's no sense of immediacy to it, so I imitate my mother's pose, and peek out. The street is empty. I watch nothing for about ten minutes. Whatever it is that draws my mother to this view of the world isn't apparent to me. Maybe it's habit, or maybe she just wants to turn her back on what's inside. Frank once told me that when he's here he feels like there's someone behind the front window of every house on the street. I look around, but I can't tell.

Someone moves upstairs, and I jump up quickly and drag the chair back to its usual place.

When my mother comes down I am sitting calmly in the kitchen, rearranging the pill bottles on the table by size, smallest to largest. She announces that we are going to Peg-Mel's. "I go every afternoon after rest time," she says.

Without waiting for a word out of me, she, and her re-turned take-charge personality, which I'm glad to see even though Peg-Mel's wasn't in my plans, go to the hall closet and get her hat, a large brown felt number with the brim turned up all the way around. It's much too big, and when she puts it on, it sinks down until it balances on her eyebrows. When she turns toward me I'm reminded of a nursery rhyme I used to read to the kids; it went something like "Under a mushroom sat a wee elf . . ."

I don't want to go with her. For one thing, I have just been to Peg-Mel's for a Snickers bar. Since friendliness and hospitality are services Peg-Mel's offers along with the fruits and vegetables, I chance an enthusiastic recounting of my recent visit. Personally I prefer a little more anonymity in my grocery stores. Besides, I want to be in the house when my father comes downstairs.

"Let's go, Lilly." My mother peers at me from under her hat. "You can carry the groceries."

So we set out; my mother lugs a large plastic purse she has had for years, and I dangle her multicolored mesh carryall like a psychedelic hair net from my index finger.

"I used to only go once a week," she says as we stroll toward the grocery, "but I need more exercise now."

I can't argue with this; who doesn't? Besides, it's something for her to do on the other side of the nylon curtain.

Peg-Mel's has not been upgraded in years. It's not dirty exactly, just dilapidated. The cans on the shelves are dusty, not because they sit there long but because no one bothers to clean them off when they stock the shelves. The vegetables are dumped, not stacked, in the slanted bins, so the mirrors above them reflect a jumble, not an arrangement, with an occasional pear in with the tomatoes, a green pepper in the broccoli. The bug-eaten outer leaves of the lettuce have not been removed. But nobody seems to care. My mother certainly doesn't. What she cares about is they all know her.

She bangs on the meat-counter call bell, and a large man appears behind the counter. He lights up when he sees her.

"Hey, Maggie!"

She beams.

I never heard anyone call my mother Maggie before.

When she introduces me I'm surprised that behind the huge aproned stomach and bald head of the butcher, are the remains of Fred Baker, a high-school classmate of mine. We went to a dance together once. He was a nice guy but we didn't have much in common. I'm amazed when my mother announces that he owns the place.

"Yep," he says, "bought it back in '78 when Peg and Mel retired. Gives me a good living." He points to some chicken breasts and my mother nods. He tears off a large sheet of brown paper and wraps them up. "So, how are you doing, Lilly?"

"Fine, just fine."

"I'd recognize that hair anywhere," he says, smiling.

I think I'm supposed to say thank you, so I do, and resist the urge to reach up and see what's going on up there.

"Still married to the same guy?" While he talks, he writes in black marker on the butcher paper.

"Uh huh. You?"

"Nope." He caps the pen. "Ellen thought I wasn't home enough," he says. He turns away and wipes off his cutting board.

Ellen Flynn bounces into my memory, a cute little cheerleader with a ponytail and eyes that blinked all the time. She wasn't one of my friends, but she was OK. They got married right after high school.

Fred looks back at me. "She's got a business in the mall now, silk flowers. Doing real well, too." He sighs and wipes his hands on his already-stained apron. "She got married again, Tommy Andrews, maybe you remember him?"

I shake my head.

Fred shrugs. "He's laid off from State Energy. Too bad. Home all the time, though, maybe she likes that."

I doubt it, but I don't say.

Fred hands the package to my mother, "Anything else, Maggie?"

"No, that's it." She hands me the chicken.

He waves as we leave. "Nice to see you, Lilly."

"You too, Fred."

We are barely in the frozen-food aisle, when my mother leans over and whispers loudly in my ear, "He's still in love with her. I guess you can tell."

I put my fingers to my lips. "Shhhhh."

"He can't hear us, Lilly. Besides, he told me straight out." She moves a little ahead of me. "Sad," she says, shaking her head.

I shrug, just to show I'm listening, and reach for an empty cart that someone's abandoned in the ice-cream section.

"Carts make too much noise," she says, and hands me a box of frozen peas to hold with the chicken. As we move down the aisles, it gets a little tough to balance the additions: three baking potatoes, a head of lettuce, a tomato, and a plastic container of nonfat yogurt.

I try to put the stuff in the carryall, but she stops me. "No, Lilly." When she touches me, it feels like a leaf has fallen on my hand. "They'll think you're stealing," she whispers.

The gray-haired woman at the checkout, who agreed with me that Snickers is the best candy bar of all time, rings up our purchases quickly, and allows my mother to introduce me to her, as if she's never seen me before.

"Nice to meet you, Lilly," she says, and winks at me.

Her name is Shirley, and she could stand to lose a little weight, but she's a pleasant person, with very pink cheeks. She reaches under the counter and pulls out a brown paper bag. "Your mother goes for the paper bags," she says. "Only paper."

I relax as Shirley bags our groceries, figuring the Peg-Mel's friendliness system is more complex than I thought. The bag goes in the carryall.

My mother shoves our purchases across to me. "Thanks, Shirley," she says.

Outside, she stops me. "I could get bagged in plastic," she says. "But I never would."

"I always ask for paper, too," I say.

"She uses too much rouge, don't you think?" She starts to move down the sidewalk.

"Shirley?"

"Yes. Too bad." She shakes her head.

I shake mine.

My mother insists on fixing dinner. "You're not a good cook," is how she explains it.

Actually, despite what Christie says, I'm good in the kitchen. I even like to do it. The truth is, my mother doesn't know whether I can cook or not; she has never let me fix a meal for her. Even when the kids were little and my parents used to visit, they either took us to restaurants, or she cooked. I thought it was because she wanted to help me. Now I find out she thinks I can't handle the nightly chicken. But I can be mature about this. In a world of crack houses and organized crime, who cooks the chicken isn't a biggie with me.

I cross the kitchen and look out the window over the sink. My father's old lawn chair is empty and he's nowhere in sight. I check the den but I can tell without going in he's not there. It's too dark, too quiet.

Back in the kitchen I ask, "Where's Pop?"

"Gone," she says, pulling the outer leaves off the lettuce and running water over it.

"What do you mean gone?"

"Gone is gone," she says, shaking the lettuce over the sink, splashing water everywhere. Her back is to me so I can't see her face.

"How do you know he's not upstairs?"

"I can feel it in the house."

This I don't question. My mother has the same sense of people that I do of direction.

"I need to call Frank," I say, and go into the hall.

"Suit yourself," she says behind me.

Upstairs I can feel what she felt from further away. He's not here. I sit on the edge of their bed and dial Frank.

"Blake, Hayes, Marsh, and Johnstone," says a voice I don't recognize.

"Who's this?" I ask.

"Sarah Walker," says the voice. "Who's this?"

"Where's Polly?" I ask.

"She just left the room, for a convenient moment," replies the girl. She's chewing gum. "I'm just sitting here for a favor. Usually I work with Mr. Johnstone."

"Oh." Outside a boy goes past on his bicycle. I'm glad I talked to Peter before Frank could let him go with the Hatchers.

"I mean I usually work with him when I work at all, which I just started to do yesterday. Polly will want to know who called I'm sure."

"Lilly Blake," I say, looking at the featureless reflection of Lilly Blake in my wedding band.

"*The* Lilly Blake?"

"What do you mean *the* Lilly Blake?" I am *the* Lilly Blake only in my dreams.

She chews her gum a little faster. "The one married to Mr. Blake?"

"Yes. Is he there?"

"Pleased to meet you. No, but Polly said, she wrote it down right here," the sound of a piece of paper being picked up, "if you called again to tell you he'll call you back."

"She always says that." I'm getting a pinched nerve in my neck and tilt my head from side to side.

"That's because she's got it written right here, I guess."

I'm sure she's holding it up so I can see. "She probably reads it off, like I did."

"Do you know where my husband is, Ms. Walker?"

"No, Mrs. Blake," she says. "I haven't met him yet. I've heard a lot about him, though. I personally don't think he's the least bit crazy—I love animals myself."

"That's nice. Just tell him I called."

"I'll do that. You have a nice day now."

This is starting to feel wrong to me, my never being able to reach Frank. But maybe I'm just throwing myself into the soap opera, to keep everyone else company.

I lie back on my parents' bed and close my eyes. Wouldn't it be funny if all the time I'm trying to figure out whether or not I should have married Frank, he's got some girl stashed in a white-and-chrome bachelorette apartment on the other side of town, distracting everyone's attention by pretending that the worst thing he does is ride around his backyard on a horse?

Maybe divorce is like the flu. Marsh and Johnstone already have it. Hayes would have it too if he weren't dead. He wasn't at home when he died, either, a major embarrassment. The partners kept his name on the door because it scared them when they thought about how easily they could take it off. Now I think they've forgotten he isn't there anymore.

But I'm off the track. My mind is restless and I need to get it back on Frank. For example, is he a victim of divorce flu? I try to concentrate on the positive aspects of all this. If I get divorced, there's still time to get to the top. Audiences would love me. My age would be a very positive factor and I could maybe even add a limp. Christie and Peter would brag about me. Frank would try to get me back.

I reach for the telephone again. I'm not sure who to call, but it'll come to me. Frank's got to be somewhere.

There's no dial tone, which really ticks me off because now I'm hot to track him down. I click the buttons up and down several times.

On the other end someone else punches buttons, and a voice says, "Hello, hello, hello."

"Frank?"

"Lilly?"

"I just called you," I say.

"I know. Just got back to the office." He rustles papers around on his desk to prove it, but he could be shuffling papers in a trash can at *her* house.

"I talked to Peter," I say. "I was surprised you weren't there." As soon as I say this I hate the way it sounds; but Frank's too innocent to see I'm being mean.

"Peter's fine. In fact, the Hatchers want to take him up to the cottage tomorrow."

"No way."

"Now, Lilly, don't be hasty, he's fine." I can hear his fingers drumming on the desk.

"No way, Frank."

"OK. No sweat. We're doing great."

"Frank, tell me this." I get up and start to pace, carrying the telephone in one hand and dragging the cord behind. "How come I can never reach you since I'm on this trip? I don't have this problem at home."

"You never call me when you're home."

"Why would I call you then?" I turn and kick the cord out of my way. "It's now I need you. You're never there."

His chair creaks. "I'm in court a lot of the time."

Ha! I think. But I play along. "How's the case going?"

"Not too great." He sighs. "Alex is crazy."

"I've been telling you that for years, Frank. What did he do?"

"He told the judge to go blank himself." Frank always says blank, when he means you know what.

"Why?" I kick the cord out of my way and go back the other direction.

"He says the judge doesn't know blank about the law." He shakes his head. I know he's shaking his head, because I've seen him do it so many times when he's on the phone.

"Why'd he say that?"

"Well, it's true, but, it's not the thing to say, under the circumstances."

"Oh."

He changes the subject. "So, how's everything?"

"OK I guess, except Pop's gone again." I sit down on the side of the bed and pull back the curtain.

"What do you mean 'gone again?'"

"Gone is gone," I say impatiently, looking as far down the street as I can see. He is nowhere in sight. I let the curtain drop back into place.

He thinks this over. I hear the chair creak as he leans back. "Where does he go?"

"That's what I'd like to know." I get up and start to pace again.

"Maybe he goes out for a drink."

"There aren't any bars within miles of here, you know that." I stop in front of the mirror over the dresser, to make sure it's still me. "He's going to someone's house."

"Have you asked him about it?"

"Be serious, Frank, what would he say? 'Yes, I'm having an affair.' Of course not. He'd lie." I clear my throat. "Besides," I add, "I think he's avoiding me."

"You should ask him."

"I can't."

"Why not?"

"I just can't, that's all."

He sighs, and for a minute he doesn't say anything.

"What are you thinking, Frank?"

"I was just thinking you never know what's coming. This is our last summer together, as a family, I mean. We should take one last family vacation."

"Frank, we never take family vacations."

"Well, that's wrong, Lilly. That's what I'm saying. This is our last chance. This thing with your parents has got me thinking."

I frown at my reflection; this sounds a lot more like me than it does Frank, and I'm worried I may be making it up.

He continues. "I think we should go to a dude ranch; ride horses, herd cattle, that kind of thing."

The good news is, I'm not crazy; the bad news is, Frank may be.

"Can we talk about this Frank?"

"Oh, sure. AAA is sending some brochures."

I don't remember the rest of our conversation, but when I come down the stairs I can smell dinner cooking already. The oven, with the chicken and potatoes in, must be jacked up to high. The peas are in a saucepan, still in a frozen block with a little water under them and a small white heap of sugar, about a teaspoonful, on the top. My mother sees me looking at this. "Sugar on peas brings out the flavor," she says.

"Remember that. It'll come in handy if you start to cook."

Since neither Peter nor Christie will eat peas, it's not as handy for me as it might be for someone else, but I look interested.

"Dinner's almost ready," she says.

"Aren't we waiting for Pop?" I look out into the backyard, but his chair is still empty.

"It's six o'clock, Lilly."

"Mom, let's wait."

She busies herself over the sink. "We have always eaten at six o'clock."

I look at my watch. The hands form one straight line down the middle; six o'clock all right. "Your watch is fast," I say.

I step into the backyard and walk toward my father's chair. There is not much left of the old green paint, and what there is, is cracked and peeling. I sit down and stretch my legs out in front of me. It's cool here after the rain, and peaceful. The sun is going down, leaving a pink arc on the horizon; the smell of damp grass rises. I can see why my father spends so much time in this chair.

Next door Mrs. Potter has come outside again. She can't see this far anymore, and I feel like a spy, but she never looks up. I watch as she touches the plants tenderly, whispers to them. Before her husband died she was as quiet as an empty room. Now she never stops talking. My father's the only one who will still call to her.

The leaves of the Lilly tree filter the fading evening light. It reminds me of the garden scene from *Faust*. I lean back and close my eyes. I wonder if my father would tell me where he's going if I were a famous soprano. People tell you things when you're famous, because they think you can help. If you're just regular like they are, they write you off.

I try to pretend for a minute to be my father. Where would I go if this life were mine? I haven't thought about this long enough to come up with anything, when the sound of a squeaky hinge on the back gate gets my attention. I sit up and watch my father as he tries to slip unnoticed into the yard. He leans on the gate to rest a moment, then turns toward the house.

"Hi, Pop," I call.

He looks surprised, then smiles. His gait is a little uneven as he walks toward me, but that may be because he doesn't have his cane with him. He only uses it when his feet hurt too bad to walk without it.

"You look good sitting out here," he says. "Wish you came more often." He smiles at me. He's not trying to make me feel guilty, he really means it.

"Me too." I get up. As we walk toward the house he brushes flakes of old paint off my back.

"Don't want to get this on Mother's floor," he says.

I agree.

"Where were you, Pop?"

"Just out for a walk."

"Where'd you go?"

"Nowhere, just in the neighborhood."

I notice that his slippers are muddy so he didn't necessarily walk the neighborhood sidewalks. There aren't many places he could have gotten muddy around here; Thomas Jefferson Elementary School, Taylor Park, and one or two vacant lots I know about. All of these places could be shortcuts to somewhere else. "Better wipe your feet off before you come inside." I point at his slippers.

He seems surprised and stoops a little to get a closer look. "Now, how did I do that, I wonder?" He steps off the walk into the rectangle of light cast by the kitchen window and slides his feet back and forth in the thick grass close to the house. He grips my arm to steady himself. Finally, he is satisfied.

He looks at me, then beyond me to the kitchen window. I turn and see my mother watching us.

"So," he says, letting go of my arm.

"So," I say.

"Do you hear those crickets, Lilly?"

I nod.

He turns me around until I face the backyard. "One calls, and one answers, but they never move. Each one stays in its own place to make music together. People hear music and they go look for where it's coming from, and when they find it, of course, it's usually the wrong sound. But, they pretend to be happy with what they've got."

By now my mother's face has disappeared from the window. I slip my arm through his and we walk toward the house. He is trying to tell me something, but I don't know what. It's too confused. And, I think he's wrong about the crickets.

"Crickets are probably happier making music than doing anything else, because it's such a good sound and it comes from way down inside. Like your singing, Lilly, you're happy when you sing, aren't you?"

"Yes."

"You could have stayed still, singing. You'd be happy."

"I am happy."

"Maybe, but could you be happier? That's the question."

"What are you talking about, Pop?"

"I'm talking about you."

"Don't you like Frank?"

"That's got nothing to do with it." He clears his throat. "You'll get old, the two of you."

"And if I sang?" I ask.

"Don't you see it, Lilly?" He shakes his head.

Before I get to feeling too sorry for myself, I have to remember I just caught this man sneaking into the yard from who knows where, and he's managed to turn the whole thing around to crickets and my lost career. He's pretty sharp. Besides, even if I were going to listen to this cricket-people thing, he's left out the most important part. That's the part where a person's got problems, and everybody's either got them or is going to get them; it's not as appealing to sing alone then. That's where his cricket idea falls down.

We walk up the back steps. He unlocks the door and lets us into the brightly lit kitchen. The screen door sags a little on its hinges but it still closes behind us with a good slap.

My mother has finished her dinner. Her plate is empty but she hasn't left her place; the other two look like plastic models of food.

"You're late," she says.

My father sits down and puts a pat of butter on his baked potato. It sits there. He eats a bite of chicken. "Good dinner, Margaret."

"Thank you." She folds her napkin beside her plate.

"Come on, Lilly, join me," he says.

I do my best but I can scarcely eat anything. It's not only that the food is cold. I've lost my appetite, and that has never happened to me before.

Chapter Ten

In the morning I know I have to visit Thomas Jefferson Elementary School. It must have been the mud on my father's shoes that reminded me of the place. Even after all these years, I remember the playground mud. Or maybe it was all that talk about crickets and singing, because it was there, in kindergarten, that Miss Ariel Hemphill showed me what I could be.

The truth is, I didn't fit in at all. For one thing, there was my hair, wild as a forest fire and just about as uncontrollable. Any kid who felt left out could be an instant hit by pointing at my hair, and everyone else would die laughing. In some ways, though, all the attention to my hair protected the part of me that was really different, the singing part. That was the part Miss Hemphill knew about.

Carole and I were in some kind of lady-training period in those days, preparatory, I can only guess, to being presented at court and marrying royal blood. Our mothers made us practice curtsies and wear ugly brown lace-up shoes for good feet. But life is filled with disappointments, especially for mothers. I never had occasion to use a curtsy except once, as Desdemona's maid, and Carole's mother should only see the palm trees her daughter's walking on now.

Since this visit is one I want to make by myself, I have to wait through a long morning of getting to rest time, the easiest time to slip away. I don't want to have to explain where I'm going, let alone why—I just want to go.

I lose a game of Scrabble to my mother, watch "Wheel of Fortune" with my father, eat lunch (chicken salad made with yogurt and oat-bran nuggets), and finally my parents get settled in their room for afternoon rest.

I wait another ten minutes, after all the noises and little movements and whatever in there have stopped, just to be on the safe side. Then I slip down the stairs and out the back door. I feel as guilty as if I'd stolen something, but most of all I feel like I'm about six years old. By the time I walk the five blocks to the school, I'm almost scared, like I used to be.

The building grows up out of the sidewalk suddenly, a big brick thing that couldn't be anything but a school. I get kid butterflies in my stomach just looking at it, but I keep on going.

There are ten wide steps that lead to the huge double front doors. They give off the same hot concrete smell as my parents' steps, but I don't have any pleasant memories of these. I try the handle on the big front door; the cool, brass thumb latch clicks down. I'm surprised, and a little unnerved to find the building unlocked, but I pull the door open anyway. It's so heavy I wonder how the children ever get inside at all.

It's quiet in here, not much like a school, but that's only because T. J. is closed for summer vacation and the kids are all making noise somewhere else. The hall is cool, and very dark, and I stand still for a minute, letting my eyes adjust. At the other end of the long corridor, a typewriter clatters, and light spreads from an open door in a cone onto the scuffed brown tile. It's a mystery to me why the building is unlocked, and even more, why anyone would be inside working on such a lovely day.

The last thing I want is to be found in here, so I'm careful to make my way along the hall quietly. What I really want to see is the kindergarten, the room where I had some of the best, and worst, moments of my life. I don't have to look far, because it's in the same place as it was when I went to school here, just beyond the lockers, to the right of the front door.

The doors into the kindergarten room have small glass panes you can look through, that is if you're an adult you can look through them. As children, all we ever saw before we pushed into the room, was solid, splintery wood. I press my grown-up face against the glass and look in.

It's a big room with shelves on all sides. The shelves are filled with books and toys; there is still a special corner for blocks, and another on the opposite side for dress-ups. The dress-ups were my favorites. They were just old dresses our mothers gave, with a few fancy things from older sisters, but on us, tiny as we were, each was a ball gown.

I step inside as quietly as I can, and close the door behind me. Just like a good little kindergartner, I walk to the center of the round braided rug that fills the middle of the room, and sit cross-legged on the floor. The rug is exactly like the one we sat on; they must like the style. The upright piano is still at the edge of the rug, and Miss Ariel Hemphill sits on the bench as clear as if she were really there, facing all our little faces. I put my elbows on my knees, and cup my face in my hands.

I loved beautiful Miss Hemphill, and music was my favorite part of the day. We sang "The Farmer in the Dell," "Row, Row, Row Your Boat," "Old MacDonald Had a Farm," and "Oh! Susanna," as loud as we could. Even then I could outsing a whole class. And I guess I was pretty enthusiastic about it, now that I look back. At the time I was just enjoying myself. And Miss Hemphill encouraged me, a lot.

She left T. J. to get married when Carole and I were in second grade. To us it seemed a pretty important thing she was doing. That was forty years ago, more or less, but I can't picture her any other way than she looked to me while she was still here, beautiful and pale. She had long blond hair that hung down her back like the still, moonlit surface of a pond, and the softest voice I've ever heard. I liked to pretend I was Miss Hemphill; when I did it, I talked real softly. Everyone just thought I was sick, but I knew who I was. I liked the hair part the best. When I was Miss Hemphill inside, no one could tease me about my hair—it didn't matter. Everybody liked her. Nobody else in the whole school, maybe in the whole world, was liked by everybody like she was.

From where I sit, the keys on the piano look as yellow as horse teeth, which makes me think this might even be the same piano. I move to the bench and touch middle C. The sound wobbles. I have scarcely pushed the key, but I can tell that the piano is still in tune. School has probably only been out for a week or two. I wish I could play something, very quietly, but I don't dare. The worst thing I can imagine happening to me right now, is to be caught pretending to be a kindergartner. One thing I know is, a lively imagination isn't as appreciated as it might be.

I go back and sit quietly in the middle of the rug. That's enough for me right now. I've just gotten myself good and settled, when I hear footsteps coming down the hall. Like the tap of old John Silver's wooden leg, they echo in the empty corridor, getting louder as they approach the door. My heart beats like a woodpecker on a drainpipe. The note I played couldn't have been heard outside this room, it was no more than a whisper of sound. I'm sure of it. So why is someone coming? Maybe my psychic side met up with someone else's and gave me away? What can I say if I'm caught?

I scramble up, and tiptoe quickly to the playhouse. It's not easy, but I squeeze myself inside. I fill the whole thing up, like Alice in Wonderland, who grew too big, too fast. My face is the same size as the little window. As I wait for the door to swing open, I pretend I'm invisible. It's easy to do that kind of thing in a kindergarten room; all you have to do is close your eyes.

But the footsteps pass by the door without hesitation. They don't even slow down, which is almost a disappointment now that I'm so prepared. A few steps further on, they stop and the hinge on the heavy outer door groans as the door is pushed out. Then, quick scraping steps on concrete as someone turns around and pulls the door shut behind them. I hear a lock twist into place with a loud click. I am locked in Thomas Jefferson Elementary School; that's not so good. But I have not been caught; that's very good.

I ooze out of the playhouse, but it takes a minute before I can unfold completely, because my legs are so cramped. Feeling comes back into them slowly. I try not to remember the story Johnny Batchelder told me in this very room, about the lady whose leg went to sleep and she dropped dead when she tried to walk on it.

I limp across the room and poke my head into the hall. The typewriter is silent and it is dark at the end of the corridor. Actually, in thinking about it, the problem of getting out is minor, and doesn't worry me a bit. I feel like the luckiest person on earth, because (a) I wasn't found, and (b) I'm alone in Thomas Jefferson Elementary School.

I always wanted to play Miss Hemphill's piano, but I never dared. I didn't know how to play, of course, but being me, I never considered that a problem. Asking for permission was the problem; I was afraid someone would laugh at me.

Today I strike up an enthusiastic version of "Old Mac-Donald Had a Farm." I half turn toward the children and smile at them as I sing, encouraging them with nods of my head to join in. My hair hangs long and blond to the middle of my back, my T-shirt is a soft blouse of the finest silk. For one wonderful moment I am Miss Ariel Hemphill, and Lilly Sawyer, the one with the beautiful voice, is in the front row. She'll go far, that girl. Sing for us, Lilly, sing "Climb Ev'ry Mountain."

My hands tire long before my voice, and I stand up and stretch. I'm surprised to see what time it is on the big round face of the clock above the bookshelf. There's no point in knocking myself out getting home; I already blew it. Rest time is long since over. I'll say I went out for a power walk since my mother approves of exercise. I say it out loud to see how it sounds—"I went out for a power walk . . . I just did a power walk . . . I love power walking, don't you?" It needs work, I'll practice on the way home, but I think she'll buy it.

I examine the rows of windows along the far wall; piece of cake. There is a wooden ledge in front of the windows, and it too shows the school must have just closed for the summer, because it's not even a little bit dusty. I pull myself up and sit for a moment dangling my legs, and feeling the quiet room become a part of me. Then I flip the lock on one of the windows, and push it out. It's easy to climb through, but I wouldn't have dared to do it when I was a real kid. I hang from the sill a moment, then drop to the ground, where I push up quickly and brush off my hands. No one has seen me.

When I get back to the house my mother's out front but she doesn't even ask where I've been, which is a little irritating. She is on a low white plastic garden chair, doubled over with both hands inside the flower bed. I sit on the ground in front of her.

"Oh, Lilly, there you are." She's pulling weeds I guess, although most of what comes up is flowers. "I'm airing them," she says.

I accept that. It doesn't really matter what she's doing; they're her flowers.

"Whatever happened to Miss Hemphill?" I ask.

"Miss who?" She peers at me over her old glasses, vaguely annoyed at being interrupted.

"Miss Hemphill, the kindergarten teacher at T. J."

"What made you think of her?"

"I just wondered." I lean toward the flowers and begin to pull out weeds.

"Don't do that, Lilly," she says. "You don't know how."

"You don't have to be a genius to pull weeds, Mother."

"I know that." She removes one of her gardening gloves and slaps it against her leg. A puff of dry earth colors the air. Then she puts the glove back on. "I'm not just weeding."

"You're not?"

"No." She turns back to her work.

I lean on my heels and watch her reach for the same weed I just had and decide that she will always be a mystery to me. I stand and brush the dirt off my hands.

"Is Pop inside?"

"Who knows?" She jabs at the ground and I leave her to it. Since she never answered my question about Miss Hemphill, I think maybe she doesn't remember her.

The air in the den is dancing with TV light, but he's not there. The house feels empty, so there's no need to look upstairs. I go down the hall to the back door and look out. My father is hunched over in his lawn chair, staring at the ground between his feet. Ants again, I bet.

I grab a Fig Newton out of the box on the refrigerator and go outside. He doesn't look up as I approach and I move quietly behind his chair to look over his shoulder. I want to see what he sees.

"Ants," he says. "I like to watch ants." His feet are planted firmly on either side of an anthill and the tiny creatures are moving sort of crazily in every direction. It doesn't look to me like they've got all that much of a plan.

"How did you know I was here?"

"I just did." He looks up and smiles. "You don't walk like an Indian you know."

"I try."

My father tried to teach me to walk without any sound at all when I was a child. I don't know whether it was for his benefit or mine, but I never could get the hang of it.

I hold out the Fig Newton. "Maybe they'll like this better than chicken."

"I do," he chuckles, and takes a big bite out of the cookie. Several crumbs drop to the ground and the ants scramble to pick them up. "Ants have lots of teamwork," he says.

I put my hand on his shoulder. His bones are small ridges under the thin cloth of his shirt. "Yes they do," I say.

"We could all do with a little more teamwork." He holds a twig between his fingers like a small wand, then leans forward and scratches his name, Gilbert, into the ground. The writing is awkward, sharply angled, like writing carved into a school desk.

"I always watch these ants." He shakes his head. "Mother says it's a waste of time, but it's much better than the TV, don't you think?" He pats my hand and his skin feels like dry tissue in a gift box.

"Seems like it would be," I say.

"Bert and I had races—put bets on 'em. Mother stayed inside, and waited for him to go. Now *that* was a waste of time." He leans forward and stares at the ground. "Watch him, Lilly," he points, "look at him go! He'd win a race all right!"

I lean on the arm of his chair, and we watch as the Olympic ant disappears into the mound. Then I turn to him. "What's going on with you two, Pop?"

"Your mother and me?" He rubs his chin.

"Yes, what's happening?"

"I don't know, Lilly. Something isn't right, is it?"

"No, something isn't right."

"Maybe we're not much of a team anymore." We both stare at the zigzagging ants.

"But why? You've been together for such a long time."

He shrugs his shoulders, and draws a circle around the anthill with his stick. "I don't like being old, Lilly."

"No."

"It's hard work."

"I know that, Pop."

He looks back at the ground. "We're just not doing it together, I guess."

When I don't say anything he says, "You know about Bert?"

"Yes, Pop," I look down on the top of his head. "I came for the funeral."

"Did you?" he says. "I don't remember. We used to watch ants, and we had a drink or two." He laughs. "Remember that Old Grand-Dad?"

I smile. "Maybe you should have asked mother to join you."

"We did."

"Pop, where do you go every evening?"

"That first bottle of Grand-Dad we had, Bert brought." He leans back. "The night Chrissie was born he brought the first bottle of Grand-Dad." He looks up and chuckles. "He thought that was real funny."

I smile.

"I was the Old Grand-Dad," he continues, in case I didn't get it.

I bend toward him. "Pop, where do you go?"

"Why here, of course, just here." He stretches his legs out in front of himself, carefully avoiding the anthill.

"No, you go somewhere else, I've seen you."

"Lilly, where would I go?"

I kneel down beside his chair. "That's what I want to know."

"Well, I don't go anywhere, you're imagining things."

Even though I am practically staring his head off, he doesn't look at me. "I am not imagining things," I say.

He looks toward the house. "I suppose your mother put you up to this."

"No she didn't."

"Yes she did. She told you I was stepping out." He shakes his head back and forth. "I can't believe she told you."

"I've seen you myself, Pop."

"No you haven't and neither has she, because I'm not going anywhere." He snaps the little twig in two and drops the pieces beside the anthill. Then he puts his hands on his knees and leans back in the chair.

"Sing to me, Lilly, sing 'Summertime.'"

"Here?"

"Why not?" One of his ragged eyebrows twitches as he looks up at me.

"I might bother the neighbors."

"Letty Potter won't hear even you, poor soul, and the Baxters are away. There's no one to bother."

It is one of the quietest days I can remember. The houses look deserted, even the breeze has died down and the birds are quiet. "OK." I swallow a couple of times to loosen up.

With his eyes closed, his face sags like an airless balloon.

"Summertime . . . and the livin' is easy. . . . Fish are jumpin' . . . and the cotton is high. . . ."

It's from *Porgy and Bess*, one of my favorites. He taught it to me. Without an orchestra to overcome I can sing pretty soft, for me anyway. Besides, I'm working my way up to the high note. By the time I get to it, ". . . standing by," he's asleep.

My mother comes rushing around the side of the house flapping her apron. "Hush, Lilly, hush, you'll bother the neighbors."

Like I said.

I go inside to call the police station on Jackson Street. If they're not all out writing tickets, I'll give them an anonymous tip about the open window at Thomas Jefferson Elementary School.

Chapter Eleven

For a minute I'm not sure I heard anything at all, and I'm sort of surprised to find myself sitting up with my eyes wide open in the middle of the night. Then, I hear it again, plop, plop, soft like the puff of popcorn but steady. It seems to be coming from my window. I slip out of bed and walk across the room in my bare feet.

At first I don't see anything out there, it's so dark, but when I pull the curtain all the way back, there's Carole in the front yard, bent over like a lawn ornament, digging around in my mother's flowers. She straightens and fires another dirt clod at my window before she notices me. I hold both hands up flat for her to stop. As soon as she sees me, I leave the window and hurry down the stairs.

Carole goes around to the other side of the house like she

used to when we were kids. I know she'll do that, so I don't even pause in the front of the house. She's leaning against the back door peering through the glass, her hands cupped on either side of her face to cut out the glare from the floodlight on Mrs. Potter's back porch. My mother thinks Mrs. Potter set it up so she could look in our house, but I doubt it. The way I figure it, unless a person could see inside my mother's head there's not much going on over here. Anyway, when I open the door, Carole practically falls in.

"What are you doing here?" I whisper.

She gives me a look right out of the movies. "Todd was a very strange man," she says.

"Was?" I whisper.

She rolls her eyes and sighs. "*Is*, Lilly, *is*." She tries to pick up where she left off, "He—"

"Shhhhh!" I say, and point at the ceiling meaning my parents are asleep. I tug at her sleeve and turn, hoping she will follow me, quietly, across the kitchen to the basement door. She follows me, but not quietly, because of those stupid shoes (she's still got on the palm trees). I think she does the best she can though, under the circumstances.

When I flick on the light at the top of the stairs, strange shadows flatten themselves against the wall, and I'm glad I'm not alone. Of course, if I were alone, I'd be in bed asleep and not down here at all, so I guess it's a moot point.

The noise she makes going down the wooden basement stairs gives me a headache right off. At the bottom, I stop and listen for the slap, slap, slap of my mother's backless slippers following us down. Nothing. Hard to believe, because my mother's ear is still the sharpest in the family, but who questions such good luck?

This is one of the last houses in America without a rec room. There's no wet bar, no paneling, no shag rug. What we have here is a genuine basement. My parents use it to store things, mainly clothes, furniture, books that may come in handy some day. It's where my mother unearthed my current room decorations from, for example. There's a little of everything down here.

The floor is concrete, very cold on my bare feet, and the walls are the foundation bricks whose paint has long since crumbled dustily to the floor. The air is at least ten degrees cooler and damp; I shiver slightly.

"Here." Carole hands me an old red sweater from a pile of clothes too large for the green plastic bag they've been stuffed in. "Put this on."

"Thanks." I pull on the old sweater and feel better. For one thing, it covers up my Mimi death-scene costume. For another, it has a musty smell, like a rented beach house. If I weren't so curious about what Carole's going to tell me, I'd close my eyes and pretend to be at the beach. It's the perfect setup for a fantasy based on, say, *South Pacific*. But first things first.

I sit in a corner on a pile of towels; Carole pulls herself up on an old kitchen table. A bare bulb hangs in the middle of the room, and swings in small motions in the disturbed air.

I wait, hoping she's so interested in her own life she won't notice my tired, unlifted face, in the mean-spirited light of this basement.

"What are you muttering about, Lilly?"

"I'm not muttering about anything," I snap back.

"Now I'm hearing things," she sighs. "Well, it doesn't surprise me, considering everything." She leans forward. "I left him there, Lilly," she continues, like this is big news. "He was," she shakes her head, "I don't know." She arranges herself like a lilly pad on the table, and clasps her hands in her lap. "Probably the English are all like that." She nods. "I'm sure it's a cultural difference." Then, with a faraway look in her eye she says, "I'll have to find another tennis coach, I guess."

"God, Carole! How can you think of that now?!" I pull a pair of black-and-white checked towels from the pile I'm sitting on, and wrap my cold feet in them one at a time. Then I lean back into the red beach-smelling sweater, and ask, "How did you get here, anyway?"

"I called a number on the bulletin board in the Union. Some kid was coming home."

"Someone else lives in this town?" I notice I've got my arms folded across my chest, and immediately loosen up.

She smiles, whether at me or at her luck in getting a ride I'm not sure. "Dropped me right at your door."

"That was nice."

She nods. "I paid for the gas."

"Oh."

"It was the least I could do." She twists her wedding rings around and around; the diamonds flash like strobe lights on a dance floor.

"What happened to the dating?" I ask.

"We did date. We went to the movies, you were there, and we went to the zoo." She stretches her legs out in front of her and twists her feet this way and that, examining the palm-tree wedgies which have certainly had a workout. "We walked all over the place. I was a little worried about it, Lilly," she says. "I don't know where I'd ever find another pair of these shoes."

"So what happened?" I ask, hoping she'll skip the kinky details, if there are any, and just come to the point.

"The zoo did something to him." She sighs. "It must have been the zoo. Something happened there."

"What do you mean?"

She looks at me for a minute and then, satisfied she's got my complete attention, she says, "He thought he was Tarzan." She licks one of her long fingernails and polishes it with the skirt of her sundress.

"He looks like Tarzan," I offer.

"Anyway," she says, ignoring my comment, "I came home is what happened."

Obviously a lot has been left out, which is fine by me. I just want to know the bottom line. "You didn't go home, you came here."

"Same thing." She smooths her hair back and smiles at me. I'm supposed to be flattered, I guess.

"Why didn't you go to your house?" I ask. My feet feel a little numb, so I reach down and loosen the towels up a little.

"Jeff's asleep," she says, and looks at her watch for my benefit.

"Oh, sure, why didn't I think of that?"

"Don't be snippy, Lilly. What could I tell him?" She thinks she has me there, I can see it in her eyes.

"Good question, since you're supposed to be guarding Christie." I lean back and give her a head-on look.

"Right." She looks away.

"Carole, I've been telling you for years, lying never helps." And I have been.

"But you're wrong. It helps a lot unless you change your mind, which I usually don't. Then it's a problem." She stares at the crumbled wall. "I'll figure it out."

"Why won't you listen to me?" I feel like I might be whining, but really, it is frustrating. Besides, it's very late, and I have a tension headache, the worst kind because it's so discouraging. I mean, things are bad enough and then you slap a headache on yourself.

To distract my attention, I concentrate on my towel-wrapped feet. They look like soccer balls on the ends of my legs. I recross my ankles, assessing the effect. Pelé would be mad with desire about now. Now, that's kinky. Peter could have him for a stepfather. He'd probably like that, once he got over the shock of Frank's getting the old heave-ho.

"Can I stay here?" Carole interrupts my fantasy with a Princess Diana, don't-leave-me-on-the-shelf look. Christie can do that one, too.

"You *are* here."

"No, I mean until Friday. Jeff won't know." Even in the harsh light of this basement I have to say it, her face job is pretty good.

"And what am I supposed to tell my parents?"

"Your mother would understand."

"No she wouldn't." My mother doesn't understand about affairs, especially now. Maybe that's where I get it from.

"I could stay down here; they'd never have to know."

"Don't be ridiculous."

I myself am not staying down here another minute. Even

with the old red sweater on I'm freezing. I'll stick Carole in the guest room and figure this out tomorrow. I lean forward and unwrap my feet. "Come on, and don't make any noise."

We start up the stairs when I remember something I wanted to ask her. "Carole, do you remember Miss Hemp-hill?"

"The kindergarten teacher?"

"Yes."

"Sure I remember her. Why?"

"Do you ever wonder what happened to her?"

"No."

"Well, I do. Maybe we can go find her, for old times' sake."

"Why would we want to do that?" Carole gives me a shove up the stairs and clumps up behind me.

"I don't know, I just thought maybe it'd be a good idea."

"Maybe, Lilly."

The kitchen seems warm after the basement, and smells of damp tea bags. I gesture for Carole to follow me, but she really has no sense of how to walk like an Indian. I may not do it very well, but at least I know you're supposed to.

In the hall I turn around. "Take those things off," I whisper. I'm pointing at the palm trees. For a minute I think she's going to tell me where to get off, but then she bends over and undoes the ankle strap. I am, after all, her only hope right now. It gives me a little power.

We climb up quietly and I leave her at the door to the guest room, one shoe dangling from each hand. She starts to speak and I put my finger to my lips. "My mother hears everything," I say, and go to my own room. "Tomorrow," I whisper from the door.

It's hard to sleep with so much on my mind. The list

grows. My marriage, a large subject; my son, who was almost allowed to go to the neighbors' beach house even though he has been very sick; my friend, who's hiding from her husband in my parents' house; my parents themselves, who are both nuts; and my daughter, whose Frisbee-eyed boyfriend is on the loose at Bolton College. They file back and forth through my head like a round of carved figures on a cuckoo clock. And over it all, a "loose widow" dressed in scarlet, spins a web around us, then dances across it on little black shoes laughing her head off.

I hear the grandfather clock strike every hour until four, then, somewhere between four and five I must fall asleep because the next thing I know the clock is bonging ten times and the sun is shining directly into my face. I'm still wearing the red sweater, and I've been dreaming about sun and sand, and I think I was singing "Bali Ha'i." Bert was there, having a nightcap with my father under a palm tree like nothing ever happened. Whoever was in my bed in the thatch hut was just a big lump under the sheet, but somehow I'm pretty sure it wasn't Frank.

I don't feel like I've slept at all. It's too much to hope that Carole was part of the dream; for one thing, there's the red sweater to account for. I try to brush some sense into my hair, but it looks like I feel. I tie my scarf on tight, sort of like a brain corset, and decide this is another day for sweatpants. The legs are wonderfully loose, but unless I'm mistaken, the bottom's a bit snug.

On my way downstairs I stop by the guest room and peer in. The old Victorian double bed looks solid, the white chenille cover is in place, the room is empty.

The TV is on in the den, and my father sits in his usual

spot. He has a cup of coffee balanced on the flat arm of his old brown chair. The surface has a dull cold look.

"Morning, Pop."

He smiles up at me vaguely. "Hello, Lilly."

"Want me to get you some hot?" I indicate the cup.

He shakes his head. "It's never hot," he says.

I'm not sure what that means but I ask, "Is Mom up?"

"She's always up." His eyes leave the television screen and focus somewhere over the corner cabinet.

"Pop, what are you thinking about?"

He shrugs. "Nothing," he says.

In the kitchen Carole and my mother are drinking tea, their heads almost touching, speaking in low voices. They stop talking when I come into the room.

"Carole," I say, "what are you doing here?" I'm using a forced heartiness they will both know is a bluff, but what else can I do?

"Please, Lilly," my mother says in her spare-me voice. "Coffee or tea?"

"Coffee, please."

She puts a spoonful of Sanka in a cup and runs tap water in. The coffee has the same flat look my father's had.

"Coffee's bad for you," she says, and hands it over. Carole nods in agreement.

I look into the cup, defeated. "Give me tea, then." I'll have another headache by noon without my coffee, but at least I'll have something hot to drink, which I need under the circumstances.

My mother gives a satisfied little 'humph' and dumps the coffee out. The steaming tea tastes like a leaf pile used by dogs, but I drink it anyway. I close my eyes and pretend to be the queen of England. Who can blame me? I have always thought tea would taste a lot better if you had a crown on.

Apparently I interrupted something when I came in, because they don't start up again right away. Since I don't know what my mother knows, it's hard to begin the conversation.

"So, what's happening?" seems bland enough.

My mother looks at me over her old glasses. She has pushed them practically to the tip of her nose, so that she can see over their round gold rims. "I know all about it, Lilly. You don't have to fake it."

Carole has always gotten along better with my mother than I have, but this surprises me because the subject, no matter how it's dressed up, is sex, and my mother doesn't do sex.

"Your mother is a wise woman," Carole says, her eyes filled with unshed tears. This makes me nervous, but my mother reaches over and pats her hand. If she's so wise, I'm wondering, how come she wasn't in the basement instead of me last night? For future middle-of-the-night emergencies, I hope Carole remembers it's my mother that's the helpful one.

"I've called Jeff," Carole sniffles. "He's coming to pick me up."

"Here?"

"Well, of course here."

"Now?"

"What's the matter with you, Lilly?"

Even I don't know the answer to that. Nothing ever seems quite rounded off is all. "But what about Miss Hemphill?" is all I can think to say.

"Who?"

It's only because I haven't had my coffee.

The doorbell rings and Savage Dog goes nuts. Neither of them pay any attention. My mother says, "I heard Carole throwing rocks—"

Carole interrupts, "It was only dirt, Margaret."

Margaret?

"Doorbell!" my father calls from the den.

"Dirt, then, at your window, Lilly." She pats her thin white curls. "I thought you'd never wake up."

"You really are a sound sleeper," Carole says like she's telling me I have VD or something.

The doorbell rings again.

My mother sucks in a mouthful of tea. "I almost forgot how old I was, Lilly. It was like all those years ago, when you were children, you letting Carole in at night, the both of you going to the basement."

I must look surprised because she adds, "Don't look so shocked. I hear everything. I always knew when Carole was over."

"Doorbell!" my father calls louder.

"You knew?" I give her credit for not being a pain about it when we were kids.

"Can't someone shut up that damn dog?" my father shouts.

"Of course I knew."

My mother sips her tea. "This morning I went straight to the guest room. Carole was up, of course. We came down here and now she's going home. Simple."

I figure unless someone answers the door, she's going nowhere so I get up. I can understand why Carole doesn't want to get it, but my mother could go, I'm thinking, and give me a minute to figure out what's so simple about all of this.

"I'll fill you in," my mother says, reading my mind.

Since I have met Todd, Jeff looks pretty good to me in a plain old guy kind of way. I guess he doesn't do much with himself, either, but he stands on the front step, solid and good-natured. I switch off Savage Dog. Jeff's hair, like Frank's would be, is a little damp from the shower. I wish it weren't, because it shows he's gotten all cleaned up to come for her. I want to dry his hair for him, I don't want her to have this advantage, even if she is my oldest friend. He hugs me.

"So, how was the trip?" he asks.

No recriminations, no blame. Naturally it makes me feel guilty.

"Carole's in the kitchen," I say.

"No, I'm not." Her voice is right beside me and suddenly so is she. "Hi, Jeff." She looks young, and innocent, and ready to go home.

"Hello, Carole." He seems hesitant, his big fingers tug at his belt.

"My suitcase is out by the tree."

"It's already in the car," he says.

She nods. "OK. I want to say good-bye to Margaret." She disappears into the kitchen.

"I like you, Jeff," I say.

He smiles at me. "I like you too, kiddo."

And then Carole is back. She takes Jeff's arm and they walk out the door.

"Carole?"

She turns around from the front walk. "Oh. Bye Lilly. I'll call you."

I stand in the door and watch them drive away. The car has some kind of tinted windows, so I can't tell if they're talking or not. When they're finally out of sight, I go back into the kitchen.

"It wasn't about sex," my mother starts right in. "It was about sensitivity."

I know this conversation is going to embarrass me. I pour myself another cup of tea, and pretend my scarf is a tiara. I reach around and tighten it a little in the back.

"While she was in the bathroom putting on her new nightgown, she bought a special one you know, this person pulled one of the beds on top of the other one."

"What for?"

"She never did find out. He made steps too, to get up there; a phone book, a trash can, and a chair."

"He did?" Since I know the room, I'm trying to picture it for the full flavor.

"She says he was real interested in the big apes. They went to the zoo, you know." She shakes her head. "Maybe that was it. It sounds like he was building a tree house to me. Carole thinks so, too."

"Maybe." I gulp my tea.

My mother goes on, like she's talking to Fred at Peg-Mel's, about chicken breasts. "Then she fell off the chair, and he ripped her new nightgown."

"Ripped it?" I've lost the sequence.

"Yes. That was the worst part."

Nightgown homicide. Carole could never take it.

"She paid a lot of money for it," my mother continues.

"Two hundred dollars."

"Three hundred dollars." She jabs the table with her index finger.

I can almost see it, Carole getting all dressed up for her big part and having Todd, a man with lots of body but no soul, rewrite the lines.

My mother continues. "She said Jeff has respect for her clothes."

"Jeff pays for them."

This makes my mother pause. She decides not to discuss it with me anymore; I'm not deep enough. Instead she asks, "Do you like my perfume, Lilly?"

"Evening in Paris?"

"Yes, do you like it?" She holds her hand out, wrist up, so I can smell it. Her pale arm has small brown shadows on it, like a bruised petal.

"Well, sure."

"I'm bored with it," she says, "I want something new. What's good?"

"I don't know, Mother. Frank's allergic."

She looks as sad as if I'd told her he had a terminal disease. "I'm sorry, Lilly."

"It's OK."

"I would have given it to you," she says.

"Thanks," I say. "I would have liked it."

"I've got so much of it, I can't throw it out." She leans back. "Who would like it, I wonder?"

I shrug my shoulders because I really don't have any ideas on this one.

She rubs her wrist. The veins are like blue thread under the skin. "Maybe the Red Cross."

"Maybe," I say.

"I think if I could change my perfume, I could change my life."

"It's worth a try," I say, because anything is, after all.

Chapter Twelve

After lunch we stay at the table, my mother and me, but we're not talking. For one thing, I've got a headache, which is no surprise. For another, we both have too much on our minds.

I'm wondering what a bachelorette apartment would be like; white and chrome is appealing in an uncluttered kind of way. It would be hard to have complications in an apartment like that. My mother is probably continuing with the theme of major changes she can make in her life, and who to give her Evening in Paris to. Whatever, we're pretty involved in our own heads when the telephone rings. That's why we both jump.

It has to be Frank. "I'll get it," I say as my mother pushes back her chair.

"It's my phone," she says.

"It's Frank." That stops her because she believes in my psychic side. I press my advantage. "I'm sure."

She must not be getting any special vibes of her own, because she only hesitates for a moment before she stands aside. I hurry to the telephone.

"Hello."

The voice at the other end of the wire is high-pitched and excited. And it isn't Frank.

"Mom, what's he doing here?"

"Christie?"

"Yes. What's he *doing* here?"

My mother is hanging on my shoulder. "You said it was Frank," she whispers.

"It's Christie," I say. "Same thing."

"Mom!"

"I'm listening, Christie. Calm down." I shift the telephone to my other ear. "Now, *who's* there?"

"Dad. Dad's here. What's he doing here?" Her voice is drawn tight in her throat.

"Your father is there? At Bolton?" My mother moves around to my other side, to get closer to my phone ear.

"Yes, here. Here, here, here!" The needle on her record is obviously stuck. "He wouldn't have thought this up on his own," she says. "You sent him." I can tell from the way she's breathing that she's pacing up and down in her room; it's in the genes.

"Christie, I don't know what you're talking about."

My mother is tugging at my elbow. "What is it?"

"Sure you don't," she says. It's the same tone she used when she found me on the floor by the bedroom window.

"I *don't*," I insist.

"I'm talking about Daddy," Christie says, "D-A-D-D-Y, here, with me. I'm so humiliated." This last comes out with a slobbering rush of tears.

"Just a minute, Christie." I put my hand over the mouthpiece and whisper to my mother, "Frank is there. Christie thinks I sent him."

"That's ridiculous."

"Of *course* it's ridiculous—but she believes it."

"Give me the phone." My mother holds her hand out. She is ready to charge up the hill for me. It's a wonderful moment. I almost do it, for both of us, and then I come to my senses.

"I can handle this, Mother." I breathe deeply and uncover the mouthpiece. "Christie, if your father is there, where's Peter?"

"Right. Great. I'm dying, and all you want to know about is where's Peter!"

"That is *not* all I want to know about. I'm trying to figure out what's happening."

She sighs. "The Hatchers have him at their cottage."

This information thunks like a spear into the floor in front of me. I stop midpace. "I said he couldn't go."

"Big deal," she says.

"Christie, let me speak to your father."

"He's not here." Bedsprings creak as she flops down. "I mean, he's here, he's just not *here*, here."

"Where is he then?"

"He's gone off with the security guard," she sobs.

"Arrested?"

My mother's eyes are huge, and she's pulling my arm to get the telephone low enough so she can hear too.

"I wish. They went out for pizza or something."

I shake my head 'no' to my mother, and she looks relieved. "Where's he staying?" I ask.

"He *says* he's staying in the hall outside my room—he brought a sleeping bag."

"Where'd he get a sleeping bag?"

"Jesus, Mom, who cares!"

"Now Christie, calm down."

"I can't believe this is happening to me."

"I know, dear."

"This is all your fault," she chokes.

"How could it be *my* fault? I'm not with you, I'm not at home, I'm at Grandma's."

"Maybe so, but you're the one who has to know what I'm doing every second."

"Christie, that's not fair."

"And now you've got Dad doing it. Why did you tell him to call me?"

"I didn't tell him to call you, but why shouldn't he, anyway?"

"Because I wasn't here, that's why, just like you knew. I shouldn't have told you anything."

"Christie, you're not making sense. No one's checking up on you. If your father called he just wanted to say hello."

"At three in the morning?"

We both stop pacing. I'm thinking about this. "Where were you, anyway?"

"Where do you think?"

"Oh."

"It was no big deal, like you said," she says, but I think she's crying. "Get him *out* of here!"

I think she's talking about Frank. "Does the school know

he's there?" My mother nods that this is a very good question.

"How should I know? He's bought off the guard, that's for sure." I hear a noise I take to be pillow punching. "He says the motel is filled, but I don't believe it. Besides, what's he even *doing* here? I'm an adult."

Right.

"Christie, get Dad to call me when he gets back, OK?" I close my eyes, but I can't bring on a Limp Lulu with my mother practically wrapped around me, and my daughter sobbing away.

"Tell him to get out of here," she moans.

"Just have him call me."

I hang up the telephone and look at my mother.

"He says the motels are filled."

She seats her glasses more firmly on her nose. "I know of a room."

"Yes, Mother, I thought of that."

Just because, I lift the telephone receiver and dial Frank's office.

"Who are you calling?" My mother hangs nervously in the background. I am, after all, her daughter.

"Frank." This is the kind of call a touch-tone phone was made for, a real button-punching call, but my parents' telephone is still the old dial kind, and I grind the numbers slowly out.

"He isn't there, Lilly. Christie just told you." She has her hands on her hips as if to say I should have paid more attention. "He's at Bolton College."

"I'm calling his *office*, Mother."

She doesn't say anything but looks at me in that way she has that makes me forget how small she is. I figure I'm doing her a favor, getting her mind off her problems. I turn away as Polly Wagoner answers the phone.

"Blake, Hayes, Marsh, and Johnstone."

"Polly, it's Lilly Blake." I curl the black telephone cord around my index finger until the loops are stacked up like a spring. "Me," I add, and feel the ball crack out of the park.

"Oh, hello, Mrs. Blake," she says.

"May I speak to my husband, please?"

Polly heaves a sigh of disappointment. "Sorry, Mrs. Blake, he just left for court."

"Polly, that's a lie." I begin to pace. My mother gets out of my way.

The girl pauses. She unwraps something crinkly. I try to bend my cord-wrapped finger and can't.

"What do you mean a lie?" she asks.

I don't answer, just let it hang.

"Can you hold on a minute, Mrs. Blake? My other line is ringing." Click. She's gone. A barely perceptible beep, beep, beep tells me I'm on hold. Poor Polly, now she's got to figure out how to deal with me. She's probably scanning her desk for ideas; dictionary, thesaurus, pencils, stapler, scotch tape—all useless. She was only doing her job, that's probably what she'll say, but I'm plenty irked.

She comes back on with a click. "I was only doing my job," she says.

In answer I start to hum, quiet soothing tunes from *The Sound of Music*, so she'll think while she was off, I had to put *her* on hold. There would be nothing unusual in this since every other household in America has call waiting; the background music is my own invention. She's chewing something. "Where the heck did she go?" she mutters.

I break off midscore of "Climb Ev'ry Mountain," flick the

mouthpiece with my fingernail, and say, "Sorry, Polly, had to take another call."

"That's OK."

"You were going to tell me where my husband is?" The no coffee, etcetera headache tightens.

"No I wasn't, I was telling you I was doing my job. I can't tell you where he is because it's," she lowers her voice, "confidential. But just between you and me, I'd be happy if I were you because where he is was first to save you worry from a hospital experience, and then because of your daughter, and I think it's nice he's such a caring person." She pauses to catch her breath. "He's a gentleman, I can tell you. Not like," she hesitates, "some of the others."

I wait.

"Besides," she goes on, "sometimes he really was in court." There's scraping in the background, as if a chair is being moved closer to Polly and someone is sitting down.

I flick the mouthpiece with my fingernail several times. "Another call. Hold on a minute, Polly." I gently move my mother aside, and open the freezer door. I hold the receiver against the fan to simulate the whir of another call being connected. Then I pick up with "Edelweiss," soft and distant into the cold telephone. Polly's chewing rapidly. "You know," she says, "she's not as dumb as we thought. She knows."

Another voice, farther away, says, "How'd she find out?" It sounds like Sarah Walker.

Polly's silence is clearly a shrug.

"She should count her blessings is what I think, considering Marilyn Monroe Jeffries works here."

"Nah. She's working on Mr. Marsh. He's got more money."

"He's a pain in the butt. If I were her, I'd go for Mr. Blake."

I've heard enough. I run my fingernail across the mouthpiece again. "Polly?"

"Yes, Mrs. Blake."

"That call was something I have to attend to. In the future you'll tell me the truth, right?"

"I can't do that, Mrs. Blake. Not if he tells me not to."

"As a woman, Polly, your loyalty is to me."

"How do you figure?"

"It's simple. It's how we got the vote."

"I've always voted."

"Polly, we're sisters."

"No we're not, Mrs. Blake. I'm your husband's secretary."

I hang up quick, before I can make it worse. My mother waits a few minutes, shaking her head, and going tsk, tsk, tsk. Then, seeing that I'm not going to make any more interesting calls, she leaves the room still shaking her head. She probably thinks I should have let it lay. After all, I might have found out something bad, like a girl in a bachelorette apartment, for example, and then what would we do? I was just lucky is what she thinks. And she thinks I took a big chance.

I clear the dishes off the table and put them in the dishwasher. She'll take them out and wash them, because she doesn't like to use her dishwasher, but I've done my part; the kitchen is clean, and I can take off.

In the hall I lean up the stairs and listen. Someone is moving around in my parents' bedroom. "I'm going out," I call. "Be back for dinner."

I snatch up my purse and car keys, before she can ask where I'm going, before she can tell me my sweatpants are inappropriate for wherever it is, before she notices they're a little tight in the rear.

Actually, I'm not going anywhere. I just want to get out for a while. If Carole's home, I'll stop by and tell her about Frank. I need another person's bird's-eye view on the situation. I may not mention about Christie's no longer being the only virgin she knows—at least, near as I can tell, that's what she was saying.

I close the door tightly behind me and hurry down the front steps. As I pass the big tree my mother's unmistakable voice sings out, "Lilly?"

She's on her hands and knees weeding her flowers, this time on the street side of the tree. And she's got her mushroom hat on.

"I thought you were upstairs," I say.

"No, I'm here." She thrusts her gloved hands into the flowers and digs around. "These plants depress me. I want something lively."

"Like what?"

"Like marigolds maybe."

"Marigolds smell bad."

"Marmalade is bitter," she responds.

"I don't like that either."

"Well, I do." She sits back and looks up at me. The quivery motions of her head seem a little more noticeable today, and I wonder if it's worry that does it, or if she's tired.

"Maybe we could plant marigolds out back where there's more sun." I start around to the side of the house to see if there's a good spot.

"No, Lilly." Her hand's up, like a traffic cop. "I want them here."

I turn around. "OK. If you want me to, I'll stop at a nursery and see what I can find out, but don't hold your breath."

"That would be nice, dear. I think everything might be fine if I could just have something bright here."

I bend down and pat her hand. "OK, I'll try."

"Where are you going?"

"Just out. I want to drive around, look at things, nothing much. I'll be home for dinner, though. Do you want me to pick anything up?"

"No, I always go to Peg-Mel's." She reaches up and pushes a thin curl of hair back under her hat.

"OK."

"They expect me."

She reaches back into the flowers and I know I'm dismissed. "See you later," I say.

The station wagon, without the two girls, Carole and me, plus all the luggage, is definitely junky-looking. I peel away from the curb.

I'm surprised my mother didn't ask more about where I was going, and even more surprised she didn't ask to go along. But I'm glad, because the first thing I have to do is get a cup of real coffee, before I die.

I drive direct to the 7-Eleven and order a large cream and sugar to go. I'm not going to drink my coffee black anymore; this is definitely a cream-and-sugar life I'm leading. With my coffee in my hand, I drive up and down the streets in a more or less organized way, trying to hit every one in town. It's important to me to see what has changed, and what hasn't, since I was a kid.

Carole's street is where the rich people lived. It seems funny to me that she lives there now. Today her house looks huge and empty. I don't think she would leave town without calling me, although the circumstances are unusual.

I park out front for a while, afraid to ring the doorbell in case they're in there patching things up. Jeff could be playing the perfect leading man, if he's figured out what that is in Carole's case. For me, I think it would be someone like the prince, someone who couldn't take his eyes off me, who brought me presents every five minutes, took me away on trips to romantic hideaways, laughed at my jokes. Or maybe it would just be someone who forgave me for doing something stupid.

I drive past St. George's, but I still don't want to go in. I just can't imagine Bert actually being there, is all. I expect to see him every time I turn a corner.

There used to be a nursery on Peachtree Street, and I find my way there pretty easily. It's just the way I remember it, large and rambling, with a huge greenhouse for indoor plants and rows and rows of outdoor plants. The place is staffed by scrubbed teenagers in green aprons. I feel conspicuous in my sweatpants with the popped-out knees and tight rear. Disneyland's the only other place I've seen so many clean, decent kids all at once. How does a person raise a preppy kid, I wonder? Information like that could be worth a fortune.

Anyway, they fill me in on flowers and they know a lot. The bottom line, as I knew, is that there isn't much choice for a yard as tree-shaded as my mother's. When I keep after them about unusual possibilities, a shiny kewpie doll of a girl chirps, "You need to talk to Mr. Carter." She leads me down a damp-smelling corridor to a large greenhouse room filled with plants, all sizes and shapes and colors. To me it looks like a Hitchcock set, but I'm sure it looks good to someone who likes plants a lot. An old man dressed in loose coveralls is bent over a green ledger book, entering figures with a pen that's swallowed up in his knuckly hand. When he looks up, he seems familiar.

He smiles at me, right off. "You're Gilbert Sawyer's little girl, aren't you?" he asks. "Remember the hair."

He has a ruddy complexion, not very much hair of his own, and a very big nose. I can tell by his eyes he's a nice person, and probably a little lonely. "Knew your daddy real well," he adds, "when we were all getting around better. Bert Foster, too." He shakes his head. "Too bad about Bert. I used to have a bourbon with them once in a while. They must have done that every night for forty years."

"At least," I say. I think I remember seeing him at the house.

"I know your yard, too. The problem with flowers there is that big oak tree in front. Tree still there?"

I nod.

"Yep, figured it would be. Those suckers never die, and when they do people don't cut 'em down anyway. Too expensive. Hope for lightning or something."

I nod.

"Wish I could help you, though." He shakes his big head. "Only two suggestions for your mother if she wants marigolds; she's gonna, one, have to take down that tree, or, two, move." He scratches his cheek. "What's she want marigolds for anyway?"

I shrug. "Don't ask me."

"They smell bad, you know." He wrinkles up his nose.

"I know."

I'm disappointed, but I thank him for his help anyway.

After all, it's not his fault my mother wants something she can't have, but it doesn't seem fair in the great scheme of things.

I drive out to the Lakeview Mall to try on hats, which is a terrific nonfattening way to cope with almost anything. And there, under a blue straw I could wear to Buckingham Palace, now I'm so practiced at tea-drinking, it comes to me. Ellen Flynn, Fred Baker's ex. Silk flowers. I pat the bunch of cherries on the side of the hat and put it back on the manikin's bald head.

The name of the shop is Green Thumb Silks. I like it the minute I walk in the door. The air smells sweet, but it's a light perfume, not overpowering, and the flowers are beautiful. Ellen sits at the back on a high stool, behind a counter. She's bent over a pile of blossoms, illuminated by a goosenecked lamp she's pulled over her work. Her brown ponytail has been replaced by a short curly perm, but I'm sure it's her just the same. I can tell by the way she holds her head, and there's something familiar about the way her hands move. She used to work over a hem like that, in home ec. Ellen always had a lot of concentration.

When she looks up she is, of course, a middle-aged woman. I don't know why that surprises me. We all look like that, except for Carole, of course.

"Ellen?"

She blinks at me over half glasses. "Yes?"

I come closer. There is some gray in her hair now, and her hands look rough and dry. "It's me, Lilly Sawyer."

She blinks several more times. "Lilly?"

"Uh huh."

She gets off her stool and comes around the counter. Then

she smiles, the old Ellen Flynn smile, "Lilly Sawyer, as I live and breathe."

"I saw Fred. He told me you were here."

She nods sadly. "Yes. Fred."

I feel sad, too.

"It didn't work out," she says, holding a red tulip between her fingers.

"I'm sorry," I say, and I really am.

"Oh, that's OK." I can tell she's gearing herself up for a cheer, but it's hard work. "I got married again. Tommy Andrews, maybe you knew him?"

I shake my head. "I don't think so."

She has run out of steam before she quite got her feet off the ground. "He was laid off at the plant, you know." She swats her leg with the tulip.

I shake my head again, because it doesn't seem like the kind of thing she would want Fred to tell me about, and if I know I could only know from him.

"So, how're things, Lilly?" she asks, going back behind the counter.

"OK, I guess. My daughter's going to college this year."

"No kidding." She sighs. "Seems like just yesterday . . ." She trails off. We both laugh.

Then I get serious. "Ellen," I say, "I'm here on business."

She's happy for a change of subject. "What can I do for you, Lilly?"

"Can you make marigolds?"

"Sure. I can make anything; in fact, let me see." She kneels down behind the counter and rummages through some boxes. "Here." She stands up holding two huge bunches of yellow flowers. "Marigolds. Don't have much call for these."

"They're perfect," I say. "Can you make more?"

"Sure. How many do you want?" She lays them on the counter and leans above them looking at me.

"I'm not sure yet. I'll let you know. I want to try these first."

"OK." She wraps the flowers carefully in layers of green tissue and hands them to me. "These smell much better than the real thing."

"You're right about that," I say.

"What are you going to do with them, Lilly?" She pushes some buttons on her adding machine and it makes a funny clickety-click sound, like a toy train.

"They're for my mother. She loves marigolds."

"Some people do," she says.

When I get home the house is empty. It's about the time my mother goes to Peg-Mel's so I'm not surprised she isn't here. I take the flowers upstairs and hide them under my bed. Then I go into the kitchen for a drink of water. I glance out the window, just in time to see my father go through the side gate and leave the yard.

Without stopping to think, I pick up my purse and slip quietly out the back door to follow him.

Chapter Thirteen

He is only a few houses ahead of me by the time I reach the sidewalk. As he moves, he jabs the ground in front of him with his cane, pulling himself forward in jerky motions like a small boat through heavy water. At home he goes from the den to the kitchen, out to the Lilly tree, and upstairs, in a way that attracts no attention at all. But outside the house he looks small and out of place. He leans a little to the left as if he's being pushed sideways, like a wind-up toy on a low battery.

I hang back and wait for him to get further ahead before I step out behind him. The trouble is, my heart's not really in this. From behind I notice things I haven't seen before, like how loose his clothes are, how little hair he has to lift in the breeze, that he wears his slippers everywhere now. From behind, he could be someone I don't even know.

I follow him at what seems like a pretty safe distance. Of course, if he happens to turn around, he can't help but see me. I slow down a little more and let him get still further ahead. Part of me's concentrated on where he's headed and what I'll do when we get there; the other part is busy making up excuses for what I'm doing on the street behind him, in case I'm discovered.

He takes a shortcut through St. George's, and my mind races ahead of him to the houses behind the church. After all, I've just been driving these streets. I can't remember anyone who lives there, but I haven't kept up with the comings and goings of the neighborhood very well. For all I know there may be a "loose widow" on that very street, waiting by her window with the curtain pulled back, and a bottle of sherry at her side. If there is, she'll see me behind him. Of course, if she doesn't know me, what's to see? A middle-aged woman walking down the street in sweatpants.

The church grounds are wet from yesterday's rain, and muddy. A black wrought-iron fence surrounds the property, about waist high; parts of it are badly rusted, and I wonder why they don't spend a little money on it and get it fixed. The front gate screeches so loudly when he opens it, that I hear it clearly even from my following distance. I hold my breath when he turns to pull the gate shut behind him, but he doesn't look up. He watches the ground and places his feet carefully, one after the other. He disappears around the side of the church.

I stand for a minute looking at the fence. It's obvious I can't go through the gate, I'm going to have to go over, which I'm not dying to do. I hoist myself to the other side gracelessly, and naturally catch my sweatpants on one of the spikes. I yank myself off and stay in the shadows, close to the church wall. The bricks smell old and damp. They smell dark green, like a wood-nymph costume I once had. I realize I'm muttering to myself about the rip in my favorite pants, so I shut up. It helps me to understand, though, why Carole concentrates on things like who will teach her tennis.

When I turn the corner of the building I see my father pass through another gate at the back of the churchyard, and move on.

Bert's marker is dignified in a pale, polished way. The letters are etched so deep in the stone they look black. I can read them clearly from here even without my glasses:

BERTRAM FOSTER
DECEMBER 23, 1901–APRIL 15, 1989

There is a huge concrete urn set into a ledge at the base of the stone, with a few impossibly bright flowers lost inside. They lean sideways in a clump. The urn is new since the funeral.

My father pauses to catch his breath. Idly he scans the church, the grounds, the houses beyond. I close my eyes and press deeper into the wall. I pretend to be one of the bricks. I think old, I think mossy. He doesn't see me, but then he isn't really looking. He turns back to the marker and slaps the big stone on the back like an old friend; then he takes hold of it with both hands and eases himself slowly to the ground.

He rubs his knees and then leans forward, stretching toward the urn. He grabs the flowers by their plastic petals and pulls. They pop out, held together at the base by a green styrofoam block. Gently he lays them aside. His hand goes into the urn again, twice, but I can't see what he's doing.

Before I get my glasses on, the Old Grand-Dad comes out, which I can see without them.

Once I bring the whole thing into focus, I see he's got two glasses leaned against the carved gray stone. He pulls them forward and deliberately sets them in a straight line with the bottle. Then, he leans sideways on one hip, pulls a limp white handkerchief out of his back pocket and wipes off his face. Breathing heavily, he stuffs the handkerchief back, and pours a hefty shot of whiskey into each glass.

The sky is bright blue, and clear today, with only an occasional cloud moving lazily by. Poppy leans back against the stone and stretches his legs out in front of him, as if he were in the old green lawn chair in the backyard. He picks up one of the glasses and sips, crosses his ankles to settle himself more comfortably, and takes another swallow. He sits there for a long time, just looking up at the trees and drinking his whiskey.

Finally, he sets his glass down and picks up the other one. He holds it to the evening sun, admiring the color, turning it in his hand. Then he lowers the glass, says something, and pours the liquid in a steady stream, like a caramel-colored ribbon, into the ground.

My mother doesn't hear me come into the kitchen behind her. She stares out the window toward the empty chair, a lettuce leaf twisted around her finger. The rest of the head is draining in a colander in the sink.

I can't see her face, but I can see the small knuckles of her spine through the thin cloth of her dress. I can tell by how still she is, that she's thinking something over. She seems to make some kind of decision, because she shakes her head, quick shakes like she's trying to clear her brain, and then she puts the lettuce leaf into her mouth.

I put my purse on the kitchen table and I can tell by her back she knows I'm here. But she doesn't turn around.

"He's gone again," she says.

"I know."

"This time, no dinner. He can eat at her house." Her voice catches like a shoe in silk. She turns and stares at me.

I move her gently away from the silverware drawer, and get out enough utensils for three people. She watches while I set the table. When I finish, she goes past me to the refrigerator. A chicken breast, neatly wrapped in Handi-Wrap, sits on the middle shelf. She takes it out and adds it to the two half-cooked ones already in the oven. When she straightens, her glasses are steamed. She plucks the head of lettuce from the sink and holds it in front of her, looking in my direction like a hollow-eyed Little Orphan Annie. "Where does he go?"

I take the lettuce out of her hands and put it on the cutting board. "Listen," I say.

She follows me to the table and sits watching, her eyes magnified behind the glasses, as I tell her. She is quiet for a long time, her mouth working. She will give nothing, I know her.

"How did you know I followed him?" I ask.

"I saw you going down the street behind him." She gets up and goes back to the sink. "Your pants are too tight."

She tears the lettuce into small pieces and puts them in a wooden salad bowl with a few cherry tomatoes. Back at the table she puts both hands to her forehead and holds her head for a moment. Then she looks up and arranges the silverware in front of her, like a soldier readying a mess kit for inspection. "What could I have done about something like that?"

She seems to be asking the place mat, and I know I'm not supposed to answer.

When my father comes home she serves dinner as if nothing has happened. She eats the half-cooked chicken breast herself.

Chapter Fourteen

In the morning I carry the marigolds to the kitchen, still in their green tissue, and hand them to my mother.

"What is this?" she asks. She picks at the paper; it sounds like a mouse scratching in a wall.

"A present." The teapot steams on the stove with two cups waiting. I pour the tea. She seems confused. "Marigolds," I say.

She bends over the flowers and sniffs. "They don't smell like marigolds."

"They're silk, Mother."

She touches the petals, examines the stems. "Silk?" Then she buries her nose in the flowers, as if insisting that they smell.

"You can plant them out front," I say.

She looks at me like I've lost my mind. "They're not real," she says with a lifted eyebrow.

"They're real silk," I reply, and struggle to lift my eyebrow in an arch even half as good as hers.

"Lilly," she says, "you have developed a tic."

"No I haven't," I say.

"I always knew you'd get a tic," she shakes her head.

"The flowers," I remind her. They are bright as butter against the green of her kitchen tablecloth.

She looks at the pile in front of her. "I like a flower with a smell."

I shrug.

"They are pretty, Lilly." She picks several of them up and examines them closely. "A person could almost think they're real."

"Thanks. I can get more. As many as you like."

She sniffs them again. "What if it rains?"

"You don't get that much rain under the tree, there are too many leaves. They should last a while." I drain my teacup and push it away. "Besides, you can replace them."

She holds one of the blossoms up to the light. "They're very good, you know."

"Thanks."

"Silk flowers, my, my, my." She picks out several of them and holds them upright on the table, her hands circling their stems like a vase.

I cross the kitchen and rinse out my cup. "I've got to go to Bolton."

She nods. "I thought so." She adds, "Frank didn't call you back, Lilly."

"No kidding."

"I wonder why."

"He knew what I would say." I come back to the table and stand beside her for a moment.

She puts the flowers she's been holding back with the others. "Maybe."

"Not maybe. Truly!" I say, looking at her.

Her hands pluck at the green tablecloth, picking up invisible crumbs. "Yes."

"I'm going to drop by Carole's on the way and make sure she's OK. Then I'll take off."

"She's fine, Lilly."

"I just want to say hello."

"All right." She has a faraway look in her eyes. "If it will help, you can tell Frank that I do not approve of what he's doing."

"Thanks, Mother."

"That's all right, Lilly. Someone has to tell him."

I'm thankful she didn't hear Christie's half of our conversation; I don't want her sending any pronouncements to Christie. I gather up my purse and keys. "We'll probably stop by here on our way home."

"All right, dear," she says, but I don't think she's listening anymore. She has sent a message to Frank. Now she's glad to see me go.

She doesn't want to talk about it. My mother thinks if you can't see what's on the other side of the curve, it's best to keep going straight. I myself am beginning to believe it's helpful to at least take a look around the bend.

Carole greets me at the door of her house with a large box from Saks Fifth Avenue in her hands. "For you," she says, shoving it at me.

"What's this for?" I ask, but I think I know.

Carole used to do this kind of thing a lot, but it's been a long time since she thought about anyone else. Inside the box is a very slick pair of designer jeans; I know they're designer, because they have someone's name stitched in the crotch.

"You could do more with yourself, Lilly," she says.

I know what she means to say is 'thank you,' so I hug her. "I'll wear them," I say.

"Good," she smiles, with a glance at my now-torn sweats.

"Melani would look great in these," I say, holding up the jeans. "Are you sure you want to give them to me?" I mean it as a compliment, but it seems to make Carole nervous and she's tearing up again, so I put the jeans neatly back in their box, with another thank you.

We have coffee on her sun porch which is about the size of my whole downstairs. The glass-top table is set with what would be my "best," but is probably her junk, since it's only me she's got over. The coffee sits in the center of the table in a bright yellow thermos. It is *real* coffee, the kind with caffeine. It's a thrill, really, considering what I expected. Instead of brown bottles of vitamin pills, there are little silver dishes with things like whipped cream, shaved chocolate, thin pieces of cinnamon bark, and a bottle of apricot liqueur which Carole dumps into both cups before pouring the coffee. Health seems to be taking a backseat to something else this morning.

This porch is designer-done, I can tell. For one thing, it all goes together; it's the kind of room that makes you feel out of place if your clothes don't match the furniture. The chairs are white rattan with summer green-and-peach polished cotton print fabric and pillows, and the tile floor is a pale green color, so pale it's almost white, but not quite, and the not quite is a definite designer touch. I feel like a chocolate-covered radish in here, and I wonder if Carole doesn't feel like that sometimes. Maybe that's why she took up tennis, when what she really needed was someone to come in and mess up her furniture.

But I've got too much on my mind to worry about if I match the chairs.

"I'm going back to Bolton," I tell her. I scoop whipped cream onto my coffee and poke it under the surface with my finger. I relate most of Christie's call.

She hands me a tiny silver spoon. "What are you going to do?" Carole is not really asking me a question, she's sympathizing with me.

"I'm going to try to get Frank out of there," I say, sucking the remaining cream off my finger and dunking what's left of the blob with the spoon. "You didn't check out of the room, did you?"

She shakes her head no. "What if he doesn't want to leave?"

"I'll work at it," I say.

"You could seduce him, Lilly," she says, now that she's so up on it.

I sigh at the thought of trying to seduce Frank if his mind is on something else.

"Don't get your feelings hurt," she says, "if he doesn't fall right in line." She adds another scoop of cream to her coffee to make up for all the time she lost drinking poppy-seed juice. "I'm sure he thinks he's doing what he should be doing to take care of Christie."

I examine my reflection in the now-oily surface of my coffee. "What makes you think he'll reject me?"

"Not reject, Lilly, resist."

"Well, he can't stay there. He *has* to come with me." This is obvious.

"I'd give you my nightgown, but it's torn."

"I know. Frank's not attracted to nightgowns anyway." As I say it, it occurs to me that Frank has never seen me in a nightgown.

Carole's thinking this too, I see it in her eyes, but she doesn't say it, which is a big step for her.

"Call the college," she suggests.

"I can't call the college on my own husband."

"It could be an anonymous call." She beams at the thought of Frank's being captured through an anonymous call.

"Carole, how could I be anonymous on my own husband?" She looks blank here. "Besides, Christie thinks it's my fault."

"Well, it's not."

"But she thinks it is, which is the same thing."

"You know, Lilly, you have a real problem with guilt."

"Maybe, but that's how I see it."

"Why do you suppose no one else has called the college?"

"Why would they? It isn't happening to them." What I think about that is, Frank provides a diversion they can all talk about, sort of the role my hair played at Thomas Jefferson Elementary School.

Carole investigates my face. I feel like she's adding up how much it would cost to renovate me.

"I hardly ever think anything's my fault." She smiles at this useful quality.

"How's Jeff?" I ask, in case she's forgotten her hands are not entirely clean.

She stretches her legs out in front of her like a cat in front of a fireplace, and smiles a smile I'm supposed to interpret as contentment. "I have forgiven him." She stares off into outer space, which is where her mind obviously is, and sighs.

I give her a look of astonishment.

"Don't give me that look." She pauses and pours herself another cup of coffee, heavy on the apricot liqueur. I want to laugh, but she'd only get mad, and besides it's probably only a nervous laugh, so I think about not-funny things like Howard Woolfe.

She stirs a spoonful of sugar into her coffee, slowly. "If Jeff had been a better husband, I wouldn't have been looking around." This is an elaboration of her previous point, and she looks, well, the only word I can think of to describe it is, smug. "Face it, Lilly," she taps my arm with her forefinger. "It's true."

I pour myself a steaming cup of coffee out of the yellow thermos and gulp it down. "Ouch," I say, sucking in air. But it calms me enough so that I'm able to stay in this conversation. "So none of this was your fault?"

She nods.

"Nothing?"

She nods again.

Just to be sure I've got it right, I go on, "Nothing at all?"

She nods again and sips her coffee.

"Does this go for me, too?"

"Of course, Lilly. Our lives have been out of our control since day one." She fixes me with a significant look. "We are only women," she finishes off.

Ignoring that, I push on. "Like it's Frank's fault I'm not with the opera?"

She considers this. "Who else's?" she asks.

I'll have to admit it's a comforting worldview. But I can't stick with it. "It's not mine?"

"Don't be silly," she says. "Besides, it wasn't only Frank or Jeff, it was the time we grew up in too. We had to get married."

"We wanted to get married."

"We *thought* we wanted to get married. It was mind control. We're products of our time, and what happened to me was because of Jeff's neglect." I am wondering if her mind's been erased along with her face.

"You want to know what I think you are?" I say it carefully, because I don't want her to get mad.

"No."

I lean forward anyway. "I think you're afraid of getting old."

"I am not." She waves a hand in the air, as if there's a cobweb in front of her face.

"Why not? Everyone else is." I sit back and look at her. "You're just fighting it a little harder than the rest of us."

"That's ridiculous." She's got her arms folded tight across her chest.

"You're letting Jeff take the blame because then you won't have to figure out why you did such a stupid thing." She pours herself a cup of apricot liqueur, without the coffee, while I go on. "Jeff probably does think it is his fault, poor guy. He's always thought you were some kind of comet."

She takes a big gulp. "You don't understand anything," she says. "Why don't you go down to Bolton and straighten out your own life?"

"Think about it," I say. I push back my chair. "Gotta go." I clutch the Saks box in my arms.

She gets up too.

At the front door I turn around. "What did the whole town know about my parents, Carole?"

She looks genuinely confused.

"You said it was a small town, remember?"

"Oh." Her face brightens. "Why, that your father was drinking over at St. George's everyday, Lilly. Some people thought it was odd."

"Why didn't you tell me?"

She shrugs. "You didn't ask. In fact," she continues, "it didn't seem to me like you wanted to know."

"Maybe you're right." I step out the front door. "Thanks for the jeans."

"You're welcome, Lilly. I think they'll look nice on you."

She's not sure, of course, because I may be the shape of my sweatpants. "I'll see you when I get back," I say.

The inside of my car is like a kiln. I drive with the windows open to blow some of the hot air out. By the time I get to the highway it's just normal hot in the car, so I close the windows and turn the air conditioner on high. I need a good sing, or I'll blow my stack. I put *La Bohème* in the tape deck, and sing along with "Che Gelida Manina," pretending it's cold in Paris and I'm there with Rodolfo, who's crazy for me after only one viewing. Frank really does fall short in the romance category, but maybe that's one of life's less necessary classifications. Hearing Carole talk about whose fault is what, and who's a product of whom, makes me a little embarrassed. I'm my own product, such as it is, and she's right; I could have done more with myself.

Obviously I'm not going to be able to concentrate on the Paris theme. My brain races between Frank, graduation, the future, Howard Woolfe, Christie, my parents, Carole, life in general. I think if I can only sort it all out everything will be fine. The only clear thought I have is that things couldn't be much worse. That's when I hear the siren.

Policemen all look alike in my experience, sort of patriotic, and tough. And they all say the same thing. "Going a little fast, weren't you, ma'am?"

This one's different. For one thing he not only keeps the flasher on, but he keeps the siren going when he gets out of his car. And he doesn't say anything, not that I'd be able to hear it—he just writes the ticket. My second ticket during this little jaunt. I haven't gotten an *actual* ticket for years; now I've got two in just a few days. It's something to think about.

This one is the most embarrassing ticket I've ever gotten. There's no point in trying to get off—he couldn't hear me. He's probably nicer than he looks, he probably doesn't even like giving out tickets, so he's figured out how to make his job easier. Not hearing isn't like not listening.

He goes to his radio to call in my license number and then comes back and hands me the ticket. I take it like it's the receipt for a ball gown, fold it neatly and put it in my purse. When I look up again he's getting into his car. He drives away with the siren still screaming.

I pull onto the highway slowly and drive a reasonable sixty the rest of the way to Bolton. I stop at the motel on the way in, to make sure the room's still free. Both keys are in the slot beneath 123, so Todd is either out or gone. I'm counting on gone.

The girl behind the desk is the same one I checked in with; the one who still lives with her parents.

"Hi, Noreen," I say.

"He's gone," she tells me. She searches my eyes to see how I'll take this news, because she can't figure how he got there in the first place.

"How do you know?" For obvious reasons, I need to be absolutely sure about this.

"He told me to use the room if I wanted." She hands the keys to me over the counter. "Said it was paid for."

"What were you supposed to do in it?"

She shrugs. "I don't know. I told you, I'm a pretty boring person."

"Probably you knew I'd be back." This girl needs confidence; a tour of duty in the dorm might not hurt.

She looks skeptical.

"Trust me," I say, "you're not boring. You just have a little ESP, is all."

"Is that good?" She holds her head a little to one side.

"Sure it's good. It means sometimes you know what's going to happen before it happens."

"I do?"

"Well? I'm here, aren't I?"

"I see your point," she says.

I pocket the keys and head for Room 123; Todd, or someone, has replaced the furniture in its traditional arrangement, but the room has sort of a depressed look to it. Maybe some flowers would help. Of course, Frank won't think the room is nice, or not nice. It'll just be a room to him, if I can get him to come with me, that is.

I figure it's me, not the room, that needs work, since I'm the lure, so to speak. I brush my hair until I can tame it back into a French twist the way he likes it. Then I struggle into

Carole's designer jeans contribution to the new me. They seem a little snug, which I consider flattering of Carole, but I'm glad my mother won't be walking behind me here. I wear a white overblouse so if I start to black out I can unbutton the waist, add gold hoop earrings and red moccasins and voilà, ready. I look young at heart and mature at the same time. A very good combination, really.

The old station wagon doesn't fit my image. For the first time in my adult life I wish for another car, a red Honda Prelude maybe—a modest request, really. I slide behind the wheel and start up. My new Honda drives a lot like the old wagon, but it's gorgeous. And so red. The prince gave it to me because I had a little cold. I remember the scene:

Take it, Lilly, he says, but drive carefully.

Thanks, I say.

He slips a contract from La Scala in the glove compartment.

I don't know if I can fit it in, I say.

The house has been sold out for weeks.

No kidding?

They're counting on you, my dear, he sighs, handing me a six-pound Hershey's bar. I will be there in my box.

That reminds me, as I go past the auditorium where I left Christie, that Howard's shack is in front of the library, very close by. Maybe this is a good time to go see what's up with Howard. Maybe if he thinks I'm crazy enough, he'll just leave. Of course, it may be a little hard to impress Howard; I never feel I have his full attention.

The shack is not attractive. It's practically pitch black in there and only an occasional flash of white, newspapers I think, disturbs the blank entry hole. He's probably making himself a nest. I bend down and look in, cutting off all light to the interior, so of course I can't see a thing.

"Yo, Mrs. B." Howard crawls out. He stands up and brushes off his clothes. He has changed out of the kilt, and has on a pair of very faded blue-and-white striped overalls, and no shirt. I can't see whose name, if anybody's, is written on his knee. He sees me looking at his clothes.

"You like these?" he asks, hooking his thumbs under the shoulder straps. "I traded for 'em."

For the first time I see how thin he is. His collarbones stand out like little wings. "You did?"

"Yeah. The kilt was from my European period. These," he says looking down, "represent the common man."

"What common man?"

"*The* common man—no ancestors at all." He pushes his hair back. "The Europeans care a lot about ancestors, but the common man didn't have any. See?"

"Sort of."

He points to the ground. "Have a seat, Mrs. B."

I spin up a silent prayer . . . if these pants stay in one piece, I'll be nice to Howard Woolfe.

"Thanks, Howard," I say and drop to the ground across from him.

"So, what's up?" he asks, crossing his legs and resting his elbows on his knees, his face cupped in his hands like an offering.

"I just thought I'd come by and see how you're doing. Maybe I'll call your mother when I get home." That, I think, is a very nice touch. Besides, I may just do it. There is a bond between mothers that somehow transcends how we feel about each others' kids. The mother of a really difficult child, like Howard, is a saint in my book. Remembering Nancy Woolfe, and the faded blue of her eyes, keeps me from wanting to do Howard any real harm. I just want him out of here.

"Oh, you don't need to call her," he smiles. "I already did, like you said. She *was* a little worried."

"Good, Howard. I'm glad you listened to me." I stretch my legs out in front of me so the blood can circulate.

"Besides," he says, "I'm going to Washington. D.C."

I shift my position. "You are?"

"Yep. We're gonna put the shack up across from the White House." His eyes are as wide as they've ever been.

"Oh."

"We're taking our protest direct to the president." He hits the ground with his fist for emphasis.

I shift to the side and bend my legs a little. "What exactly is it that you're protesting, Howard?"

"Everything," he grins. Then, leaning forward, he says, "Will you say good-bye to Christie for me? The stars said midnight, but I have to leave this afternoon by three o'clock, no later."

"Do *I* have to do it at midnight?"

He laughs. I really crack him up. "No, you can do it anytime. They're only my stars."

"I see." I shift to my other side and try it with the legs straight out again.

"You OK, Mrs. B.?" he asks. "You seem a little restless."

"Coffee, I guess."

He nods sagely. "Bad for you, isn't it?"

I agree. "How's Samanda?" I ask.

"Who?" He looks genuinely puzzled.

"The girl you were with at Big Banana's." I struggle to my feet and brush my pants off.

"Oh, *Samanda*." He stands up too. "Great. She's a poet you know. Doing a reading this afternoon in the Union. I'll have to miss it, though."

We shake hands. "Have a good trip, Howard," I say. I wave to him from the car, then turn away quickly, and shift into gear.

Christie's room is in a seven-story brick building that looks like a prison. The elevator seems especially unfriendly so I walk, knowing I need the exercise and hoping this will make the jeans a little looser. As soon as I open the fire door I see Frank. He's sitting on the floor, leaning against the one closed door on the entire hallway, playing cards with a scraggly, mean-looking old man who's wearing a blue shirt with a cloth badge on the sleeve.

"Frank?" He's concentrating on his hand. "Frank?" He looks up with a little frown, but when he sees it's me he smiles warmly.

"Lilly!" He turns to his companion. "That's my wife," he says, so he must like the way I look.

I saunter forward as the other man discards a seven of diamonds with a slap to the brown linoleum.

"This is George," says my husband. "He's the security guard."

It looks to me like he's playing cards with Frank. "Is he on duty?" I ask.

"Yep." Frank scoops up the stack of cards between them.

George's fingers on his cheek are like sandpaper on the sidewalk. "That does it," he says. "You got me."

"Yep," says Frank and lays his cards in small stacks on the floor. "That about does it."

George struggles to his feet and thumps me on the back. "Good to see you, Lilly," he says. "Back to work, I guess."

"Back to work," says Frank.

George salutes. "Thanks for the book, amigo." He holds up Frank's much-read copy of *Last of the Breed*, by Louis L'Amour.

"It's a great book," says Frank, "a real classic."

"Adiós," George calls over his shoulder, and walks away.

"Adiós," says Frank. He turns to me. "Can you believe it, Lilly? He never heard of Louis L'Amour."

He stacks the cards, rubber bands them with red and blue rubber bands he gets from his pocket, and puts them in the briefcase on the floor beside him. I catch a glimpse of shaving cream and a toothbrush. "George is taking Spanish lessons for when he moves to Mexico. He wants to be a hired hand." He looks up at me. "What brings you here?"

"As if you didn't know. What are you doing, Frank?"

"I'm taking a stand, Lilly." He pulls a yellow rubber band from his pocket, stretches it out, and fires it off at the wall across from him. "Got 'im," he chuckles.

I notice there's a squirmy pile of spent rubber bands on the floor. "Frank?"

"Yep?"

"Are you OK?"

"Never better." He slaps his thigh. "Action suits me."

I look at him leaning back, with his briefcase beside him,

killing the wall with rubber bands, and decide I'm dreaming. I turn and head back down the hall.

"Where are you going, Lil?"

Lil? "I'm starting over, Frank." By the fire door I turn around and retrace my steps, but I put a little hitch in my git-along, if you know what I mean. I'm a dance-hall girl in the Cow Skull Saloon. "Howdy pardner," I say.

"Huh?"

"How's about we go for a quick one?"

"A quick what?" he asks.

That I'm not sure about, I just thought I was using the right lingo to move him out. "A quick anything," I finish lamely.

"I can't leave here, Lil," he scratches his head. "Little gal needs me."

"Little gal wants you to take a hike," I say.

"There's nowhere for me to go." He looks pleased with himself, and more than that, I think he expects me to be happy about all this.

"I've got a place. You don't have to be here."

His eyes say I've lost my mind. "She wasn't in her room when I called."

"So what?"

"So what? It was three o'clock in the morning."

"That didn't seem to bother you a couple of days ago when Howard came to call. Besides, why did you call her at three o'clock anyway?"

"I just wanted to say hello. What's wrong with that?"

"At three o'clock in the morning?"

"I'm not a clock watcher, Lilly," he says all disgusted.

I'm thinking, male menopause.

"Don't say that, Lilly."

"I didn't say anything."

"You definitely did."

"I did not."

He looks at me. "I came here to put your mind at rest," he says. He gestures to the floor beside him. "Have a seat."

"That's what Howard said, Frank." I begin to pace. For one thing he'll expect it. For another, I don't want to push my luck with the jeans.

"You are *not* putting my mind at rest." The cowgirl persona is slipping a little, but this is serious. Besides, only one of us can be crazy at a time. "You are torturing our daughter," I say. "She's embarrassed to death."

Frank seems relaxed. He leans against the wall. "She's embarrassed us plenty," he says.

"That's no excuse, Frank."

"Why not?"

"It's expected. Where is she anyway?" I pause in my pacing and look down at him.

"Who?"

"Don't be coy, Frank."

He indicates the closed door. "In there."

I knock on the door.

"Go away."

"Christie, it's Mother."

Nothing. I know she's behind the door, probably leaning toward me listening. It's a little like dealing with my mother. I start to hum and the door flies open.

"Stop it, Mom! Things are bad enough."

She looks pale even without her Kabuki makeup, which is, thankfully, gone. Her eyes are desperate.

"Howard's gone," I say, getting right to point number one.

"It figures." She leans against her door.

Behind me Frank says, "Howard who?"

"You're not being funny, Daddy." Her mouth quivers at the corners.

"She's right, Frank," I say.

"How do you know?" she asks me, one foot on top of the other.

"I saw him on my way over. He said to say good-bye." I put my hand on her shoulder and she lets me keep it there.

"Where'd he go?" she asks, looking at the floor.

"To Washington. The shack is going to the White House."

She pats my hand and moves away. "It figures." She looks at both of us. "And I'm not sorry about anything; I was practically a freak. No one here could believe it."

Frank fires off another rubber band. "Believe what?"

"Never mind, Frank."

"And you should be perfectly happy. Howard's gone, just like you always wanted. Now, I want Dad to be gone, and you too," she adds unkindly. Her lip trembles.

"Washington's the perfect place for him," says Frank. "He'll have a great time."

Christie turns her back on him.

"It's the murder capital of the world," he gloats.

I stare him down.

"There's nowhere for me to go," he says.

"Oh yes there is," I pull the key out of my purse.

"Where'd you get that?"

"Never mind." I turn Christie around and give her a hug— I get real pressure in return. "We'll pick you up day after tomorrow, sweetheart."

She nods and walks back in her room, but the door stays open.

Frank snaps down the latches on his briefcase and picks it up. "OK, Lilly," he says. "If it means that much to you I'm willing to cooperate. I only hope you know what you're doing."

"I do, Frank."

At the front desk he leaves a note for George. "Mexico sounds good. We may come down there. Keep in touch." And he writes out our address.

Chapter Fifteen

For the first few minutes I feel triumphant, like I'm ten and I've won at Capture the Flag. Frank's my flag, of course, but what to do with him now, is something else again.

As we approach the motel, I realize there's no way to get to the room except through the lobby, which means Noreen will see us. Not only do I feel guilty, as if Frank is someone I just picked up in a bar, but I feel a little responsible for Noreen's worldview. She's seen a lot these last few days.

She is bent over something behind the counter, writing her little heart out, so I grab Frank's hand and hurry him across the lobby. We've almost made it when she looks up and blinks a couple of times.

I stop in my tracks, and Frank bumps into me.

"Hi," I say.

She says nothing, so I float my hand in Frank's direction like I'm introducing a new line of car. "Husband," I say.

She nods and points to what she was working on. "Term paper," she says.

We move on across the lobby to the hall door. Frank is huffing and puffing behind me. "What was that?" he asks. "Some kind of code?"

"No, Frank," I smile. "That was a simple exchange of facts between two women."

This shuts him up.

In the room we put our things away; Frank has a new Louis L'Amour for the bedside table, *Crossfire Trail*. He pats it as he lays it down. We look at each other, but we're not talking a sexy look here, nothing to buy a three-hundred-dollar negligee for. No, it's more a what-should-we-do-now look. After all, we're stuck in a time warp somewhere between the O.K. Corral and here.

"How'd you get here, Frank?" I ask, closing the dresser drawer.

He sits on the edge of the bed. "Plane."

"You just made up your mind and hopped on a plane?" This is a new Frank for sure.

"Yes, I did." He looks longingly at *Crossfire Trail*, which is definitely the old Frank. "I took Hooker back and came on out."

"Hooker?"

"My horse."

"Where's Peter?" I press on. This isn't entrapment. I really want to hear it from Frank's own mouth.

"He went with the Hatchers."

"I said he couldn't go, Frank. I told both of you." I get up and start to pace.

"Did you?" He scratches his head.

"You know I did."

"Lilly, he was perfectly fine. Dr. Felcher said to let him go." Frank has on his soft voice, the voice that's supposed to calm me down. Usually it makes me crazy, but this is pertinent information.

"You took him back to Dr. Felcher?" I stop midpace.

"Of course."

I hold my hands behind my back and begin to move again. "Well, what does he know?"

Children are often the root of marital unrest. I wonder if Rodolfo would have been so crazy about Mimi, say in twenty years, if they'd had kids; or Cavaradossi, Tosca; Radames, Aïda; Siegfried, Brünnhilde; Othello, Desdemona —now that I think of it, none of them made it to that point. Even so, I can't picture any of those couples being alone in a motel room and the tenor wanting to read a cowboy book.

There's just too much stuff hanging off us, stuff we accumulated after those first days when we were just Lilly and Frank, that's what it is. It's like being one of those doomed people on the Saturday "Creature Feature," who catch a virus and grow moss all over. The virus is a metaphor for life, I finally figure out. A lot of people around me aren't dealing with it all that well. Like Carole for example, she's just erased it. And my father, he's bent down by it; my mother's pretending it isn't there. I don't want to do any of those things. I want to accept my moss, and still be able to stand up under the weight, and see out some little green hole on my fuzzy face.

Frank flips on the TV, but that must feel wrong even to him, so after checking out the channels he turns it off again, and he looks a little embarrassed. The light slips back into the screen. It's awfully quiet in here.

"So, what happened with Alex and Maxine?" I ask.

Frank kicks off his shoes and puts his feet up on the bed. "Judge threw the case out."

"I thought the judge was mad at Alex."

Frank sighs. "He was, but then he met Maxine."

"What did she do?"

He leans back like he's in pain. "She told the judge he didn't know blank about the law."

"I thought that's what Alex said." I try to sit cross-legged on the bed, but my jeans say no.

"He did." Frank closes his eyes. "It's the first thing they've agreed on in a lot of years."

"That's nice."

"I guess so. It changed everything."

"They're back together?"

"Yes," he opens his eyes. "We'll have to go through this every few years. Maxine hates me now."

"Of course. How's Melinda?"

"Fine. She's real surprised they got back together."

"I'll bet."

"What do you mean?"

"Oh, Frank, everyone knew about Melinda and Alex."

"What about Melinda and Alex?"

"They were sleeping together."

"Don't be silly, Lilly."

"They were."

"No they weren't."

There seems to be little point in pursuing this, besides, the whole thing is making me hungry. "Hungry?" I ask.

He doesn't look hungry, and he doesn't bother to answer. He's sort of roaming around the room.

"How about a movie, then?" I'm thinking popcorn. "*Fatal Attraction*'s here."

"Are you sure you want to see that, Lilly? It's supposed to be scary."

Scary movies aren't a patch on real life as far as I'm concerned; but Frank's better at the day-to-day than he is at movies, so probably we should skip it. The thing is, it would have passed the time and the action would have been someone else's problem. Being by ourselves is going to take practice. Since I was pregnant with Christie when we got married—didn't I mention that?—we've never really been by ourselves.

And then I remember Samanda. "Frank, I know what we can do. We can go to Samanda's poetry reading."

This seems like such a good idea to me, I can hardly sit still. I dial the college activity information number right away, and wait while it rings. All the time Frank's asking, "Who's Samanda? Who's Samanda?" But I don't want to have to break off right in the middle of reminding him, so I don't answer.

Finally someone's on the other end of the line. It seems to be a big problem that I don't know Samanda's last name, but I tell the woman she's supposed to be in the Union sometime today, and that she's a poet. It sounds like she's wading in papers, but finally she says, "Samanda Outrage? Would that be the individual?"

It's not likely there are too many people named Samanda

around here, and Outrage sounds about right, but I need to be sure. "What does it say after her?" I ask.

"Poetry reading," she answers, "four-thirty P.M. in the Dove Room at the Union."

"That's it!" I'm very excited. "Thank you so much."

"My pleasure," she says, and hangs up the phone.

Frank tries again. "Who's Samanda, Lilly?"

"She's the girl Howard picked up."

"Howard Woolfe?" He can't believe anyone who had a chance to be Christie's boyfriend would even look at anyone else.

"I told you about her on the phone, Frank."

"Oh, yes." He shakes his head. "Did Christie know?"

I shrug. "She called him 'Arthur.'"

He's frowning at me. "Who called whom 'Arthur?'"

"Samanda called Howard, 'Arthur.' He says it's his middle name," I say.

"Well, it's not. He must be crazy." Now he gets up. "Did you say anything to him, Lilly? I mean, did you confront him?" He begins to pace.

"Calm down, Frank." I reach for his hand. "I can't believe you're going to have a chance to see Samanda. This is so great," I say. "It'll make you feel good about Christie."

He looks surprised. "I already feel good about Christie."

"I mean her clothes and all, you know. You're going to love Samanda."

Frank doesn't look all that convinced. He checks his watch. "Maybe we should go eat instead," he says. "You're hungry."

"We can eat after, Frank."

"OK," he says, clearly puzzled. "If that's what you want."

Basically Frank's a pretty good-natured person, and I guess he figures if I want to see Samanda it's all right with him, but since neither of us like poetry, he can't imagine why I want to go.

Four-thirty doesn't seem like a hot time for a performance, but there's quite a crowd in the Dove Room, and no empty seats, by the time we arrive. In fact, two people in black armbands give us their places the minute we walk in; they must be hosts or something. I guess it's a courtesy thing, since we're clearly older than the rest of the audience. Probably Carole would have had to stand; it's something to think about.

There's a podium up front, and two chairs facing the audience. In one of them, a tweedy-looking man crosses and uncrosses his legs so many times you can't help but think he's nervous. He's small, with thin white hair and pale cheeks. The other chair is empty. A young man sits in a corner playing some kind of howling music on a flute. He's wearing a pink sweatshirt that says BOYCOTT ANYTHING PICKED, and Howard's kilt.

Samanda makes her entrance midhowl, and sits in the empty chair in the front. There's a lot of shuffling as people settle in their places, but pretty soon it gets quiet. She is wearing a sheet held together at the top with duct tape. Her feet are bare and her silver-rimmed glasses sparkle like bubble wands dipped in soap film.

Frank leans over to me. "This is Samanda?" he asks.

"Shhhhh, Frank," I say.

"But is it Samanda?" he asks.

"Yes," I whisper.

He shakes his head.

"Don't worry, Frank," I pat his hand, "she doesn't live in the dorm."

"Good," he says. He's a little conservative, I believe I mentioned.

The tweedy man steps up to the microphone and pauses. The audience gets quiet and waits. Just as he's about to begin, he changes his mind and moves away from the podium. He stands instead, to the side of it, and leans against it casually. "We don't need a microphone in here, do we?" He smiles at all of us. "They're so formal, don't you think?"

"What?" someone shouts from the back.

"I said I won't use the mike," he says, still smiling.

There's rustling in the back. "What's he say?" someone asks.

The gentleman beams at us. "Hear me OK in back, can you?"

"Nah, man."

"No way."

"Samanda, get that guy back on the mike," someone shouts.

Samanda rises from her chair and moves forward. She touches his elbow. "Dr. Eflin, would you mind using the microphone, just this once?"

The little man looks embarrassed. "But can't they hear?"

"No, I don't think so," she assures him.

"Well, of course, if that's what you want, Samanda."

He walks back to the podium, folds his arms and leans forward on it. He waits for us to quiet down again. I notice he's too short to really pull this off. I don't think he knew it himself until he tried it, but two bad starts wouldn't look good so, he's standing on his toes back there. Most people can't see that. I feel sorry for him, because I can tell he wants to be a part of this group.

"Samanda," he begins, "is a poet of extraordinary quality. She sees the world as no one else sees it, and she has agreed to share her vision with us this afternoon." He looks behind him and smiles at Samanda. She smiles back.

"As most of you know, Samanda is a graduate student, working on her master's degree. She is the *only* graduate student we have here, but I think we may say thank you for that, to all of you out there who participated in the sit-in at the president's house last year." He clears his throat and continues. "Some said it was only because Bolton College did not offer a master's degree, but *I* say it was discrimination. Samanda," he turns away from us and beams at her, "is a woman."

"What's he say?"

"Talk into the microphone, Jack!"

"He says she's a woman."

"So what?"

Dr. Eflin turns back toward the audience. "The women's struggle has been hard," he pauses, and shakes his head, "but Samanda went to the wall, and she conquered!" His finger points sternly at the ceiling. "To commemorate the struggle, Samanda has taken as her last name, a word that sums up what the administration tried to do to her last year. Ladies and Gentlemen, Samanda Outrage."

Everyone claps loudly, several people cheer.

"Let's go," says Frank, pulling at my arm.

"Shhhhh," I say, and pat his hand.

Samanda comes to the podium and puts some papers on the upper shelf. Then she waits for silence.

Frank tugs at my arm, but I smile at him.

"Thank you, Dr. Eflin. Thank you my brothers and sisters." She reaches under the shelf and takes out a glass of water and proceeds to drink the entire thing. We wait. When she's finished, she picks up her papers and looks at us. "I will begin," she says, "with 'To Hunter Creek.'"

"That's where Samanda lives," I whisper, "at Hunter Creek."

To Hunter Creek

Once a babbling brook
Hunter Creek's now full of shit,
I live there
In a box.

"C'mon," says Frank.

I start to shush him, but this time I see he means business. He's already on his feet and he's got my wrist in a grip like handcuffs. Everyone turns to look at us. I've never seen so many frowns in one place in all my life. I smile apologetically at all of them, and wave at Samanda as we leave.

It's not that I don't see Frank's point; it's just that I have a personal interest in Samanda. Once outside, Frank puts his arm around me. "You can sure pick 'em, Lilly," he says.

I like being under his arm. Maybe we will figure out what to do at the motel later on. I remember that Madame Butterfly's kimono is still under the front seat. He's probably tired of the Norn look by now.

Chapter Sixteen

In the morning I find myself sorry to leave this little motel room. It doesn't look nearly so depressing now. I look at Madame Butterfly's kimono with affection. Frank's imagination seems much improved. He'll really love my costume from *The Girl of the Golden West*; I don't know why I never thought of it before.

I get Frank to check us out, because I don't want to face Noreen today. Besides, the checking-out process is something a real husband does. A gigolo would send his woman, I figure, and if I figure that, I'm sure Noreen does.

So he takes care of it and comes back to the room, without, apparently, getting into any conversation at all, or at least if he does, it's not worth repeating to me. He's not much at small talk, so my guess is he just checked out, pure and simple, which is really the best way to do it.

By the time he gets back, I've pitched the designer jeans, at least I've mentally pitched them. They're back in their box, neatly folded; I'll give them to Christie or maybe the Red Cross. The important thing is I'm in my sweats, and happy about it. Frank isn't a noticing kind of a guy, it's one of the best things about him, so he won't even know what I have on. It's a trait that lets me be the me I dream of, no matter what I look like, sort of like the steamed-up bathroom mirror.

Outside, the day is beautiful and sunny. Frank opens the car door for me, which I appreciate. Samanda Outrage would probably drop him with a kick to the back of the knees.

I close my eyes and lean against the seat. Music is everywhere in my mind, and I leap from one aria to the next, but it's all so sad. My beautiful friends all come to such bad ends: Tosca, Lucia, Desdemona, Aïda, Mimi, Brünnhilde, Carmen, Butterfly, Gilda, Manon. But they get there so romantically a person tends to forget the bottom line. When you take the time to think about it, they don't have such a hot deal, really.

"There's the dorm," says Frank.

"There's the dorm," I agree.

We pull over to the curb and wait for Christie and Melani. Kids are milling about all over the place, parents are hanging back like we are. This is a very different scene from the one a few days ago where each kid was paired with at least one parent and they eyed each other with so much suspicion. Now they relate like mad, hugging and kissing, exchanging addresses. It's like a railway scene in a war movie.

Finally Christie and Melani break tearfully from one of the larger groups, and drag their suitcases along the pavement toward the car. Frank gets out to open the back, but he doesn't make a move to help carry their bags.

"Hey, Dad," says Christie, as if she has completely forgotten their recent problem.

"Hey, Christie," he beams and gives her a hug. He even turns to Melani the garage burner, and says "Hi, Mel." Then he gets out of the way.

I can't look while they heave the stuff into the back, for fear they'll strain some necessary part, but they grin at Frank like he's passed the test of manhood. They kick the door shut and lean against it, huffing and puffing and totally content.

"Hi, girls," I call, leaning out the window.

They smile at me, and then come around to get in the car. When they're finally settled in the backseat, we drive away with both girls sniffling and waving out the window.

"There's Sean," says Melani, waving her hand practically off.

"He's a fox," says Christie. It sounds a little forced to me, but I give the kid credit.

"I am in love with that school," says Melani as she dabs at her eyes with the seat belt.

"Me too," sighs Christie. She is wearing a new Bolton College T-shirt, and some faded out jeans I don't remember seeing before. She sees me looking at them. "I traded with a girl down the hall, for Mimi's hat," she says.

"That's fine, dolly." I'd rather have her wearing old jeans than the strange little hat from *La Bohème* any day.

Melani has the Kabuki makeup on, and Christie has braided her hair with gimp. It seems we got the best of this deal, but they both look pretty good. Besides, I think the Kabuki period's a short one.

"They're going to let us room together," beams Melani. "Isn't that great?"

"Great," says Frank, but he's smiling like he means it.

"So," I say, resting my chin on my arm as I look over the backseat, "you had a good time?"

They both look at me with surprise.

"Of course," says Christie. She pulls her new T-shirt away from her chest. "Isn't this a great shirt?"

"Great," I say. "And you registered for classes?"

She sighs deeply, and lets the shirt snap back. "That's what we were here for, Mom."

She leans back against the seat and I can almost feel the energy draining out of her. "Was it easy?" I ask.

"Was what easy?"

"Getting registered. That's supposed to be the worst part." My college friends used to complain about standing in line to register. Since I was standing in audition lines, it was something we had in common. But the question sounds stupid even to me; I'm just trying to find a connection.

Melani blinks her bright blue eyes at me. "Bolton's very advanced," she says. "They use computers for everything."

"Yeah, everything's done by computer," Christie chimes in. "It's the only way to go." Christie herself hasn't been within ten miles of a computer before. Her high school is not on the cutting edge in this area.

"I use computers," says Frank.

No one pays attention.

"They were really stupid not to use them before," says Christie.

"They didn't have them," I venture.

"No, they had them," she says. She proudly hands me a

thin rectangle of paper. "Here's my printout. I got all the classes I wanted."

"So did I," says Melani, passing hers over.

I look at the schedules they've handed me. The letters are faint as all get-out on this print thing, but I don't want to say. It's probably part of the charm. I fish out my glasses and try to make out Christie's list of classes: Fr 101B, Eng 101B, Hist 101B, Biol 101B, Ck 612. Ck 612? "What's Ck 612?" I ask.

"That's my elective," she says, swatting her nose with her braid.

"But what *is* it?"

"It's a cooking class, for restaurateurs." She reaches to take her schedule back.

"It's for senior honor students," Melani offers. "Very advanced."

I look at Christie and she returns my gaze as an equal. "Put your eyebrow down, Mom. It's *my* schedule."

"You don't know how to cook," I say, handing her schedule back to her over the seat.

"I'm here to learn, aren't I?" The discreet sprinkling of bronze freckles on her nose is new.

"Sure, but why'd you take an *advanced* course?" This seems, to me, to be a good point.

"Because it's in desserts."

There's a certain logic I can understand here, but I see some problems ahead. "How'd you ever get in?"

She smiles. "I told them I had a catering business at home."

"Christie, that wasn't true."

"It was creative. We're supposed to expand our creativity— that's what they said." She pats her cheek contentedly with the soft end of her braid. "I may take acting, too," she adds.

"You don't need it, Chris," says Melani with admiration. "You were great."

"Melani's taking the class with me," says Christie. "It's the only one we have together. I said she ran the Illinois branch of the business," Christie chuckles.

Since I know Melani is as accomplished in the kitchen as Christie, the class should be great. I wonder how many other hungry freshmen are registered for Ck 612.

I'll let the school deal with Ck 612. With every passing day, I understand the separation thing a little better. And how it can work to a person's advantage.

I look at Melani's schedule, which is similar to Christie's except she's taking sociology instead of biology, and each number is followed by an A instead of a B.

"What does the A mean?" I ask, smoothing out the folds in the paper so that I can see the faint gray letters better.

"Advanced," Melani says, "I want to push myself." She stretches her legs out as far as she can, which is not very far, because Frank and I have got the front seat all the way back.

"At least she didn't take forestry," mutters Frank; no one hears him but me. He laughs away to himself, happy as can be.

I ignore him and turn to Christie, the meaning of the B on her schedule suddenly clear. She smiles. "I don't," she says.

"I wouldn't have taken all easy classes," I say.

"You didn't take any classes," she says.

Now, I'm sort of immune to teenage superiority, but Frank's not. "Christina," he says sharply, looking back at her, which is not such a good idea since he's the driver and the road is flying by.

"Slow down, Frank," I say. "I know about this road." I

open the glove compartment and show him the two tickets I have collected over the last few days. He already knows my theory about the crime problem in this country, so I don't have to say anything. "Besides, I *didn't* take any classes—not this kind anyway."

He slows down but he's still irritated. "Who cares?"

"Christie does," I sigh.

"No one can sing like you, Lilly," says Frank.

"I do not," Christie says.

"Why, thank you Frank."

"I mean it," he says patting my knee.

Christie grabs her neck. "Aaaaargh!" she says, and pretends to faint. She falls against Melani.

Melani giggles. "I love you guys. You're so much fun," she says.

Christie sits up and shows her eye whites. "You should live with us," she says.

Melani can hardly contain herself. "Show me how to do that, Chris," she says. "I've always wanted to learn how to do that."

I turn back and watch the road disappear under our car like one long gimped braid. I wait for Frank to mention my speeding tickets, but he doesn't. He probably doesn't want to hear about muggers and crack houses. I think it was very honest of me to mention them, since usually I just pay up quietly. Even in the old days, Frank was only aware of my ticket-getting ability in a tip-of-the-iceberg sort of a way. By coming clean just now, I've probably saved him from getting one, which would have bothered him a lot; he's just not used to it.

As soon as we pull in the driveway to the Williams's house,

we see Carole sitting on the front steps. It looks like she's been waiting for us. And she's got something in her lap that resembles a huge tomato. When we get closer she looks up and then waves at us with whatever it is she is so concentrated on. Closer still, she stands up and comes down the steps. She is carrying two enormous knitting needles in her hands, with about two rows of bright red knitting accomplished. The needles are attached to a loop of yarn that swings twenty feet back to the stoop, where a red ball rolls around crazily at the top of the steps. A booklet flutters white pages against the concrete.

She hugs us all and then keeps her arm, with the knitting, around Melani's shoulder.

"What's that?" asks Melani, pointing to the knitting needles inches from her neck.

"I am knitting your father a sweater," says Carole.

Melani breaks out laughing, which is pretty mean, but I can tell she can't help herself. I touch the two rows on the needles.

"They're soft," I say.

"I think it will be nice," says Carole.

"Why don't you just buy him a sweater, Mom?"

"I wanted to do something special for your dad," she says. She gives me a significant look.

I arch my eyebrow. "It's a nice idea," I say.

"Sure is," says Frank, who is totally confused by the whole thing. "Where *is* Jeff?"

"She doesn't know how to knit," Melani whispers loudly to Christie.

Christie rolls her eyes.

"He had to go in to work. Cars can be a problem," Carole

says, hardly able to keep herself from looking at the station wagon. "But," she turns to Melani, "he'll be home soon. He wants to hear all about it." She pauses. "And I *can* knit."

"OK." Melani looks at Christie and tries to do the eye-white trick, but she's still an amateur.

"I wore my new jeans yesterday, Carole," I say, "they look terrific."

"What new jeans?" asks Christie.

"Carole gave me a pair of designer jeans. If you hadn't been so mad when I was at your dorm, you'd have seen them."

Melani looks first at her mother and then at me. "Did they come from Saks?" she asks.

I look at her with a smile. "They were in a Saks box."

"Mom!"

"Now, Melani."

"Mom, you keep doing that!"

"No I don't. I don't keep doing anything."

"Were those *my* jeans?" she asks.

"They were much too big for you, Melani," Carole says, without looking at me.

"Mom!" Melani lets out a really good moan.

"She gives away your clothes?" Christie is genuinely shocked.

"First it was a pair of shoes her friend Sheryl's kid wanted to wear for Halloween. That got her started. She's like a kleptomaniac in reverse; last week she gave my math teacher my favorite scarf."

"She passed you, Melani, and I didn't have time to go to the store."

"But my jeans!"

"You wear my clothes all the time," Carole answers, which

even *I* can see is not the same thing. "Besides, they were much too big."

"They're *supposed* to be like that."

Carole's looking a little embarrassed. "I'm going to pay you for them, Melani."

"That's not the point." Melani's blue contacts are afloat.

The sad thing about all this is, I don't even want the jeans. "Tell you what," I say, "how about I give them back?"

Melani lights up, but then she looks over at her mother.

"No, Lilly, they were a gift," says Carole.

"Ha!" says Melani, under her breath.

"I appreciate it, too, Carole, I do. It was very thoughtful of you, but really, I want Melani to have them back."

"She only wears sweatpants anyway," says Christie.

"She could do more with herself," says Carole.

"I do as much as I can," I say, thrilled with my nerve. I get the box out of the car and hand it to Melani. "I hope I didn't stretch them."

"Thanks, Lilly," she says. "I love these jeans. If you stretched them, it's OK."

Carole has started to knit, standing up. I mean, what else can she do? I give her a pat. "I'll call," I say.

The minute we turn out of the Williams's driveway, Frank says, "What happened to her face?"

"Whose face?" I ask.

"Carole's. Didn't you notice?"

"What do you mean, what happened to it?"

"She looks different," he says. "I don't know what it is."

"Younger?" I suggest.

He shrugs. "It doesn't look like Carole."

the air of flowers and dust—and of course, now, a heavy dose of Evening in Paris perfume. I'm neither happy nor unhappy, I'm just sort of me, Lilly Blake, getting along. The immediate problems seem resolved, but something will come up; that's just the way life is.

And it's OK because it looks like we're all in it together, floating down the good old river of life. I close my eyes and picture the river of life where the street was a minute ago. I know a lot about this river—it's got a current that only goes one way, fast, and there are rocks and rapids, falls that can sneak up on you, things that make the trip overexciting at times. But there are the smooth patches, the quiet beauty of the places you pass through that makes it all worthwhile. The main thing is, you can't just float, you've got to work at it, and it takes practice; sort of a paddle here, paddle there approach. The only choice is, a person can sit the whole thing out, like on this curb, or a person can jump in and get a nick or two—but what a ride! It's what the kids call 'going with the flow'; it's what I call adjusting for life.

I've never been to a dude ranch before, for example, but it's probably not all that bad.